THE CHALLENGE

"I'm flattered to think you fear me as a rival," Linnet told Judith Jordan.

A flush entered Judith's cheeks. "I wished to get the measure of you, Miss Carlisle, and I rather think I have. We will be meeting again."

"I sincerely hope not, for yours is the sort of society I abhor," Linnet said.

"Oh, I feel the same way about your society, Miss Carlisle, but you have become something of a thorn in my side of late, and I'm afraid I'm going to have to deal with you," Judith said. With that she walked away.

Linnet gazed after her. Maybe it was gratifying that the Bird of Paradise was jealous, but what wasn't so gratifying was that Judith was also gloriously beautiful, fascinating, worldly, witty, and stylish.

Against such a creature, what chance did dull little Linnet Carlisle have competing for the attention of so sophisticated a lord as Nicholas Fenton? Linnet had to find out. . . .

SANDRA HEATH was born in 1944. As the daughter of an officer in the Royal Air Force, most of her life was spent traveling around to various European posts. She has lived and worked in both Holland and Germany and now resides in Gloucester, England.

The Pilfered Plume

Sandra Heath

A SIGNET BOOK

NEW AMERICAN LIBRARY

A DIVISION OF PENGUIN BOOKS USA INC.

SIGNET TRADEMARK REG. U.S. PAT OFF. AND FOREIGN COUNTRIES
REGISTERED TRADEMARK—MARCA REGISTRADA
HECHO EN DRESDEN, TN.

SIGNET, SIGNET CLASSIC, MENTOR, ONYX, PLUME,
MERIDIAN and NAL BOOKS are published by New American
Library, a division of Penguin Books USA Inc., 1633 Broadway, New
York, New York 10019

First Printing, October, 1989

1 2 3 4 5 6 7 8 9

PRINTED IN THE UNITED STATES OF AMERICA

1

Ivystone House was the lakeland residence of Miss Edith Minton, an elderly lady of excellent family and comfortable means. It was set picturesquely on a wooded, west-facing slope between the high fells and beautiful Grasmere Lake, in the heart of the Lake District, and enjoyed matchless views over the brooding, romantic countryside that made this part of northwest England the resort of poets, artists, writers, and travelers alike. But it hadn't been the fashionable scenery that had brought heiress Linnet Carlisle so far away from her mansion in Mayfair, it had been a broken heart, and the desperate need for the comfort and understanding offered by her great-aunt, Miss Minton.

A year had passed since Linnet's flight from London, it was June again, and the new nineteenth century had begun, but still she lingered in the quiet and seclusion of Ivystone House. She was loath to return to the capital, for it was full of painful memories that might still prove too much to endure. In London she'd again encounter the man who'd broken her heart and betrayed her trust, Nicholas Fenton, Lord Fane. Time was said to be a great healer, and there was now a new love in her life, but there were still nights when she dreamed of all that had befallen her the year before, and the hurt clung to her when she awoke the next morning.

Nicholas was undoubtedly the most dangerously attractive man in London. He possessed looks, wit, charm, and wealth enough to lure any woman he chose, and was horseman, swordsman, and shot enough to make him much liked and respected by his own sex; but to Linnet he'd proved faithless, callous, and totally without principle, and finding out the cold truth about him had been the most devastating experience of her life.

She'd already been grieving over the sudden death of her beloved uncle and guardian, Joseph Carlisle, and then had suffered the humiliation of Nicholas's affair with a certain Judith Jordan, a notorious demimondaine who was known throughout society as the Bird of Paradise because of the dyed and decorated plumes she always wore in her golden hair. And, as if all this had not been enough to endure, there had been the revelation that Nicholas had cheated her uncle in a game of cards and had acquired the Carlisle family estate in Essex, Radleigh Hall.

However, it was one thing to know that Radleigh Hall had been stolen by sleight of hand, but quite another to prove it in a court of law, and all Linnet had had was her late uncle's word. She'd adored Joseph Carlisle, but he hadn't always been a paragon of virtue, having led a rather dissolute life in his youth. He'd been involved in at least two duels, escaping from both by chance rather than accuracy as a shot. The first had been with a cuckolded husband, the second with a guards officer who'd accused him of dealing from the bottom of the pack. Inevitably, this latter incident had immediately sprung to society's mind when the matter of Radleigh Hall came to light, and Linnet had known that without substantial and irrefutable proof, her late uncle's word would never be accepted above that of Nicholas, whose honor had, until then, never been in question.

She'd faced Nicholas with her accusations, but he hadn't deigned to reply, a fact which in her eyes damned him completely. If he was innocent of an affair with the Bird of Paradise, and innocent of cheating over Radleigh Hall, why hadn't he said so? Society's attitude made her position impossible, for it chose to take his side over Radleigh Hall, and was much amused that he may have deceived her with an infamous Cyprian. It had all proved too much for her, and on impulse she'd fled to her great-aunt in the Lake District, there to try to overcome the misery that had so cruelly engulfed her.

There had been those who'd taken her side, however, especially her closest friend and confidante, Venetia, Lady Hartley. At twenty-two, Venetia was one year Linnet's senior, and was also very much a woman of the world. At nineteen, she'd made a dazzling match with Lord Hartley, a very wealthy gentleman, but it had been an unhappy marriage, and on his death a year later, his young widow hadn't grieved for long before setting out to enjoy her wealth and freedom to the full. One of her great pleasures was being the hostess, and her select dinner parties were among the most *recherché* in London. She was lovely, lighthearted, and vivacious, and was much sought after by a string of hopeful suitors, especially a very wealthy young Cornish landowner called Freddy Grainger.

To Linnet, Venetia had been a jewel among friends, frequently making the tedious journey north in order to pay a visit at Ivystone House. During these stays she'd acquainted Linnet with all the latest gossip, and had endeavored to persuade her to return to London, but in this latter purpose she'd always been defeated. On one visit, however, she'd brought with her her half-brother, Benedict Gresham, who'd recently returned from Madras, and he had very swiftly become the new love in Linnet's life.

Benedict was thirty years old, dashing, good-looking to a fault, and flatteringly smitten with Linnet from the first moment he'd seen her. He'd hesitated to court her, however, for his financial affairs were in confusion because of immense legal difficulty is transferring his affairs from Madras, and he was forced to reside under Venetia's roof while everything was sorted out, but Linnet had been drawn to him, and in the end he'd confessed his love for her. She'd welcomed the confession, and had gladly granted him permission to call upon her whenever he could.

On a particularly fine June afternoon, when the sun shone down from a flawless blue sky, Linnet strolled in the terraced gardens of Ivystone House. She was deep in thought because Benedict and Venetia were due to arrive again that very day, and she knew they'd press her to return to London with them. She also knew that her great-aunt would counsel her to remain where she was, for the old lady didn't think Linnet was ready yet to resume her place in society. There was bound to be conflict, and Linnet knew she had to decide for herself. She had to make a sensible decision, and not succumb to the some-times impetuous side of her nature, a side that went only too well with the fiery shade of her hair.

Her long-sleeved gown was made of delicate white muslin, and had a low, scooped neckline. There was a wide yellow ribbon around the high waistline, immedi-ately beneath her breasts, and the gown's train was held up from the grass by a dainty golden cord that was fixed behind her right shoulder. It was last year's gown, but still very modish, for fashion hadn't changed much over the past twelve months. Her long chestnut hair was swept up beneath a straw gypsy hat that was tied on with an-other yellow ribbon, and she carried a closed white para-sol in her white-gloved hand.

She walked slowly, her brown eyes downcast as she considered the problem from every angle. Her great-aunt's roses were in their full summer glory, filling the warm air with scent, and the hill stream flowing down through the garden babbled contentedly. The water was cold and clear, and reflected her slender figure moving along the grassy bank. She found that her thoughts were becoming just as clear. Nicholas didn't matter to her any-more, but Benedict did, and it would be Benedict who'd be at her side now if she returned to London. Perhaps such a return was the very thing to restore her spirits . . .

Near the end of the garden the land dished slightly, causing the stream to form a pool before spilling over a ledge of rock and plunging down toward Grasmere Lake far below. From here the view was at its most spectacu-lar, and could be enjoyed from a wrought iron bench on the other bank, where climbing roses formed an arbor. Stepping stones had been placed in the shallow water, and Linnet gathered her skirts to tiptoe across.

She'd almost reached the other bank when the cord supporting her train gave way suddenly and her hem fell into the water. With a cry of dismay, she hurried over the final stones, reaching the safety of the bank and then picking up the train to try to wring it out. As she did so, she revealed an improper amount of leg and the daringly low scoop of her neckline.

"Upon my soul," drawled an amused and appreciative male voice. "It's worth dragging myself up here to the sticks if I'm to be afforded glimpses of such rare and delectable lakeland views!"

She straightened, at once embarrassed and delighted. "Benedict! I didn't think you'd arrive quite as early as this."

"So I see," he murmured, allowing his gaze to move slowly over her.

She quickly dropped the hem, conscious of a swift flush warming her cheeks.

Sketching an elaborate bow, he smiled. He was a little above medium height, with dark-brown curly hair and warm, long-lashed hazel eyes. His coat was sky-blue, his waistcoat of an excellent gray silk, and his gray cord breeches of a particularly tight fit. The pearl pin on the knot of his starched neckcloth shone as he nonchalantly tossed his top hat onto the grass and then stood facing her, his expression a little reproving. "I called you three times, madam, but you failed to hear me."

"I—I was thinking," she replied.

"That much is obvious. Well, since you are now well and truly aware of my presence, and since you are, er, decorous again, shall we observe the civilities? Good afternoon, Miss Carlisle."

"Good afternoon, Mr. Gresham."

"Are you pleased to see me?"

"Very," she admitted frankly.

"Then I shall be very bold and presumptuous, and not ask permission before joining you." He swiftly crossed the stepping stones, taking her parasol and placing it on the bench. Then he seized her hands, looking ardently into her soft brown eyes. "I've missed you," he said, his voice warm with longing.

"And I've missed you."

Slipping an arm around her waist, he pulled her close and kissed her on the lips. It was a passionate kiss, filled with desire, and she responded, linking her arms around his neck.

His eyes were dark as he drew back. "How long are you going to languish up here in the back of beyond? Haven't you been able to put Fane behind you once and for all?"

"He is behind me."

"Then, don't I matter enough to you?" He cupped her face in his hands.

"You know that you do."

"Prove it by coming back to town with me this time."

"I—I think I may do just that," she said slowly.

His eyes brightened, and he stroked her cheeks with his thumbs, still cupping her face. "Do you really mean it?"

"Yes."

He lowered his hands, his joy fading a little. "But what of the dreaded Great-Aunt Minton? She will do her utmost to dissuade you."

"She has my best interests at heart."

"Does she? Or is it simply that she loathes me, and likes Venetia little better?"

Linnet felt uncomfortable, for what he said was only too true, her contrary great-aunt *did* dislike them both. The old lady didn't believe a word he said, and viewed poor Venetia as some sort of snake in the grass, even though Venetia had been so strongly supportive over the past year.

Benedict drew a long breath. "It's very disagreeable to know that your one and only relative views me as being little better than Fane."

"She just wants to protect me. You must understand that."

"Protect you from what? I'd never treat you as he did,

and, to be honest, I rather resent her constant insinuations that I would."

"She'll come around when she knows you properly."

He smiled, pulling her close again. "I love you, Linnet."

"And I love you."

Thoughts of Nicholas swept over him again. "Damn the fellow's eyes! Whenever I encounter him in town, which is often, it's all I can do not to call him out for what he did to you."

"You mustn't think about him, and you certainly mustn't call him out, he's . . ."

"A better swordsman and shot than me?" he interrupted.

She smiled a little ruefully. "Something of the sort."

"You do mean it when you say you're over him, don't you?"

"Of course I do. Now, then, come and sit down." She went to the wrought iron bench, sitting down carefully, and arranging the damp train of her gown. "I trust Venetia is well?"

"She is, if a little exhausted after the journey," he replied, joining her.

"How are the improvements coming on at Berkeley Square?"

He hesitated. "They aren't."

"Aren't? What do you mean?"

"She doesn't reside there anymore. She moved suddenly two weeks ago to a new house in Fane Crescent."

Linnet's brown eyes widened. "Fane Crescent?" she said slowly.

"She did it against my advice."

"She's free to live wherever she chooses, Benedict," Linnet replied, wondering why Venetia had made such a move without saying anything to her. The crescent was undoubtedly one of the most exclusive addresses in Mayfair, and was built in the grounds of Fane House itself. The entrance was guarded by gates and a lodge, and no one was permitted to pass unless authorized to do so. The crescent and house faced each other across a large sunken garden of considerable beauty, and to have purchased a residence there must have cost Venetia a small fortune.

Benedict looked uncomfortable. "She now resides at number sixteen, which is in the very center of the crescent, facing directly across at Fane House. I don't know why she felt she had to reside there, for she must have known it would hurt you."

"It really doesn't matter, Benedict. As I said, Venetia is free to live wherever she chooses."

"She showed little thought when she chose that of *all* addresses, but then, given the way she's been behaving of late, I suppose I shouldn't be surprised."

Linnet looked at him in surprise. "Whatever has she been up to for you to speak of her like that?"

"She's been treating poor Freddy Grainger very badly, and he has no idea what, if anything, he's done to deserve it. It first began at a ball at Holland House. Freddy confided in me that he'd proposed to her the night before, and she'd intimated that she might well accept him. At the ball, however, she virtually cut him, and after a while I noticed that she was spending a great deal of time with a gentleman I didn't then know anything about."

"But you do now?"

"Oh, yes, I do now." He got up from the bench, going to look at the view. "Can you see Town End from here?" he asked suddenly.

Startled by the apparent change of subject, she gave a quick laugh. "Why, no, it's just around that headland over there. How on earth have you heard of such a tiny hamlet?"

"I understand a Mr. Wordsworth lives there."

"The poet? Yes, he does. He and his sister, Miss Wordsworth, took the old Dove and Olive Branch Inn just before last Christmas. It's just a cottage now." She thought of the rather unconventional and odd poet. "You surely aren't saying that *he* was the gentleman at the ball?"

"No, not quite. He and a certain Mr. Coleridge wrote

a collection of verse entitled *Lyrical Ballads,* which has become very fashionable, did they not?"

"Yes. It's really very good. I have a volume myself."

"Have you ever seen Coleridge? I understand he visits Wordsworth quite frequently."

"Yes, as a matter of fact, I have. It was on a Sunday morning outside Grasmere church. Everyone at the Wordsworths' cottage had been at an all-night picnic on the island in the lake, and he was with them." She called to mind the pale, rather slender, intense-looking young man.

Benedict looked at the view again. "Well, *he* was the man at the Holland House ball. You will admit that he is an attractive enough fellow?"

"Yes," she said slowly, "but as to whether she would turn away from Freddy on account of him . . ."

"She certainly acquired a copy of *Lyrical Balads* after the ball, *and* she began to subscribe to the *Morning Chronicle,* for which newspaper he just happens to be the theater critic." He paused. "I am also of the opinion that on a number of occasions she chose the times of her visits here to you to coincide with visits he happened to be paying to Wordsworth. I have every reason to believe he's there now."

Linnet sat back, a little bemused. "Well, if you're right," she said after a moment, "there isn't a great deal you can do about it. She's a widow and a free agent, and he's hardly all that unacceptable, is he?"

"You obviously don't know, do you?" he said softly, returning to stand before her.

"Know what?"

"The knave's married, and has a family."

Linnet stared at him in dismay. "No, I didn't know."

"Now perhaps you see why I'm so concerned. I can't believe she's actually turning her back on a catch like Freddy Grainger in order to indulge in a liaison with another woman's husband. Linnet, I know my half-sister can be difficult, scheming, single-minded to a fault, and as stubborn a creature as ever lived, and I know, too, that you're the last person to interfere in anyone's private affairs . . .''

"But that's exactly what you're going to ask me to do?" she finished for him.

"I know it's a great deal to ask, but you *are* her closest friend."

"She won't thank me—or you for telling me."

"All I want you to do is talk to her."

"I'll try, but I can't promise anything."

He smiled, reaching down to take her hand, and drawing her up into his arms again. "You're the most adorable creature in all the world," he murmured, kissing her again.

She pulled determinedly away. "I think we'd better return to the house, before my great-aunt begins to wonder what we're up to."

He sighed, and nodded. "Oh, very well. I vow I can't wait to spirit you away from here, and leave the old besom to her own devices."

Still holding her hand, he retrieved her parasol, and then they stepped back over the stones to the other side. A few minutes later, they were walking up toward the house.

2

Linnet didn't have an opportunity to do as he asked until just before dinner that evening, because when she and Benedict entered the house they were told that Venetia had decided to rest in her room until then.

Great-Aunt Minton was a very particular person when it came to observing custom and etiquette, and the fact that her home was in remote lakeland, two hundred and fifty miles from London, didn't deter her from insisting upon dressing properly for dinner.

Linnet chose one of her favorite gowns, an apple-green silk embroidered with tiny sprays of white flowers. It only had little sleeves, and since there was an unexpected chill in the evening air, she carried a white woolen shawl. Her maid, Mary Kelly, had dressed her hair up into a becoming knot, with one long chestnut ringlet tumbling down from the back. The knot was adorned with a golden comb, and she wore pearl earrings and a three-string pearl choker. Her skirts rustled as she went downstairs to the large wainscotted parlor where everyone would gather before proceeding to the dining room.

Venetia was the only one to have arrived before her. She was seated in Great-Aunt Minton's favorite chintz-covered armchair, and was so engrossed in a book that she didn't at first hear Linnet enter. Outside, the sun was beginning to sink toward the western horizon, and shafts of rich evening light shone through the windows, past the pots of ferns and white geraniums cluttering the sills.

Linnet paused in the doorway, observing her friend for

a moment before drawing her attention. Venetia was very like Benedict, with the same long-lashed hazel eyes and curly dark-brown hair, which she wore fashionably very short. She was tall, with a willowy, almost boyish figure which tonight was shown off to great advantage in a slender mauve taffeta gown. A black lace shawl was tossed idly over the back of the chair, and the evening light picked out the amethysts on her bracelet as she turned a page.

Linnet moved softly across the room, leaning over the back of the chair to suddenly read aloud from the page. *"I pass, like night, from land to land; I have strange powers of speech; The moment that his face I see I know the man that must hear me; To him my tale I teach,"* she intoned dramatically. "Good heavens, isn't that a little grim and indigestible just before eating?"

Venetia started, and gave her a cross look. "Linnet Carlisle, it's beastly of you to creep up like that!"

"I was intrigued to see what was absorbing you so completely. I didn't realize *The Rime of the Ancient Mariner* was to your liking."

"This volume happens to be all the rage in town this year."

"In the provinces, too. I have a copy." Linnet moved around to a chair opposite, and sat down. "I've never seen you reading poetry of any kind before."

Venetia eyed her suspiciously. "My dear brother Benedict has been telling tales, hasn't he?"

Linnet nodded ruefully. "He's worried, Venetia."

"It's none of his business."

"He's your brother, and he cares about you. I care about you, too." Linnet paused. "Is there any truth in what he tells me?" she asked, deciding upon a forthright approach.

"No." Venetia got up crossly, her taffeta skirts rustling. "I do wish he'd keep his nose out of my affairs. I managed perfectly well while he was in Madras, and yet he seems to think I'm helpless."

"He's anxious about your reputation, and he's concerned that you'll throw away your chances with Freddy Grainger.''

"Oh, to perdition with Freddy-Wretched-Grainger!'' snapped Venetia.

Linnet look at her in surprise. "I thought you were fond of him.''

"I am, but not to the point of wishing to rush into marriage.''

"After over a year, it's hardly rushing,'' commented Linnet dryly. "Besides, I'm told he proposed to you, and that you led him to believe you were going to accept, but that the advent of Mr. Coleridge at the Holland House ball put paid to it.''

"My dear sibling *has* been clacking, hasn't he?'' Venetia sighed, going to place the book on the mantelpiece. "Well, he's wrong about Mr. Coleridge, who is most definitely *not* my lover. Oh, I admit to finding him attractive, for he's everything romantic, but I've yet to clamber into his bed.''

"Venetia!''

"If I'm being too worldly for your sensibilities, I apologize,'' replied Venetia sharply.

"I only want to help,'' protested Linnet, a little hurt.

Venetia was repentant, and smiled sheepishly. "Forgive me, it isn't fair to bite *your* head off when it's Benedict's fault.''

"I admit I *can* feel your teethmarks,'' answered Linnet, pretending to rub her neck.

Venetia grinned, sitting down again. "I'm just tired after the journey. Believe me, Linnet, I'm not indulging in a liaison with Mr. Coleridge, or with anyone else for that matter, more's the pity. I admit that I changed my mind about Freddy that night at the Holland House ball, but it wasn't because of Mr. Coleridge.'' She paused, becoming a little uneasy as she abruptly changed the topic of conversation. "Linnet, there's something I have to tell you.''

"Yes?''

"Has Benedict told you that I've moved from Berkeley Square?''

"To Fane Crescent? Yes."

"I hope it won't make any difference to our friendship, for I'd hate that. I bought the house because Fane Crescent is *the* most desirable address in town, and properties there don't often become available. When Lord Faverholme died so suddenly two months ago and his sister decided to sell . . ."

"You don't have to explain, for I do understand."

"I didn't want you to think I'd deliberately kept the move from you, it just happened so quickly." Venetia looked anxiously at her. "You don't see it as a slight of any kind, do you?"

Linnet smiled. "Of course not."

Venetia was relieved. "Oh, I'm so glad, for I value your friendship very much indeed." She hesitated, looking quickly at her. "Actually, I saw Nicholas himself four days ago, at the grand unveiling ceremony."

"What grand unveiling ceremony?"

"Oh, didn't you know? He's put an equestrian statue of his late grandfather in the sunken garden between Fane House and the crescent. I gather it's something he's wished to do for some time now."

"Yes, it is," replied Linnet, who knew the immense regard Nicholas had always had for the third Lord Fane, who'd brought him up from boyhood after the tragically early death of both his parents in a fire at the Fenton country seat in Kent.

"If the statue is anything to judge by, the third Lord Fane and the fifth are virtually identical in appearance," went on Venetia.

"My great-aunt assures me that they are peas from the same pod," agreed Linnet, who'd often wondered if the third Lord Fane had been more than a mere friend to Miss Edith Minton. Indeed, the thought had occurred to her that such was her great-aunt's admiration and regard for that gentleman, that there seemed a great likelihood that he was the reason she'd never married.

Venetia was changing the subject again. "I saw Benedict just before I came down. He tells me you're almost certainly returning to London with us this time."

"Yes, that's right," answered Linnet, expecting to see a delighted smile break across the other's face, but instead, Venetia became very serious.

"Linnet, I don't think you should. You're just not ready yet."

Linnet stared at her, and then laughed in disbelief. "But, you've just spent the last year trying to persuade me to go back!"

"I know, but that was before I spoke properly to your great-aunt. She and I had a talk when I first arrived this afternoon, while you and Benedict were in the garden. She told me that in spite of your obvious deep affection for Benedict, you still have upsetting dreams about Nicholas."

Linnet looked away. "She shouldn't have told you."

"No, and Benedict shouldn't have told you about his suspicions concerning Mr. Coleridge, but he did, because he's worried about me," replied Venetia, reminding her that no one's private affairs are completely inviolate.

"Well, just because I occasionally dream about Nicholas, it doesn't mean I'm not ready to go home to Carlisle House. What happened a year ago was truly horrid, and is bound to have left its mark, but Benedict means everything to me now."

"Does he?"

Linnet looked curiously at her. "Venetia, what is all this? Don't you want me ever to return?"

Venetia smiled quickly, putting a reassuring hand over hers. "Of course I do, you ninny, it's just that I don't want you to be hurt all over again. You're bound to see Nicholas all the time, for he's very much in evidence. He . . ." She broke off, changing her mind about what she'd been on the point of saying.

"Yes?"

"He spends a great deal of his time in the company of that tawdry Bird of Paradise person—in fact, he actually took her to Radleigh Hall a month or so ago. I wouldn't have told you, but if you're going to return, it's important that you know what to expect."

Linnet lowered her eyes. It was painful to know that Nicholas had so little regard for her that he'd taken the Cyprian to the estate that had once been the country seat of the Carlisle family.

Venetia watched her. "You see? It hurts you to think of it. He still has the power to reach you, Linnet, in spite of what you feel for Benedict, and you aren't going to find it at all easy if you go back to town. Nicholas Fenton is the devil in disguise, for although he's outwardly the most handsome and attractive of men, inside he's all that's base and callous."

Linnet nodded. "I know, Venetia, and I've accepted that that's how he is. He really doesn't matter to me now, and I'm quite set upon going home."

Venetia was about to say something more, but at that moment they heard steps, and the door opened to admit Benedict and Linnet's great-aunt.

Benedict was dressed superbly, in a purple velvet coat, white satin waistcoat, and white silk breeches, but although he looked the picture of fashionable masculine elegance, his face was dark and angry. So was Great-Aunt Minton's, and Linnet knew immediately that they'd been having words, most probably about her contentious decision.

Giving Venetia a disapproving look for daring to occupy the favorite armchair, Great-Aunt Minton sat on a sofa, taking particular care about the arranging of her charcoal satin skirts. She was a small, neat person, her graying hair powdered and curled in the old-fashioned style that was so favored by ladies of her generation. In her youth she'd been considered a beauty, and her wealthy Carlisle connections had made it certain that she'd be able to snap up a suitable husband. But she'd turned down all offers, and had quite abruptly retired from London to take up residence in the seclusion of Ivystone House.

Snapping open her fan, she eyed Linnet. "Mr. Gresham informs me that you've elected to return to London."

Linnet lowered her gaze guiltily.

"I see from your manner that it is true. Would it not

have been courteous to have informed me yourself? After all, you have been residing beneath this roof for a year now.''

"I'm sorry, Great-Aunt Minton, I didn't mean to cause offense.''

"Nevertheless, that is precisely what you *have* caused, and in quantity. You came here in considerable distress, and in my opinion you have a long way to go before you are completely over that distress.''

"I have to go sometime, and I feel that now is as good a moment as any.'' Linnet glanced at Benedict.

Her great-aunt sniffed. "With all due respect to Mr. Gresham, I don't think his presence is going to protect you from the undoubted pain of confronting Lord Fane again.''

Venetia sat forward. "Your great-aunt is right, Linnet. I do wish you'd stay.''

Benedict was caught completely off guard by his sister's change of heart. "Venetia! What are you saying?''

"I'm sorry, Benedict, but Miss Minton has made me see things differently now. If we have Linnet's best interests at heart, then we must persuade her to remain here.''

Great-Aunt Minton was no less surprised than Benedict. She looked quizzically at Venetia. "Well, Lady Hartley, I didn't imagine that you and I would ever be on the same side in this.''

Venetia met her gaze a little unwillingly. "I've given the matter considerable thought, Miss Minton.'' She turned to Benedict. "Forgive me, but it really is how I feel now.''

"Well, thank you very much, sister mine!'' he replied bitterly. "I thought that you, at least, were my ally in this, but you've let me down with a vengeance!''

Linnet rose suddenly to her feet. "Will you all stop talking as if I'm not here? I do have a mind of my own, you know, and I've decided to go back to Carlisle House.''

Great-Aunt Minton's lips twitched. "And how, pray, do you intend to go on once you're there?''

"Go on? I don't understand.''

"May I remind you that your late uncle was your guardian, and that therefore you were under his protection? If you go back now, you will no longer have that protection. At the very least, you need a chaperone."

Benedict turned quickly to Venetia. "You'll gladly undertake the role, will you not?" he pressed, fearful that the old lady was about to propose herself.

Venetia was flustered by being placed on such a spot. "Why, I . . . Yes, of course. Linnet, you're more than welcome to live with me, in Fane Crescent," she added awkwardly.

Great-Aunt Minton snorted. "And how, pray, would that protect my great-niece's reputation? I can hardly consent to her residing beneath the same roof as Mr. Gresham!" She gave Benedict a baleful look. "You *are* still residing with Lady Hartley, are you not?"

"Yes. My financial affairs aren't yet in order."

"So it seems. Mr. Gresham, if I may say so, your bankers and lawyers appear to be taking an *unconscionable* length of time sorting matters out. Are they incompetent, or are your finances in the greatest tangle imaginable?"

"I'm in their hands," he replied shortly, dull color touching his cheeks.

She raised an eyebrow archly, and then returned her attention to Linnet. "My dear, not only can Lady Hartley not be considered as your chaperone because of Mr. Gresham's presence, but also because her address is quite out of the question. It must be clear to you that there would be very unwelcome talk if you were to live in such close proximity to Fane House. There is only one sensible solution, and that is that I return to London as well, thus offering you *my* protection."

Benedict was appalled. It was too awful a prospect to contemplate, and he looked pleadingly at his half-sister, but Venetia could only shrug, for there was nothing she could do.

Linnet appreciated her great-aunt's offer, and gladly accepted. "But are you sure you wish to return to the hurly-burly of London life after all this time?" she added.

"It isn't a case of what I want, my dear, but a case of where my duty lies. You are my dear sister's grandchild, and I am your only remaining relative, and it is therefore incumbent upon me to watch over you, as I have been doing for the past year."

Linnet went to her, bending to hug her warmly. "I do love you so," she whispered.

"You don't deserve me, that's for sure, you little minx," replied the old lady fondly, patting her arm.

Benedict groaned inwardly. *He* didn't deserve the old biddy either! She'd always been as obstructive as possible where his suit with Linnet was concerned, and she'd made it embarrassingly clear that she didn't give much credence to what he said regarding his financial problems. She'd continue to stand in his way in London, constantly gnawing away at Linnet's resistance. Oh, plague take the woman!

Great-Aunt Minton rose to her feet. "I think it is time to adjourn to the dining room. I trust you will enjoy the meal, for the main course is Grasmere trout." She swept out in a rustle of charcoal satin.

Benedict gave her retreating figure a dire look. Trout? He abhorred trout, and the old harridan knew it!

3

It was pouring with rain one week later when two carriages set off from Ivystone House *en route* for London. The first, Venetia's handsome maroon traveling carriage, contained Venetia herself, Linnet, Benedict, and Great-Aunt Minton. The second vehicle, Linnet's private carriage, conveyed the servants, three maids, and Benedict's valet. Word had been sent ahead to the staff at Carlisle House, warning them to expect their mistress's return from her long absence, and all that remained now was to accomplish the long journey without mishap.

There was little conversation in the first carriage, for the atmosphere was strained. Linnet endeavored to appear carefree, but the truth was that she was filled with trepidation now that the moment was upon her. Was she really ready to face London again? How would her friends react? How much of the previous year's story would be dredged up and recirculated? Above all, how would it be when she inevitably came face to face with Nicholas?

She'd dressed with care, determined to put on a brave front. Her gown was a brown-spotted cream muslin, and with it she wore a tightly-fitted brown velvet spencer that came exactly to the gown's high waistline. A froth of chestnut curls framed her face, and the rest of her hair was pinned up in a knot beneath her high-crowned straw bonnet. The bonnet was tied beneath her chin with wide, wired ribbons she'd had woven specially for her, in a design of the little brown birds after which she'd been named. She strove not to fidget with the strings of her reticule, for that would have alerted her hawk-eyed great-aunt to the extent of her secret uncertainty. She was glad of the carriage's close confines, for it meant that she could feel Benedict beside her, and occasionally touch his hand, without her great-aunt noticing.

The past week had been a trial, for the old lady hadn't wasted an opportunity to try to dissuade her from returning to London, citing various excellent reasons for remaining in the Lake District. First of all there was Linnet's personal well-being, which her great-aunt was convinced would suffer from such an unwise move. Next there was the apparent mystery surrounding Benedict's financial affairs. The fact that it wasn't a mystery at all, but a legal tangle that he could do nothing about, made no difference to the old lady, who was of the opinion, only just concealed from Benedict himself, that it was Linnet's fortune, and not Linnet herself, that was proving the real attraction as far as he was concerned. Finally there was Venetia, who apparently shouldn't be trusted on any account. Linnet had endured it all, for she knew her great-aunt was concerned only for her, but it was very difficult holding her tongue when there was constant criticism both of the man she loved and of her closest friend.

Beside her, Benedict sat gazing out of the rain-washed carriage window. One arm rested along the ledge, and his gloved fingers drummed on the polished wood. He wore a dark-green coat, a green-and-white-striped waistcoat, and white corduroy breeches. The tassels on his Hessian boots swung to the motion of the carriage as it swayed down the narrow lane, where rivulets of water trickled along the ruts. His top hat was pulled well forward so that he wouldn't catch Great-Aunt Minton's baleful eye, and his expression was dark. The devil take the old woman for foisting herself upon them; and take Venetia too, for deserting his cause and endeavoring to make Linnet stay in this godforsaken corner of the realm. He stole a brief glance at his elderly adversary. If she imagined that she was going to prevent him from courting her niece, she was very much mistaken. Linnet was his, and he wasn't going to relinquish her because an obstinate and unreasonable old biddy had taken a dislike to him.

His fingers continued to drum, the sound barely audible above the rattle of the carriage and the noise of the rain on the roof. If he was honest, the dragon's presence was the only cloud on his lakeland horizon, for his other purposes had been accomplished. Linnet was returning to London at last, and Venetia hadn't been caught out in any indiscretion with Coleridge, whose stay at Town End had, according to investigation, lasted only two days. The tendency of the occupants of the former Dove and Olive Branch Inn to walk on the fells in the dark, or stay on the Grasmere island until dawn, had meant a possibility that Venetia might slip from her room at night in order to be with her unsuitable lover. He, Benedict, had spent several sleepless nights on guard against such a happening, but Venetia hadn't stirred from her room at all, emerging bright and fresh in the morning while her brother had been tired and irritable.

Venetia sat opposite him, well aware of his watchfulness over the past week. At first she'd been very angry, but then had decided to ignore him, for if he wished to spend sleepless nights, that was his concern. She was more concerned about Linnet's determination to go through with this return to London. Venetia didn't think the time was right, and intended to support Great-Aunt Minton in any attempt to make Linnet reconsider, even at this late hour. Not that it would be easy supporting the old lady, whose vague antagonism hadn't gone unnoticed. Venetia didn't know in what way she'd sinned in the other's eyes, she only knew that Linnet's great-aunt was an ally only on the matter of the departure from Ivystone House; on every other front there was no trust or liking at all.

Venetia sighed, looking out at the dripping trees as the carriage passed. She felt very out of place in her bright apricot lawn gown and matching full-length frilled pelisse. There was a posy of silk forget-me-nots pinned to the underbrim of her cream hat, and another posy on her right shoulder, giving her a summery look that just didn't go with such miserable weather. The warm sunshine and flawless skies of a week before might never have been. Was it an omen? Was Linnet's return to London going to be as disagreeable? Venetia rather feared it was.

Next to her, Great-Aunt Minton was very precisely and properly turned out in a bottle-green linen pelisse and green-and-white sprigged-muslin gown. A discreet number of powdered ringlets peeped from beneath her wide-brimmed hat, and there was a warm shawl around her shoulders, to protect her from the drafts she was sure would percolate the carriage in such inclement weather. She didn't think much of Venetia's elegant carriage, which was handsome enough but had fussily pretty lamps and excessively ornate blinds. And its crimson upholstery had been especially chosen to flatter the owner's brunette looks, thus showing her to be guilty of a certain unbecoming vanity. The former Miss Venetia Gresham had done very well for herself, marrying into the peerage and emerging very quickly as a wealthy young widow, and there was no doubt that she was a very attractive person, but there was something about her that Miss Edith Minton simply couldn't take to. It was quite an irrational dislike, and as such not to be approved of, for one always had to have a reason for disliking a person, but where Lady Hartley was concerned, there didn't seem to be any explanation for the vague feeling of distrust.

Where Mr. Benedict Gresham was concerned, however, there was a great deal more to go on. Behind his handsome, engaging exterior, the old lady felt certain he was not what he seemed to be. His charm was just a little too easy, and his smile a little too ready. And then there was this business with his financial affairs. He'd been back in England for some time now, lodging with his half-sister, and in all that time he seemed no further forward than he had at the very beginning. There were tales of tortuous legal tangles, and the withholding of funds, mention of an estate in the north of Northumberland which was being improved to his very exact specifications, and of various London town properties he'd inspected and found lacking, and even of a Newmarket stud of thoroughbreds he was considering purchasing. It was all a trifle unsatisfactory, lacking substance, and Linnet's great-aunt required a little more in the way of fact before she'd ever consider him even remotely suitable for her niece.

Turning her attention to Linnet, Great-Aunt Minton sighed inwardly. The child looked so tense, but was pretending to be light-hearted. She'd suffered so much at Nicholas Fenton's callous hands, and would suffer more when she saw the blackguard again. To think that his grandfather, the third Lord Fane, had been such a paragon of every virtue . . . She sighed aloud. Linnet Carlisle had execrable taste in gentlemen; her first love had been a total disaster, and her second seemed little better. Why, oh why, couldn't she fix her affections upon a deserving person, instead of a succession of rogues and villains?

The carriage reached the foot of the hill, turning south onto the main Kendal road. Grasmere village loomed across the meadows to the northwest, almost lost in the gloom and rain. The coachman brought the team up to as smart a pace as possible, maneuvering them along the rain-washed road as it meandered beside the gray, glinting waters of the lake. The second carriage followed, its occupants laughing and joking together, but in the first, the uncomfortable silence continued, and promised to do so for the next three days or so.

It stopped raining at last on the afternoon of the third day, as the two travel-stained carriages drove into the yard of the Turk's Head Inn, in the town of Barnet, just north of London. Barnet was the first stage out of, and last stage into, the capital, and was consequently very busy. Its long main street was lined with hostelries, for there were not only numerous stagecoaches to cater for, but also at least seven northbound mails, including the important Holyhead coach.

As the two travel-stained vehicles from Ivystone House drew to a weary standstill and ostlers hurried to change the teams, Linnet looked out at the noisy, teeming yard. Doors opened and closed constantly, bells rang, customers called to waiters, servants seemed to come and go from every doorway, and porters carried luggage to waiting coaches. A barber's boy ran by with some razors in a bowl, and a washerwoman carried a huge basket of clean linen toward the kitchen doors. The smell of cooking hung in the air, as did the familiar odor of stale ale, which had permeated every establishment they'd stopped at during the past three days.

Another private carriage pulled into the yard, halting alongside, and Linnet recognized the crest on the gleaming panel. It was that of her good friend Lord Morpeth, and he'd already noticed her, smiling as he flung open his door to come and greet her. He was a tall, pleasant-looking young man, with a lazily nonchalant appearance that accurately defined his whole character and outlook.

For a moment Linnet's heart sank. This was her first encounter with one of her old friends. Would it pass off easily? Or would it become evident that the events of twelve months before were still uncomfortably fresh in society's mind?

He opened the door of Venetia's carriage, hastily removing his hat to speak to them all. "I trust I'm not intruding, but seeing a face that has been absent for far too long has made me a little bold." He smiled warmly at Linnet.

Linnet hastened to introduce him to her great-aunt, who wasn't acquainted with him. "My lord, allow me to present you to my great-aunt, Miss Minton, of Grasmere in Cumberland. Great-Aunt Minton, this is Lord Morpeth."

"Madam." He bowed.

"My lord." Great-Aunt Minton surveyed him for a long moment. "Yes, I can see you are your mother's son."

"You know my mother?"

"I do indeed, sir, she is a very charming and agreeable lady. Pray remember me to her."

"I will be sure to do that, Miss Minton." He looked at Linnet again. "I trust this means you are returning to the fold?"

"I am."

"And not before time. We've missed you."

Linnet smiled. "I understand from Venetia that you have formed a lasting *tendresse* for Lady Georgiana Cavendish. Is it true?"

"Yes, very true indeed."

Linnet reached over to squeeze his hand. "I'm very glad for you. Shall we soon hear an announcement?"

"I sincerely hope so, but you know how the financial details tend to drag on."

Great-Aunt Minton gave a sniff. "Oh, we do indeed, sir," she said, looking deliberately at Benedict.

Linnet quickly spoke again. "I trust you will invite me to the celebrations, my lord."

"Naturally. Well, I must take my leave now, for I'm on my way to Chatsworth."

"To haggle with the duke?" inquired Venetia.

"I prefer to call it conducting a very civilized discussion," he replied, putting on his hat. "If he's to be my future father-in-law, I intend to walk on eggshells in order to stay on his right side." He smiled at Linnet again. "It really is good to see you once more. Everyone will be very pleased to see you again."

"*Every*one?" She raised an eyebrow, thinking of Nicholas.

"Well, does *he* count? I vow the fellow don't deserve it if he does. Ah, I see I'm holding you up, for your team's been changed. I look forward to seeing you again soon. Good luck." He closed the door, calling to the waiting coachman to drive on.

As the carriage swayed forward once more, Great-Aunt Minton looked out approvingly at Lord Morpeth. "What a very *pleasing* young man, a true credit to his parents. And so eminently suitable, in every way." She forbore to actually look at Benedict, but she didn't need to, the barb was very evident indeed.

Benedict glowered at her, and Venetia rather irritably twitched her skirts away, to show her profound annoyance with the old lady. Linnet gave her great-aunt an equally cross look, and as the two carriages emerged once more into Barnet's main street, the silence of the past three days was restored to the one in the lead, while the servants' good-humored chatter continued in the other.

The closer they drew to London, the busier the road became. There was a great deal of traffic, from covered carts and wagons, to chariots, chaises, gigs, curricles, and phaetons. Stagecoaches thundered to and from the capital, and drovers moved their slow herds toward the markets. Now that the rain had stopped, the predominant sound was that of hooves and wheels crunching on the graveled surface.

Linnet gazed at the horizon ahead, where the remembered spires marked the skyline. Soon the first villas appeared, and then it seemed no time at all before they'd reached Tyburn and were turning east along Oxford Street. It was good to see the shops again, their windows displaying such an abundance of fine wares. Then Oxford Street was behind them, as the carriages turned south into the elegance and grandeur of Mayfair. They negotiated Grosvenor Square, and then struck south once more along the cobbles of John Street.

Charles Street, and Carlisle House, lay at the end of this thoroughfare, but halfway along it, on the western side, stood the gates and lodge guarding the drives into Fane House and Fane Crescent. Linnet steeled herself, little realizing that in a moment she was about to see not only the gates and lodge, but also Nicholas himself.

4

The tall wrought iron gates, their posts surmounted by the Fane lions, appeared quite suddenly on the right. There were two pairs of gates, one to admit traffic to Fane House, the other to allow access to the crescent itself, and in between stood the little lodge, where the gatekeeper took his duties very seriously indeed, never allowing any vehicle or person in unless authorized.

Beyond the gates, Linnet could see the crescent. It was very fine indeed, curving grandly away from the gates, its windows looking south over the large sunken garden toward Fane House on the other side. The crescent was a masterpiece of symmetry, three stories high, with stone facings and pedimented doors, and Fane House, while far from the largest mansion in Mayfair, was surely the most beautiful. Its windows were tall and airy, and the central bay was crowned by a fine classical portico with Corinthian columns. The main entrance was approached up a wide flight of ten steps, and the drive before it was large enough for a carriage and six to turn with ease. Linnet gazed at it, and then looked at the sunken garden, where the newly erected equestrian statue of Nicholas's grandfather stood among the trees.

The gatekeeper had hastened from his lodge suddenly, hurrying to open the Fane House gates, and her attention was drawn to him immediately. He snatched off his hat, standing deferentially aside for a horseman to enter. It was Nicholas.

He rode one of the superb Arabian horses he and a few

other discerning gentlemen kept especially for riding in
Hyde Park, and he was accompanied by two rust-colored
greyhounds, which padded obediently at his horse's heels.
He was more darkly handsome than she remembered,
with an aristocratic profile that was both fine-boned and
strong. His lips were firm, neither too full nor too thin,
and there was a cleft in his chin that gave him a rugged
look. His eyes were a clear, piercing blue, dark-lashed
and penetrating, and his complexion was tanned, for he
wasn't one to languish overlong in stuffy drawing rooms.
His hair was thick and wavy, and so dark it was virtually
black, making Benedict's seem pale in comparison. A
fawn top hat rested at a rakish angle on his head, and he
wore a light brown coat with a high standfall collar. The
frills of his white shirt protruded through his partially
buttoned gold brocade waistcoat, and his fawn silk neckcloth was tied in an intricate knot. Cream cord breeches
clung to his hips and legs like a second skin, and there
were gleaming spurs at the heels of his shining topboots.

He rode with effortless ease, making little of controlling his spirited and nervous mount. He'd been riding in
the park, and for some time, for the horse was sweating
a little from the exertion. The greyhounds bounded ahead
as the gates swung fully open, and he was about to ride
after them when some sixth sense made him look directly
at the passing carriages.

His glance settled unerringly on Linnet, and he reined
in, turning in the saddle to watch her. If he was startled
to see her again, he gave no hint of it. She was conscious
of how blue his eyes were, and she saw how his lips
twisted into a faintly mocking smile, as if he found her
vaguely amusing. Slowly he removed his hat, sweeping
her an exaggerated bow, then the carriage carried her
from his view.

Her pulse was racing, and she knew there were telltale
spots of color on her cheeks. She was trembling, for she
hadn't expected to encounter him quite so quickly. The
past was all around her suddenly, and her treacherous
senses recalled the warmth of his kisses, and the softness
of his whispered words of love, but then she remembered

the falseness that was beneath everything. She had to look past his beguiling exterior and see the blackness within. Ignoring her great-aunt, she openly took Benedict's hand, curling her fingers tightly in his.

But the old lady's thoughts were still on Nicholas. "How like his grandfather he is—indeed, he could be James all over again—but how regrettable that a man of such noble appearance should be such an unprincipled villain."

Venetia moved uncomfortably, clearing her throat and catching Linnet's eye. "Why, I do believe I forgot to tell you something very important."

"You did?"

"Mr. Sheridan's *The School for Scandal* is your favorite play, is it not?"

"Yes."

"And Miss Pope is your favorite actress?"

"She is. Why?"

"Well, it so happens that you can see both tomorrow night at the Theatre Royal. I thought perhaps we could all go together. My private box offers such a splendid close view of the stage."

Linnet smiled. "I'd like that very much."

"Good." Venetia looked at Great-Aunt Minton. "The invitation does, of course, include you."

"Mr. Sheridan's works are not to my liking, Lady Hartley. Besides, after this journey, I shall require a day or so to recover, but I'm sure my niece's presence is all that you really require, and that you, as a widow, can undertake to chaperone her properly for one night."

Benedict sat back, satisfied that for one evening at least he'd enjoy Linnet's company without her great-aunt breathing down his neck. But then his thoughts turned to Nicholas. Damn the man for being there at the very moment they passed by. Pray to God he stayed well away from Linnet from now on.

The carriages reached the bottom of John Street at last, turning right into John Street at the corner by the Berkeley Chapel. Charles Street was one of the few thoroughfares in Mayfair to be solely residential, for nearly all the others possessed a sprinkling of superior shops, from perfumiers and saddlers to circulating libraries and confectioners. All that Charles Street could boast, apart from its handsome lines of brown brick houses, were some taverns, for Mayfair's great houses supported large numbers of menservants, and such numbers had a thirst to quench.

Carlisle House was a plain mansion, set back from the southern side of the street behind a boundary wall and courtyard. A flowergirl was on the pavement outside, her calls carrying clearly into the carriages as they swept through the gateway into the courtyard.

Hearing the hooves, the butler, Sommers, hastened outside to greet his mistress. He was a little elderly now, having long been in Joseph Carlisle's service, and he presented a quaintly old-fashioned appearance, in a gray wig and a full-skirted dark blue coat. His breeches had silver buckles, as did his black shoes, and beneath his white silk stockings, his calves were padded. He hurried to open the carriage door.

"Welcome home, Miss Carlisle. Welcome home."

"Thank you, Sommers." She held her hand out to him, and he assisted her down. "Is all well?"

"It is indeed, madam. The house is ready and aired."

Benedict alighted, turning to help Great-Aunt Minton down, and then Venetia.

Linnet paused, looking at the main door of the house. When last she'd been here, a black wreath and ribbon had adorned the varnished panels, and all the shutters had been closed. The house had been in full mourning for her uncle.

Benedict offered her his arm, and they mounted the steps to the door, going into the great entrance hall, where the floor was tiled in black and white and the walls had been cleverly painted to resemble the palest of green marble. The various doors possessed fine gilded architraves, and there were two sofas placed on either side of the black marble fireplace. At the far end of the hall rose the staircase, parting at a half-landing to rise to the gallery on the floor above. Beyond the staircase, screened by a fine row of Ionic columns, was the entrance to the ballroom, which lay across the rear of the house, and was one of the grandest in London.

The servants were lined up, waiting to greet Linnet and her great-aunt, and as this custom was observed, Benedict and Venetia waited by the fireplace. As the servants dispersed, Great-Aunt Minton instructed Sommers to serve a restorative dish of tea in the drawing room without delay, and then she went up to her room to change, accompanied by her maid.

Linnet went to rejoin Benedict and Venetia. "I can hardly believe I'm back here after so long," she said, looking around the hall.

"Well, you are, you may take my word for it," replied Venetia, smiling. "We won't keep you now, for you must be tired. Is it a firm arrangement for the theater tomorrow night?"

"Yes, of course."

"Good. We'll call for you at about half-past seven." Venetia was about to turn toward the door, when she hesitated. "Linnet, I'd love you to dine with us one night soon. I know you shrink a little from the address . . ."

"I do, rather," admitted Linnet.

"Just think about it, then, and I'll issue a proper invitation soon. For the moment, however, I'll just say *à bientôt, ma petite.*" She quickly kissed Linnet on the cheek, and then hurried out.

Benedict didn't follow immediately, but turned Linnet to face him. "Did it bother you much to see Fane again so quickly?"

"It unsettled me, rather than bothered me."

"If you like, I'll call on him, and . . ."

"No!" she said quickly. "No, that wouldn't do at all. Just leave things as they are."

"If you're sure . . . ?"

"I'm quite sure."

He smiled into her eyes. "I do love you," he whispered.

"And I love you."

Glancing quickly around, and seeing no one in evidence, he pulled her close, embracing her as he kissed her on the lips.

She returned the kiss, slipping her arms around him, but then she drew gently away. "You're keeping Venetia waiting."

"She deserves it, for attempting to make you stay in the back of beyond."

"Don't be ungrateful. She's giving you a roof over your horrid head."

"So she is. Well, maybe I'll forgive her, then." He kissed Linnet's nose. "I'm so glad you're here in London again, for now I won't have to wait an unconscionable time before seeing you again. Roll on tomorrow, even if it does mean watching my sister ogle Coleridge!"

"Benedict, I think you're wrong about her. She made no attempt to see him at Ivystone House."

"Perhaps because she knew I was watching."

"Or because she had no intention of seeing him in the first place. I think you're wrong, and it won't do if you mutter about it tomorrow night at the theater."

"Are you ordering me, Miss Carlisle?"

"Yes, Mr. Gresham, I do believe I am." She smiled. "Until tomorrow, then."

He made to kiss her again, but she resisted. "If Venetia drives off and leaves you to walk back to Fane Crescent, it will serve you right."

Grinning, he pretended to capitulate, walking quickly to the door and out to the waiting carriages. The second carriage, still containing his valet and Venetia's maid, to say nothing of luggage, would accompany the first back to Fane Crescent, and then return to the Carlisle House mews, behind Charles Street.

Linnet didn't watch the carriages leave, but stood alone in the entrance hall, gazing at every remembered corner. She recalled her precipitate flight from the house, before dawn, when she'd hurried down the staircase in her traveling clothes, hardly seeing anything for her tears. Well, all that was behind her now.

She turned to look at the Ionic colonnade by the blue-and-gold ballroom, and began to walk slowly toward it.

At the top of the marble steps leading down to the ball-room floor, was a magnificently decorated archway, and the foot of the steps was flanked by two black-and-gold statues of African princes, each holding aloft a many-branched candlestick. The dance floor itself was surrounded by royal-blue velvet sofas, all at present draped in white cloths. The wall opposite was lined with tall French windows that opened onto the garden terrace, while all the other walls were hung with immense gold-framed mirrors. These mirrors made the ballroom seem much brighter and more spacious than it actually was, reflecting everything from the chandeliers suspended from the golden hipped-roof to the orchestra's ornate apse high on the eastern wall. A number of doors opened off the room, mostly into little antechambers where fires were lit on winter nights to warm the chill feet and hands of the elderly spinsters, dowagers, and assortment of chaperones who always attended balls, but one double door opened into the adjacent conservatory, where breakfast was always served.

The late afternoon sun shone obliquely through the French windows, lying in shafts across the pink-and-white-tiled floor, and the covered sofas looked ghostly. Linnet hesitated for a moment at the top of the steps, then went slowly down, untying her bonnet's ribbons as she went.

Turning back one of the sofa sheets, she sat down, tossing the bonnet beside her. Then she sat back, surveying the great room and remembering balls she had attended there. There had been so many. One on each of her birthdays after the age of seventeen, and one to celebrate her presentation at court, just as there had been one recently at Devonshire House for the presentation of Lord Morpeth's beloved, Lady Georgiana Cavendish. There were always Christmas balls, too, and it had been on just one such festive occasion, the Christmas before last, when she'd first met Nicholas, a recent acquaintance of her uncle's at their mutual club in St. James's.

She'd never forget seeing him for the first time. He'd arrived late, and she'd been dancing with Lord Granville

Leveson-Gower. Nicholas had caught her attention immediately, for he was so breathtakingly handsome and few men could have appeared to better advantage in formal evening attire. The dance had ended, and he'd claimed her from Lord Granville. The next dance had been a ländler, which was possibly the most intimate of the dances at present fashionable, involving the partners facing each other, their arms entwined. She hadn't simply danced that measure with him, she'd floated on air. His touch electrified her, and his piercing blue eyes seemed to gaze right into her soul. She'd loved him straightaway, and had foolishly believed that he'd loved her. Oh, so foolishly.

"Miss Carlisle?" Sommers's voice echoed as he spoke from the top of the steps.

She turned. "Yes?"

"A running footman has just delivered a message for you." He descended to the floor, carrying a little silver salver on which lay a sealed letter.

"An invitation already?" she asked, smiling, but as he lowered the salver her smile faded, for the writing and seal on the letter belonged to Nicholas.

The butler recognized the writing as well, and avoided her eyes. "The footman has instructions to wait for a reply, madam."

Slowly she took the letter, breaking the seal.

Miss Carlisle. Since it seems you've at last deigned to return to London, I feel that sufficient time has now elapsed for us to at least be civil to each other, and since I have matters of considerable importance to discuss with you, I think it advisable that we speak soon. Allowing for your need to rest after such a rigorous journey, I will, unless you send word to the contrary, call upon you tomorrow evening at seven. Fane.

Fane. Miss Carlisle. How formal and remote, when once they'd been so intimate and close. She didn't think they had anything to discuss, for there was nothing left to say, and for a moment she considered telling him to go to perdition, but then she thought better of it. She had to face him sooner or later for they moved in the same circles, and at least if he called the first meeting would be private. Besides, he intended to call at seven, and Benedict and Venetia would call for her shortly after that, thus curtailing the interview.

She nodded at the waiting butler. "Tell the footman I will expect Lord Fane at the time he suggests."

"Yes, madam."

5

It was five minutes to seven, and Linnet paced restlessly up and down in the drawing room. She was alone, for her aunt hadn't emerged from her room all day, having been more than a little wearied by the long journey. In a way, Linnet was relieved, for her aunt's presence would have made the forthcoming interview even more difficult.

Fingering her carved ivory fan, she felt almost sick with apprehension. What did he wish to say to her? He surely didn't imagine they could set the past aside and meet as friends? Oh, if only Benedict were here to give her the support she needed.

Catching a glimpse of her reflection in the great mirror above the fireplace, she paused to inspect her appearance. Tonight she needed to look her very best, her pride wouldn't endure anything less. Her chestnut hair was swept up into a Grecian knot which was fixed with a turquoise-studded comb. A circlet of the same stones lay across her forehead, and there were more in her earrings. Her evening gown was made of the sheerest ivory silk, with a very low-cut square neckline and dainty petal sleeves that fluttered at the slightest movement. Elbow-length fingerless mittens made of ivory lace encased her arms, and there was a knotted shawl, woven in a turquoise-and-gold design, resting lightly around her shoulders. The train of the gown dragged richly behind her, the tiny ivory sequins adorning it sparkling in the early evening light that poured in through the courtyard windows.

It had been another glorious summer day, and the windows stood open, allowing the light breeze to drift refreshingly into the room. The drawing room of Carlisle House was a handsome place, its walls hung with pale-gray brocade, and the furniture was upholstered with plum velvet. There were touches of gold everywhere, and a honeysuckle design that was repeated on the cornices, the architraves, the arms of the chairs and sofas, and around the elegant fireplace.

The ormulu clock on the mantelpiece began to strike the hour, and as it did, Nicholas's dark-blue landau turned into the courtyard, the team of roans stepping high as the coachman drove them toward the house.

Linnet hurried to the windows, glad of the lace drapes that allowed her to look secretly out. The landau's hoods were down, and she saw him stand up to alight. He was dressed formally, and was evidently going on somewhere after seeing her. He stepped down, pausing for a moment to remove his black tricorn hat and tuck it under his arm. He wore a black velvet coat, very tightly cut, white silk breeches, a white waistcoat, and a shirt that was lavishly trimmed with lace. For a moment her thoughts winged back to the Christmas ball, when he'd claimed her for the ländler. There was something compellingly attractive about him even now, and in spite of the destruction of all her foolish illusions, he still had the power to affect her. She wished him in Hades, for he was surely a devil that was going to haunt her for the rest of her days, even though she now loved Benedict. She drew back from the window, for he was approaching the steps to the main entrance of the house.

She moved quickly to a sofa by the fireplace, picking up a book she'd taken at random from her uncle's library. She hadn't bothered to glance at the title, but she did so now, and saw to her dismay that it was a work on the origins and rules of the noble game of cricket!

Steps approached the double doors, and Sommers entered, standing aside to announce Nicholas. "Lord Fane, madam."

As Nicholas came in, she feigned deep interest in the book, closing it at last, as if his arrival had caught her completely unprepared. Her glance was cool, but the palms of her hands were hot. "Good evening, Lord Fane," she said in a tone devoid of cordiality.

"Good evening, Miss Carlisle." He sketched a brief bow, and then came to take her hand, raising it to his lips.

She quickly moved her other hand to conceal the title of the book, but his sharp glance had already perceived it. He straightened, smiling a little cynically. "Cricket? I had no idea you found it interesting."

"You wished to see me, Lord Fane?" She trusted her manner was suitably chill, and that he couldn't see how much he'd already managed to fluster her.

"We're to get immediately to the point? The lakeland air evidently didn't give you an appetite for polite conversation."

"Polite conversation? Very well. How is Radleigh Hall, my lord?" she replied coldly.

"Prospering, thank you. How thoughtful of you to ask."

"I trust Miss Jordan found it to her liking."

"She hasn't had the opportunity to either like or dislike it."

"That isn't what I've been told," she replied, setting the book abruptly aside and rising angrily from the sofa. "If you've come to toy with me, sirrah, you're wasting both our time. What is the purpose of this visit?"

"Well, among other things, I wished to see you again." His glance moved over her. "I prefer you in yellow, but you're looking very well for all that, so perhaps the lakeland air didn't entirely disagree with you."

"The lakeland air proved a sovereign remedy for my malady, sir, and I promise you that I'm fully recovered now."

He smiled a little. "I'm glad to hear it. I take it from your togs that you're sallying forth this evening?"

"I am."

"Let me guess. The theater? Yes, that will be it. The Theatre Royal, to see your favorite actress in your favorite play."

"I'm flattered you remember."

"I remember a great deal about you."

"As I do about you, sirrah, particularly your insincerity and villainy."

He sighed. "You haven't improved after all," he observed dryly.

"Your *belle de nuit* evidently has much to answer for, sirrah, for although she may have convinced you she finds your small talk entertaining, I find it the end in tedium so will you please come to the point of this?"

"My *belle de nuit?* Are you by any chance referring to Miss Jordan?"

"With how many such persons do you consort, my lord?"

"What a very improper question for a lady to ask."

"No doubt you imagine your wit to be the dryest of things," she retorted, turning away.

"It wasn't wit, madam, it was an entirely suitable response to your continuing ill manners. Your conduct a year ago was reprehensible in the extreme, and you seem set to continue in the same vein now you've come back."

She whirled around, her breath catching sharply. "*My* reprehensible conduct?"

"Yes."

"How dare you!"

"How dared *you*, madam. You should not have questioned my actions last year, and if I chose not to dignify your demands with replies, then you have only yourself to blame."

She stared incredulously at him. "I can't believe I'm hearing this," she said then, turning away again. "You said in your note that you have things of importance to discuss."

"We haven't finished about last year yet."

"Oh yes we have. Or are you going to tell me you didn't cheat my uncle out of Radleigh? And that your tawdry Bird of Paradise is a figment of my imagination?"

"I still have no intention of humoring your wounded pride, madam. I just wish you to know that I regard what happened as your fault, not mine."

It was too much. "Please leave immediately," she said, her voice shaking.

She reached for the little bell to summon Sommers, but Nicholas stopped her, putting his hand quickly over hers so that she couldn't take the bell.

"Very well," he said, "I'll come to the point of my visit. When I saw you yesterday, you were in Lady Hartley's carriage. Was Gresham with you?"

She twisted her hand away, turning furiously to face him. "And if he was? What business is it of yours?"

"It's very much my business. So, he *was* with you?"

"Yes."

"And had been to Grasmere?"

"Yes."

"Not for the first time, I know." His eyes were very penetrating. "What is he to you, Linnet?"

"That is none of your concern, my lord," she breathed, her whole body quivering with anger, and with a confusing tumult of other emotions.

Another carriage was arriving outside, and he turned quickly, seeing Venetia and Benedict in Venetia's town barouche. He looked at Linnet again. "Your escorts for the night, I take it. I asked you what he is to you, Linnet, and I would be much obliged if you gave me an answer."

"Why are you so concerned? You made your choice a year ago, my Lord, and what I do now really isn't anything to do with you."

"I'm fast losing patience, madam. What is Gresham to you?"

His tone was flint-sharp, and she drew back a little. "A very close friend," she said.

"How close?"

"Close enough. And that's all I'm going to say." She seized the bell, ringing it loudly. "Please leave, Nicholas, before I have you thrown out."

"Oh, I don't think you need to be so uncivilized, madam," he said softly, "for I intend to leave. I came here tonight to see if you were improved enough to be rational, but that's evidently not the case. What I had to say, therefore, will remain unsaid. For the time being. Good night."

She didn't reply, nor did she look at him as he crossed the room. Sommers opened the doors, standing quickly aside as Nicholas passed.

"You rang for me, Miss Carlisle?"

"Please see Lord Fane to the door, Sommers."

"Yes, madam."

But Nicholas had already gone. As the butler hurried after him, Linnet moved quickly to the window, looking through the nets to see Venetia and Benedict standing in some consternation by their barouche, having recognized Nicholas's landau.

Nicholas emerged from the house, and they turned. He paused to briefly accord Venetia a nod, but he looked right through Benedict. A moment later he was in the landau, being driven swiftly away across the courtyard.

Benedict hurried into the house ahead of Venetia, and Linnet moved from the window, waiting for him to enter the room.

He didn't pause to hand Sommers his tricorn, but came straight into the drawing room, snatching the hat off and tossing it on to a table. He glanced around, and saw that she was alone. "What was Fane here for?" he demanded. "Did he bother you?"

"I'm quite all right, Benedict, and as to what he wanted, well, I have to confess that I really don't know."

"Are you sure he didn't upset you?"

She managed to look composed, but the truth was that she was very upset indeed. She smiled. "Of course he didn't."

He relaxed then, coming quickly over to take her in his arms. "I can't bear to think of him anywhere near you," he whispered, tilting her lips to meet his.

She clung to him, needing his comfort and strength, then she smiled a little ruefully. "Well, at least I've had my first encounter with him."

He drew away. "An encounter that took place when you were alone. Where is your great-aunt? I thought she was determined to protect you from such things."

"She's in her room, still resting after the journey. It isn't her fault, Benedict, for she didn't know anything about it. Nicholas sent a note to me yesterday, and I chose not to say a word to her. I'd be grateful if you'd do the same, for there's no need for her to know he called, it would only bother her."

Venetia spoke from the doorway, where she'd been waiting at a discreet distance. "It's Linnet's prerogative, Benedict, not yours."

Reluctantly he nodded, smiling at Linnet. "Forgive me, I didn't mean . . ."

She stopped his apology by hugging him briefly. Then she turned to survey Venetia, who wore a pale-pink satin gown, a dazzling array of Hartley diamonds, and a Grecian stephane in her dark hair. A white feather boa trailed casually to the floor, and she looked very lovely, the satin of the gown perfectly outlining her figure, but without the sort of impropriety that would have raised eyebrows.

Linnet went to her, taking both her hands. "You look absolutely wonderful."

"And you, you wretch, look divine. I wish more than ever that you'd stayed in the Lake District. Perhaps I won't invite you to dinner after all, for you'll steal all the praise, and when I hold one of my famous dinner parties, *I* like to be the center of attention." Venetia smiled at her, but then looked more serious. "You are sure Nicholas didn't upset you?"

"Perfectly sure. Don't let's talk about him, or it will spoil the evening. Tell me, are we to be a threesome tonight?"

Venetia cast a cross look at Benedict. "No, it seems my dear brother has seen fit to include Freddy Grainger in our party. We're to be joined at the theater, and no doubt the bonds of matrimony will be rattled in my ears again." She tweaked the boa, glancing at the clock. "Isn't it time we left? The streets near the theater always become such a crush on first nights."

Benedict retrieved his tricorn, putting it on, then he turned to his sister. "Venetia, you may speak airily about Freddy's wish to marry you, but he *is* a fine catch, and if he should see you giving glances to that damned hack of a poet . . .''

Venetia's hazel eyes flashed angrily. "I intend to manage my life as *I* see fit, Benedict, and I suggest you stop worrying about my affairs and turn your full attention to your own.'' Turning, she walked away across the entrance hall and out to the waiting barouche.

An awkward silence fell on the drawing room, then he gave Linnet a rather sheepish smile. "*Am* I overstepping the mark?''

"Well, look at it from Venetia's point of view. She's a free agent, her own mistress, and you suddenly come back into her life after years of absence, expecting her to toe *your* line. It's hardly likely to go down well, is it?''

"She should accept Freddy.''

"In your opinion.''

"And in yours, if I'm not mistaken.''

She smiled. "I happen to think she and Freddy would do well together, but I don't make the error of pressing her on the point. Now then, are we going to the theater, or not?''

"We are.'' He offered her his arm. "And I promise to hold my tongue tonight, Coleridge or no Coleridge.''

Linnet said nothing more, and together they emerged from the house to join Venetia in the barouche.

6

The Theatre Royal stood on the corner of Drury Lane and Russell Street, and was the third building to be given the illustrious name, its two predecessors having suffered the fate of so many London theaters, by being burned to the ground. It was an imposing building, with a colonnade, a tall roof pillar surmounted by a statue of Apollo, and rows of windows that made it resemble a barracks.

There was a jam of carriages, for both the play and the leading actress were popular. As the barouche at last drew to a standstill by the main entrance, Linnet prepared for her first encounters with old friends, although she wasn't as nervous as she might have been had it not been for the chance meeting with Lord Morpeth in Barnet. His attitude had gone a long way toward reassuring her.

Benedict alighted, turning to assist both ladies down, and almost immediately they were hailed by a party that had arrived a moment before. It was a group from Devonshire House, and included young Lady Georgiana Cavendish, who was now so much the object of Lord Morpeth's affections, and her elderly great-uncle, Lord Frederick Cavendish, whose penchant for famous actresses of matronly years, Mrs. Siddons in particular, was well known throughout society. It was said that he only attended the theater in order to gaze upon the latest object of his affection, and Linnet could only presume that Miss Pope was at present the apple of his eye. Lady Georgiana was delighted to see Linnet again, and said so in a charmingly shy manner, but Lord Frederick saw no point in saying anything unless one went directly to the heart of the matter. He took one look at Linnet and declared that it was a damned shame about Fane, but that Benedict's frequent visits to the Lake District must surely be interpreted as a sign that there'd soon be a very welcome announcement concerning the future.

Both parties lingered for a while in idle conversation, the gentlemen discussing a forthcoming match between horses owned by the Prince of Wales and the Earl of Sefton, while the ladies discussed Lady Georgiana's recent presentation at court and the subsequent celebratory ball given for her at Devonshire House. Then it was time to go in, and the two groups parted.

Benedict drew Linnet's hand tenderly over his arm. "There, it wasn't so bad, was it? Lord Frederick may have mentioned last year, but it was only fleetingly, and he was much more concerned with trying to draw me into a wager on that horserace."

He turned, offered Venetia his other arm, and they proceeded up the theater steps and into the crowded, glittering vestibule.

There was a terrible press, and a loud babble of refined conversation. Their progress up the staircase was slow, not only because of the sheer volume of people, but also because they knew so many of those they met. Linnet felt more and more at ease, for most people greeted her warmly, with only those who were close friends of Nicholas behaving more coolly. But it was her own friends who mattered, and they were all glad to see her again, so that by the time they were approaching the box, she found herself wishing she'd returned to London long before now. She hadn't realized how much she'd missed the noise and excitement only the capital could provide.

The horseshoe auditorium of the Theatre Royal was delicately beautiful, with a magnificent vaulted Gothic ceiling and an array of handsome chandeliers. It was a vast area, boasting four rows of boxes and eight of those boxes, including Venetia's, were almost directly above the stage.

Freddy Grainger was waiting for them. He was a lanky young man of twenty-nine, with thinning sandy hair, and a freckled face. He was far from handsome, but possessed a winning charm that made him very endearing, and he was so good-natured that he was much turned to by all those friends who needed a shoulder to cry on. Much liked throughout society, his lack of success with Venetia won him a great deal of sympathy, and there were many who, like Linnet, hoped he would triumph in the end.

He was seated in one of the box's crimson velvet chairs, and as Linnet entered, having left the other two outside in conversation with an acquaintance she didn't know, he rose quickly to his feet to greet her.

"Linnet! How glad I am to see you again. You've been away for far too long."

She smiled. "How are you, Freddy?"

"Managing."

"And how is Cornwall?"

"Profiting, at the moment. I wish I could say the same of my endeavors with a certain lady."

"Don't give up."

Freddy took her hands. "Well, I'm sure that in you I have a staunch ally."

"You do indeed."

Benedict and Venetia entered the box at last, and Freddy turned immediately to greet him. He smiled warmly at Benedict. "Good evening, I trust you are well?"

"I am." Benedict returned the smile.

Freddy then turned to Venetia, and as he did so he nervously straightened his white silk waistcoat, a gesture always brought on by having to face the woman he adored to distraction. "Er, good evening, Venetia," he said tentatively.

She nodded coolly. "Good evening, Freddy." Then she calmly took her seat, deliberately looking away across the auditorium to avoid any chance of catching his eye.

Freddy lowered his glance uncomfortably, and Linnet felt desperately sorry for him. Venetia's attitude verged

on the cruel, and it would serve her right if he took his
affections elsewhere, for he deserved better than this.

She sat down in the chair Benedict drew out for her
and glanced again at Venetia's averted face. A year ago,
Venetia wouldn't have dreamed of behaving so ungraciously, but now she did it without hesitation. Was Benedict right? *Had* something occurred at the Holland
House ball? Venetia denied that it was anything to do
with Mr. Coleridge, but did admit that she'd changed her
mind about Freddy that night. Why? What had happened
that had altered her?

Linnet glanced around the dazzling auditorium, taking
note of the occupants of the various boxes, and endeavoring not to look at one box in particular, that usually
taken each season by Judith Jordan. It had always been
the accepted thing for fashionable Cyprians to take boxes
at the theater, so that they could display their charms and
attract the attention of gentlemen. For the moment, however, the box was empty, and Linnet was conscious of a
deep sense of relief. Seeing the Bird of Paradise, with
her eye-catchingly tall plumes and even more eye-
catchingly revealing gowns, would have ruined any enjoyment of this first excursion into society after so long.

After a slight delay, the play commenced, and she settled back to enjoy it. Miss Pope hadn't lost her touch,
although elderly now, and she soon had the audience
laughing at the subtle humor that was so much the mark
of Mr. Sheridan's writing.

As the first act ended, Benedict leaned close to Linnet.
"Coleridge is down there," he whispered. "Do you see
him? To the right, in the very front row of the pit."

She leaned forward a little, and recognized the poet
immediately. He was in his late twenties, with a wide
forehead and long, half-curling dark hair. His eyes were
large, and his eyebrows finely drawn and almost black.
He was dressed well, if not exactly in the very pitch of
high fashion, and there was a pad of paper and a pencil
resting on his lap as he lounged in his seat; evidently, he
was present in his capacity as theater critic for the *Morning Chronicle*. There was an air of *ennui* about him, and

it wasn't at all unbecoming, which forced Linnet to concede anew that the author of the intriguing and rather frightening story of the ancient mariner was a very attractive gentleman.

Benedict eyed the poet. "That fellow has a great deal to answer for, I fancy."

"He may be entirely innocent."

"I think not."

She glanced uneasily past him to where Freddy and Venetia sat. "Hush," she whispered, "or they might hear you."

He gave her a quick smile. "Don't worry, I'm mindful of my promise."

"Good, for I'm holding you to it."

"Not an indiscreet word will pass my lips."

The second act began, and Miss Pope's great talents soon had the theater enthralled again. She stole every scene, and when the intermission arrived, the audience showed its enthusiasm for the actress by stamping, clapping, and calling her nickname. "Popie! Popie!" She made a hurried curtsy in front of the curtain, and then withdrew to prepare for the second half of the performance.

The intermission was always a signal for much coming and going, and the box was soon filled with people. Freddy endeavored in vain to engage Venetia in conversation, but she determinedly excluded him. He sat disconsolately, his eyes downcast, and Linnet felt most dreadfully for him. Then something occurred that convinced her that Mr. Coleridge was indeed the source of his troubles. By the merest chance, she happened to glance at Venetia at the very moment she turned to look down into the pit, directly at the poet. As if he sensed her gaze, he immediately turned his head and rose to his feet. He smiled, and accorded her a gracious bow, then he resumed his seat again. Venetia returned her attention to the people in her box, and the whole incident was over in a second or so, but it set Linnet thinking. Had the exchange of glances been a mere coincidence? Or had there been more to it? The more she thought about it, the more credence she gave to Benedict's suspicions.

Shortly after that the bell rang to signal the end of the intermission, and there was much shuffling, coughing, and whispering as the audience settled to watch the stage again. Linnet prepared to do the same, but then something made her look across at the hitherto empty box belonging to Judith Jordan. Her heart almost stopped, for two people had at that very moment entered to belatedly take their places: one was Judith Jordan herself, the other was Nicholas.

The notorious Cyprian had seldom looked more a bird of paradise, for the striking plumes in her corn-colored hair were tall and magnificent, shimmering with spangles and sequins. She was a curvaceous creature, and her full figure looked as if it had been poured into her low-cut golden silk gown; indeed, as she bent to take the seat Nicholas drew out for her, her creamy bosom threatened to pour itself out again unaided.

There was no question that she was a very beautiful woman. She had large dark-blue eyes and a sweetly formed face, and her lips possessed a permanent pout, as if inviting a kiss. She took her time about arranging the soft folds of her gown, and then sat back a little, wafting a fan that was made of the same magnificent plumes as those in her hair. It moved softly to and fro, its sequins and spangles flashing.

Nicholas sat next to her, and looked directly across at Linnet. He made no acknowledgment, but his glance flickered contemptuously toward Benedict for a moment before he turned his full attention to the stage.

His arrival with the most infamous demimondaine in London hadn't gone unnoticed by certain sections of the audience, nor had the fact that his former love was seated in the box opposite. There were whispers, and raised quizzing glasses, and Linnet felt suddenly on trial. She knew the whispers were about events of the year before, and that there was speculation as to which story was the correct version, hers or Nicholas's.

Benedict knew how she was feeling and his hand crept

to enclose hers. She was glad of the gesture of comfort, and her fingers curled gratefully in his. She didn't intend to give Nicholas the satisfaction of seeing how upset she was by his latest hurtful action, and steadfastly refused to look at the other box again. But inside, hidden from view, she was trembling with pain and anger. When he'd called earlier at Carlisle House, he'd known full well that he was escorting his wretched Cyprian to the same play, but he'd deliberately said nothing. It was just another instance of his callous and cruel disregard for her feelings.

The play proceeded, and Linnet pretended to be engrossed, but in truth her thoughts were of the occupants of the other box. In the end, she gave in to temptation, and looked across; with a jolt, she found herself looking directly into Judith Jordan's coldly speculative gaze. The Cyprian's eyes didn't waver, and her sequinned fan continued to waft softly to and fro in an almost menacing way.

There was immense ill will in that long, chill gaze, and in those few moments, Linnet knew that an invisible gauntlet had been flung down.

7

Linnet looked away first, and almost immediately the Cyprian passed from her mind, because a boxkeeper brought an urgent message for Benedict.

The man came in very discreetly and whispered in Benedict's ear. What he said seemed disturbing, for Benedict looked quickly up at him. "Are you certain?" he demanded in a sharp whisper.

"Yes, sir. They said it was imperative that they see you now."

Venetia looked at her brother. "Is something wrong?" she inquired softly.

"No," he replied, "but I have to slip out to see someone for a moment."

"Who?"

"No one you know."

"Can't it wait?"

"No."

Linnet was becoming concerned, and as he rose to his feet, she touched his hand anxiously. "Are you sure everything's all right?"

He gave her a quick smile. "Quite sure. Don't worry, I won't be long." He followed the boxkeeper out.

Venetia leaned across his empty chair to whisper to Linnet. "What do you think it's about?"

"I have no idea. Venetia, I have a feeling that all is not well."

"Oh, don't worry about him, he's a big boy now," reassured Venetia, tapping her arm with her fan.

Linnet fidgeted a little, turning frequently to look at the box entrance. The final minutes of the play ticked by, and as the curtain fell, rapturous applause broke out, but still Benedict hadn't returned. Miss Pope had been called to the curtain three times before he at last came back into the box. Linnet looked quickly around. His face seemed rather pale, and she was sure he had to fleetingly compose himself before meeting her eyes.

He came to stand by her chair, bending to be heard above the applause. "I'm sorry about that. I hope I haven't spoiled your enjoyment of the play."

"What's wrong, Benedict?"

"Nothing."

"Truly?"

"Truly."

She searched his face. "You seem a little . . ."

"Yes?"

He was smiling at her, but something in his manner precluded further comment, and she fell silent.

Miss Pope couldn't be persuaded to return to the stage for a fourth time, and gradually the applause dwindled away. The orchestra played the national anthem, and then the audience prepared to leave.

Freddy turned to the other three. "I was wondering if we might all go on to Ranelagh? There's a fireworks display at midnight, and they provide a handsome supper . . ."

Venetia coldly snuffed the invitation. "I'm *much* too tired to go on anywhere," she said in a bored tone.

Freddy struggled to hide his disappointment. "Perhaps it was thoughtless to suggest it," he said, preparing to draw her chair out for her.

Linnet pleaded with her. "Oh, Venetia, won't you reconsider? It would be good to go to Ranelagh, and I *know* you like fireworks."

"I don't want to do anything except go to my bed," replied Venetia shortly, rising to her feet, and arranging the boa over her arms.

Linnet was cross with her for again treating Freddy poorly, but knew that now wasn't the time to take her to task. Eventually something would have to be said, however, for it really wasn't necessary to be so hurtful.

Benedict contained his anger with his sister, turning to Linnet to draw out her chair. As he assisted her with her shawl, he whispered a little ruefully, "Unfortunately, now is not the moment to ask a favor of my dear sister, but ask it I must."

"A favor?"

"Yes, a very important one indeed." He faced Venetia. "Sis, would you do something for me? Well, you and Freddy, actually."

Freddy smiled. "Anything to oblige."

But Venetia was suspicious. "I don't trust you when you smile so engagingly, Benedict Gresham. What, exactly, is it that you want me to do?"

"Allow Freddy to drive you home, and leave me to take Linnet back alone."

Linnet was acutely embarrassed. "Oh, Benedict, how *could* you!"

He looked quickly at her. "It's really very important, Linnet. I must speak alone with you, and your great-aunt is mercifully absent."

Venetia shifted uncomfortably. "Yes, she is, and in her absence *I'm* supposed to be the chaperone."

"I wouldn't ask you if it didn't matter a great deal," he pressed. "And is it so very much to ask? If the barouche's hood is raised . . ."

"I will know, so will Freddy, and so will Linnet herself. You're asking her to break the rules, and to deceive her great-aunt. It's wrong of you, Benedict."

Freddy remained tactfully silent, for although he knew that she was right, he also knew that if Benedict had his way, he, Freddy, would have Venetia to himself for a while.

Benedict looked beseechingly at Linnet. "Please tell her that you wish to do as I ask. Forgive me if I've approached this clumsily, but I really do have to speak to you alone."

The boxkeeper's mysterious message came back to her,

and the anxiety returned with it. "Benedict, you'd tell me if there was something wrong, wouldn't you?"

"Most definitely. Nothing is wrong—far from it, in fact. Please, Linnet, just tell my obstinate sister that there's nothing more you'd like than to drive home alone with me."

She smiled, and looked at Venetia, who capitulated with a cross sigh. "Oh, very well, but if this gets out, and Miss Minton breathes fire and brimstone over me, I'll never forgive either of you. However, no doubt I can survive a little singeing. Linnet, I was going to suggest a drive in Hyde Park tomorrow morning . . ."

"I'd like that very much."

"I'll call at the usual time, then. Come, Freddy, act the gallant escort." Giving him a haughty look that warned him not to hope for anything more than a polite farewell at the door of her house, she took his arm and allowed him to walk her from the box.

When they'd gone, Linnet turned reproachfully to Benedict. "I wish you hadn't done this."

"It was a spur of the moment decision," he replied softly, putting his hand to her cheek, "and once made, it was impossible to deny."

"I trust it is indeed as important as you insist."

"Oh, it is, believe me." He raised her hand to his lips. "Shall we leave?"

As she took the arm he offered, she looked briefly across the auditorium at Judith Jordan's box. It was empty.

But if she hoped that she'd seen the last of Nicholas and his Bird of Paradise that evening, she was mistaken, for they were talking to a group of gentlemen near the head of the theater staircase. Linnet's heart sank as she saw them, but at least Nicholas was looking the other way. Judith, however, perceived their approach immediately, and a feline gleam came into her eyes.

She waited until Linnet and Benedict had almost reached the staircase before murmuring something to Nicholas, who immediately drew her hand over his sleeve and prepared to escort her down to the crowded vesti-

bule. It was inevitable that they should all arrive at the
top of the steps at the same moment, just as the Cyprian
intended.

Nicholas saw Linnet at last, and a light passed briefly
through his eyes. He acknowledged her with the faintest
inclination of his head, and then led Judith to descend
first. The demimondaine's train slithered after her, and
the sequins in her plumes and fan sparkled in the light of
the chandeliers. She cast a single mocking glance over
her shoulder, her lips twisting into a taunting smile, then
she swept regally on down.

Linnet hesitated at the top of the staircase, but Benedict made her descend. "Don't let the creature affect you
so, and don't give Fane the satisfaction of knowing he
can so easily reach you."

Linnet endeavored to hold her head high, managing a
smile, and to her relief Nicholas's carriage arrived almost
straightaway, and both he and his odious *belle de nuit*
left. Linnet wasn't at all sorry to see them go.

Venetia's barouche came to the theater steps a few minutes later, and Benedict instructed the coachman to raise
the single hood at the rear. Then, when he and Linnet
were safely inside, their figures mere shadows to any ob-
servers, he ordered the carriage to drive not to Carlisle
House but to Gunter's in Berkeley Square.

The square was lamplit, and there were already a number of carriages drawn up beneath the trees, for it was
very fashionable indeed to enjoy one of Gunter's famous
ices in the comfort of one's private vehicle.

As the barouche drew up, Benedict leaned forward,
looking for a waiter, and one materialized straightaway.

"May I be of assistance, sir?"

"Yes. What ices are you serving tonight?"

"Raspberry, orange, and gooseberry cream ice, and a
very refreshing lemon water ice, sir."

Benedict looked at Linnet. "Which one would you
like?"

"I'm rather fond of gooseberry cream ice," she replied.

He turned to the waiter. "Gooseberry it is, then."

"Sir." The man bowed, and hurried away.

As Benedict sat back again, Linnet glanced at him. "Did you engineer all this simply to ply me with cream ice?"

"No, but you have to admit that such an evening as this does cry out for utter indulgence."

She glanced up at the clear, starlit sky, and then at the other carriages, their panels and harness gleaming in the lamplight. A warm breeze stirred through the plane trees, and a woman laughed somewhere nearby, a light, summery sound that carried clearly. She nodded, smiling at him. "Yes, it *is* a Gunter's night," she agreed.

"And a little spoiling will do you good after having had to endure the Bird of Paradise's unwelcome presence."

Linnet lowered her eyes. "I don't really want to talk about her."

"If not about her, then maybe about Fane himself?"

"No, not about him, either."

He studied her in the dim lamplight. "Linnet, forgive me if I press, but I need to know exactly what Fane means to you."

"He means nothing."

"Are you quite sure?"

"Yes. Benedict, it's all in the past, so why are you . . . ?"

He interrupted. "Because you were obviously very affected tonight when he came in with the Jordan woman."

"I was angry. He knew he was taking her to the theater when he came to see me, and yet he said nothing. At the very least he could have given me the option of crying off, but he preferred to deal me another . . ."

"Blow?"

"Yes."

"I thought you said he didn't mean anything to you any more," said Benedict softly.

"He doesn't."

"Then his actions shouldn't bother you."

She was silent for a moment, and then smiled a little. "Benedict Gresham, my aunt's verbal barbs bother you, but I don't interpret that as meaning you secretly love her.''

He grinned. *''Touché.''*

The waiter returned, bearing aloft a small tray on which lay a silver dish of pale-green ice cream and a spoon. ''Your gooseberry cream ice, madam,'' he said, presenting the tray.

She took the dish, and Benedict put some coins on the tray, then the man withdrew again. Benedict sat back again, watching as Linnet tasted the ice cream. ''I trust it is as good as it looks?''

''Definitely.''

''How long is it since you last did this?''

''Too long.'' She thought for a moment. ''Actually, it was spring last year, and I was with . . .'' She broke off, taking a long breath.

''Fane?''

''Yes,'' she admitted reluctantly.

''The fellow's name crops up with monotonous regularity,'' he observed quietly.

She didn't finish the ice cream, but put the dish and the spoon down on the seat opposite her. ''Yes, his name does seem to be cropping up, so perhaps you'd better tell me what it is that you really wish to discuss.''

He looked away for a moment. ''I think I've handled everything badly so far tonight, so much so that I'm not sure that this is the time to say what I was going to say. I'm afraid I'm still very jealous.''

''Jealous? Of Nicholas?''

''Who else?''

''You have no need.''

''Do you really mean that? I mean, in your heart of hearts?''

''Yes.''

''I love you so much, Linnet, that I can still hardly believe that you're really here in London instead of hundreds of miles away in Grasmere. I like to flatter myself that I am part of your reason for returning south.''

''You know you are.''

He took her hands, his thumbs caressing her palms.

"In a short while I will instruct the coachman to drive to Carlisle House, and there I will take my leave of you. I will return to Fane Crescent and endure the hours until I see you again. Those hours apart will be eternity."

Her fingers curled in his. "It will not be for long, for I'm sure we will see each other at the subscription ball at Almack's tomorrow night."

He smiled a little, his thumbs still moving gently against her palms. "Oh, I'm sure we will, and I'm equally sure that our social calendars crisscross like a game of hopscotch, but it isn't our social calendars that are concerning me, it's our whole lives. Linnet, I love you, and I want to be with you constantly, every day, every week, and every month of every year. I want to marry you, for nothing less will suffice."

She stared at him, her eyes shining in the lamplight from the windows. "And I could want for nothing more," she said softly.

His fingers closed firmly around hers. "You accept?"

"Did you think I wouldn't?"

"I didn't know what to think." He gave a short, incredulous laugh. "You really do accept?"

Smiling, she bent closer, kissing him softly on the lips. "I accept, Mr. Gresham, and I long for the moment when I become Mrs. Gresham."

He swept her into his arms, kissing her passionately on the lips. He crushed her close, as if he feared she would suddenly melt away, and his fingers moved softly in the warm hair at the nape of her neck.

At last he drew away, cupping her face in his hands. "I don't want to wait, I want you to be mine as quickly as possible."

"You surely aren't suggesting an elopement?"

"Why not?"

"Because I don't wish to appear clandestine."

"But elopements are romantic," he pressed.

"And cause a great deal of chitter-chatter. I want it all to be done properly, with a betrothal ball at Carlisle House and then a grand wedding at St. George's. Nothing less than a Hanover Square wedding will do. I want the world and his wife to not only see our happiness, but share it with us.''

"A betrothal ball *and* a St. George's wedding? My sister will be unbearable, and will constantly badger your great-aunt for a hand in all the arrangements. She has great ambitions as a hostess, and *recherché* dinner parties are no longer enough. She's long been pining to organize a ball, and has had her scheming eye upon your ballroom.''

"I know, and I'm sure my great-aunt will be only too delighted to allow her to attend to the arrangements. I fear my lady relative loathes being the hostess, and won't relish the thought of arranging anything as large as a ball.'' Linnet spoke lightly, but inside she had grave reservations concerning Great-Aunt Minton's reaction to the betrothal. It was true that the old lady didn't like being the hostess, but it was also true that she didn't approve of either Benedict *or* Venetia. Still, that was a bridge to cross when it was reached, and not at this wonderful moment when she, Linnet Carlisle, was utterly happy for the first time in what seemed an age.

Benedict still cupped her face in his loving hands. "If you want a betrothal ball and a St. George's wedding, then have them you shall. All I ask is that both take place as soon as possible, for I cannot bear to be apart from you any longer than absolutely necessary. Will you promise me that?''

"Willingly.''

"Weeks, not months?''

She nodded, and he kissed her again, an ardent kiss that was warm and tender, and as she gave herself to the moment, she knew her happiness lay with this man, whose strength and comfort had helped her through the misery of the past twelve months.

But as her lips parted beneath his, the past was all around her, and for the space of a heartbeat, she thought she heard Nicholas's low, mocking laughter.

8

The journey from Grasmere had evidently taken a great deal out of Great-Aunt Minton, who did not put in an appearance at the breakfast table in the conservatory the following morning, and so the awful moment of telling her about the betrothal to Benedict was put off for a little while. Linnet returned to her room to change for her drive with Venetia, and then sat at her dressing table while Mary combed and pinned her hair.

Her bedroom was a very feminine chamber, with pink-and-white floral oriental silk on the walls, and deep pink draperies at the two tall windows overlooking the courtyard. The four-poster bed was hung with white brocade, ornate and gold-fringed, and the coverlet was made of ruched pink taffeta. There was a white marble fireplace, screened by a panel of tapestrywork Linnet had made as a child, and a mantelpiece on which stood a glass-domed clock of some antiquity, two pairs of silver-gilt candlesticks, and a number of miniatures, including likenesses of her parents and Uncle Joseph. A handsome gilt-framed mirror graced the chimney breast, and there were two comfortable chairs, upholstered in golden velvet, standing on either side of the polished brass fender.

The dressing table stood against the wall between the two windows, to catch the best of the light. It was a fine piece of furniture beneath its covering of frilled white muslin, and its top was cluttered with all the paraphernalia so necessary to a young woman of fashion. There was a triple mirror, several more silver-gilt candlesticks, an array of trinket boxes, scent bottles, pin dishes, phials, cosmetics, and combs, two hairbrushes, and a T-shaped stand over which Linnet's many ribbons were draped. The colorful lengths of silk and satin fluttered a little in the light draft that crept beneath the raised window sashes, and the rattle of a carriage was heard as it drove slowly along Charles Street toward Berkeley Square.

Linnet was looking forward to the drive in Hyde Park with Venetia, for they would have so much to talk about this morning. She'd elected to wear a cherry muslin gown and matching full-length pelisse, and when her hair was finished, a straw gypsy hat would be tied on with the ribbon she was idly rolling and unrolling in her hands. It was one of the ribbons she'd had made, white silk with a pattern of her namesake bird, and she'd spent several minutes selecting it from the dressing table stand.

She glanced at Mary in the mirror. The maid was busy twisting her long chestnut hair into a knot, and then stretching forward to select some pins from the dish on the dressing table. She was a small person, very neat and clean, with a wide-mouthed face and attractive brown eyes, and when she spoke her voice had an Irish brogue that told of her Dublin origins. She was in Linnet's employ because her father had been Joseph Carlisle's head groom at Radleigh, and her mother the housekeeper, and when they'd moved on to grander things, lured to the Duke of Devonshire's employ at Chatsworth, Mary had elected to remain with Linnet, whom she loved very much.

Feeling Linnet's glance upon her in the mirror, Mary paused in her work, smiling at her mistress. "It's good to see you so happy again, Miss Linnet."

"Thank you, Mary."

"It's a fine thing that Mr. Gresham has done, bringing the roses to your poor cheeks after so long." The maid hesitated, and then spoke a little boldly, "You *are* sure about him, aren't you?"

Linnet was a little surprised. "Yes, of course I am. Why do you ask?"

"Because of Lord Fane. I know he made you cry, but you loved him so very much, and . . .''

"That's just it, Mary, I *loved* him."

"And now you love Mr. Gresham as much?"

"Yes." But Linnet looked away from the mirror. She loved Benedict, but it wasn't the same, not even now that she'd accepted his proposal.

A few moments later the gypsy hat was in place, and the ribbon tied in a big, flouncy bow beneath her chin. Mary was just handing her her gloves, reticule, and parasol, for Venetia would call at any moment, when Great-Aunt Minton at last put in an appearance; and a very disapproving, condemnatory appearance it was, too.

The old lady came into the room without announcement. Her gray hair hung in plaits down her back, and her head was encased in a frilled night-bonnet that was somewhat crumpled. She wore a nightgown beneath a green brocade wrap, and she'd evidently come straight from her bed.

Linnet turned in surprise, for it wasn't like her aunt to dispense with ceremony, nor was it like her to abruptly dismiss Mary, but this is precisely what she did.

"Leave us, girl," she commanded, waving the startled maid away.

Mary hurriedly put down the comb and pins, and gathered her skirts to almost run from the room.

Linnet rose slowly from the dressing table. "Whatever is it, Great-Aunt?" Had her unchaperoned return last night been detected?

"I'm very angry with you, my girl, very angry indeed. I do not appreciate hearing important news via the servants!"

"Oh." Linnet realized then that it wasn't her return alone with Benedict that was the cause of her aunt's wrath, but that Mary must have told the other servants about the betrothal.

"Well? What have you to say for yourself, missy? Is it true that you've been coerced into accepting the execrable Mr. Gresham?"

Linnet drew herself up. "Benedict is not execrable, nor has he coerced me into anything."

"But you *have* accepted him?"

"Yes."

Her great-aunt exhaled heavily, going to sit in one of the fireside chairs. "That was very unwise of you, Linnet, very unwise indeed."

"I don't agree."

"That much is patently obvious. I'm sorry, my dear, but I think he is a scoundrel, bent only upon acquiring your fortune."

"You think wrongly."

"Do I? Tell me, is it true that the betrothal *and* the wedding are to take place with indecent haste?"

"They are to take place quickly, but not with indecent haste," said Linnet a little stiffly.

"Why? What possible need is there for such a rush?"

"We just wish to be together. Is that so very strange?"

Her great-aunt's eyes were shrewd and bead-bright. "Would it be more correct to say that Mr. Gresham is the one to be anxious for an early celebration?"

Linnet lowered her eyes. "He does, but . . ."

"But nothing. I am still firmly of the opinion that he is pursuing you because his purse is uncomfortably thin. He may claim to have made his fortune in India, but I'm a little uneasy about his seemingly never-ending financial and legal problems. Since arriving in town he's lived off his sister, and hasn't made any move to find himself somewhere else to reside—unless, of course, his calculating eye is upon this house, which would indeed suit his pretensions to be one of London's finest gentlemen. Believe me, Linnet, he's seeking to emulate his sister, who made a very advantageous marriage, thus lifting herself considerably in society. The Greshams are nothing, merely inconsequential country squires, and I'm sure that pretty Mr. Benedict thinks that what is sauce for the Gresham goose, is most definitely sauce for the gander as well. Delay this betrothal, I beg of you. Give yourself time to think."

"I've had time to think."

"Ah yes, a year in Grasmere," replied her great-aunt caustically.

"Yes."

"During which period Mr. Gresham made a timely appearance."

"Timely? Why do you say it like that? He merely accompanied Venetia when she pressed him. She doesn't like traveling alone."

"Is that what he told you?"

"Yes."

"Then I suggest you speak to Lady Hartley on the matter, for she told me that it was *he* who pressed to do the accompanying. Now why, I ask myself, would a gentleman go to such trouble merely to accompany his sister on a tedious visit to a friend he doesn't know? Methinks the pounds, shillings, and pence of the situation were the be-all and end-all of his actions, and if you've any sense left, you'd admit that there's at least a chance that I could be right."

"You wrong him."

"Delay the betrothal."

"No. Forgive me, Great-Aunt, but I've given my word to Benedict that things will be done as quickly as possible, and I see no reason to renege on that promise. I love him, and I'm seeing him again tonight when he and Venetia escort me to the subscription ball at Almack's."

"Very well, since you will not be moved on the matter, there's nothing I can do about it. I may be your elder and better, but I don't have jurisdiction over your life. If I did, make no mistake that I'd forbid the match completely and under those circumstances, I've no doubt that the hard-pressed bridegroom-to-be would urge you to elope with him, *anything* to get his grasping hands upon your fortune as quickly as possible."

Linnet didn't reply, remembering uncomfortably that he had indeed seemed to favor an elopement; but it had only been in jest, not in seriousness.

Her great-aunt rose and went to the door, pausing there to look back at her. "Given my opinion of the prospective bridegroom, and my dislike for arranging social functions, I'm sure you will understand if I do not play a prominent part in the forthcoming ball, or, indeed, of the subsequent wedding. Besides, I have no doubt that Lady Hartley will leap at the chance. I will not embarrass you by making my displeasure public, it is my earnest hope that something will happen to prevent this betrothal from taking place, and if I should discover anything about Mr. Gresham that will convince you of the error of your ways, then I will most certainly face you with it.'' She went out, leaving the door open behind her, so that Linnet could hear her steps fading away.

Linnet stared after her. She'd known that her great-aunt disliked Benedict and Venetia, but not that the dislike went quite so deep. She roused herself then, for she could hear Venetia's barouche in the courtyard. With a heavy heart, she began to put on her gloves, and then took up her reticule and parasol before leaving the room. A little of the shine had been rubbed from her happiness, but she hoped that her great-aunt would come around.

None of the shine had been rubbed from Venetia's happiness, however, for that lady was quite obviously overjoyed by the news. She hurried into the entrance hall, her bluebell silk gown bright in a shaft of sunlight. Her gray hat was set at a jaunty angle, and she was twirling her fringed pagoda parasol. She came to meet Linnet at the foot of the staircase, seizing her hand and almost laughing with pleasure.

''Oh, I'm so delighted! I've been longing for you and Benedict to marry, and now it's going to happen! I've always thought of you as more my sister than just my friend, and soon you really will be!'' She drew back, her eyes shining. ''And Benedict said that I might be able to help with the arrangements. Is that true?''

Linnet smiled. ''Yes. My great-aunt is quite prepared to leave it all up to you.'' Oh, how prepared.

''Really? How absolutely wonderful! I've already got so many ideas for the ball *and* the wedding that I shall not know where to start!''

Linnet glanced back up the staircase, and then linked Venetia's arm. ''Let's go, and we can drive around and

around Hyde Park while you tell me about all these won-
drous ideas.''

Venetia hadn't missed the glance. ''Is there a little
more to your great-aunt's willingness to let me do the
arranging than you've said?''

''A little,'' admitted Linnet reluctantly. ''She disap-
proves of the match.''

''Well, she has made her opinion of Benedict a little
plain, has she not?''

''Yes. Still, I'm sure she'll come around in the end,''
said Linnet, with more optimism than she really felt.

''Yes, of course she will,'' soothed Venetia, and together they left the house to enter the waiting barouche,
which had its hood down because of the sunshine. Venetia settled back, her parasol twirling again. ''Why is
your great-aunt so against poor Benedict? He's been a
positive angel.''

''I know he has.'' Linnet didn't want to tell the truth,
for Venetia would be deeply offended if Great-Aunt Minton's outright accusations about fortune-seeking were
voiced.

''Why doesn't she like him?'' pressed Venetia.

''I think it's simply a clash of personalities,'' replied
Linnet tactfully.

The barouche drove off across the courtyard, turning
west into Charles Street, in the direction of Hyde Park.
Reaching Park Lane, it turned north, entering the park
through Grosvenor Gate, where a number of other carriages were arriving and leaving. There were riders, too,
for it was very much the thing to show off one's equestrian skills in London's most fashionable area of open
land, especially in the melée of Rotten Row. Inexperi-
enced or indifferent riders made use of the Gloucester
Riding House, just inside Grosvenor Gate, where expert
tuition could be received in the handling of the spirited
blood horses that were *de rigueur* in the superior circles
of London society.

As the barouche passed through the gate, coming up
to a smart pace across the park, the contretemps with
Great-Aunt Minton faded a little, and Linnet prepared to

enjoy the drive. She had little idea that before the circuit of the park was complete she would again encounter Nicholas, or that shortly after that, she would be forced to speak to the Bird of Paradise herself.

9

Hyde Park was renowned for its trees, many of them laid out in fine avenues. There were oaks, chestnuts, and elms, and they cast leafy shadows over the ground where the *beau monde* sallied forth on display.

As the barouche bowled along south and then west in the wake of a landau containing four rather superior matrons, Venetia smiled at Linnet. "Benedict would have moved heaven and earth to come with us today, but I refused to countenance it. I told him we had a great deal to discuss, and that he'd be a definite hindrance. He was quite a sulky bear when he couldn't have his way, but he was a little consoled when I reminded him that it wasn't all that long until he'd see you tonight at Almack's."

"How hard-hearted you are."

"I'm not hard-hearted, I'm practical. Men are absolutely useless when it comes to organizing social occasions; the only events to which they apply themselves with any success are horse races, hunts, prize fights, and wars." Venetia gave a philosophical sigh. "They're really exceeding tiresome creatures, but it's our lot not to be able to go on without them."

Linnet eyed her, deciding that this was an opening for the subject of Freddy Grainger to be raised. "You certainly seem to be able to go on without them at the moment," she observed, "or, at least, you seem prepared to run that risk."

Venetia stopped twirling the parasol. "You're referring

to Freddy, I suppose.'' It was a statement, not a question.

''Yes. I thought you were very unkind to him last night.''

''I don't ask him to dance such excessive attendance on me,'' replied Venetia a little testily.

''His conduct was hardly excessive, but I rather thought yours was. If you find him that abhorrent, you should let him know, and put an end to his hopes. I felt very sorry for him, for he really didn't deserve to be treated like that.''

Venetia looked resentful for a moment, and Linnet thought she was going to take offense, but then a contrite expression entered the lovely hazel eyes. ''I suppose I *was* a little harsh.''

''You were.''

''In fact, I was a downright *chienne*, was I not?''

''Well, now you come to mention it . . .'' Linnet smiled.

Venetia sighed. ''Oh, I know I was horrid, and I'm sorry. I wish I could make my mind up about him, but I just can't. I really meant to accept him that night at Holland House, but . . .'' Her voice died away.

''What really happened that night, Venetia?'' prompted Linnet, anxious to find out in order to be able to help, if she could.

''Nothing.''

''Oh, come on! *Something* happened, otherwise you'd have given Freddy the answer he wanted. Instead, you virtually cut him, and made him utterly miserable.''

Venetia met her gaze. ''Nothing happened, and if you think I'm still hiding an affair with Mr. Coleridge, you can put the notion from your head, for it simply isn't so. I promise not to treat Freddy so badly in the future—indeed, I'll do my utmost to behave properly. Will that do?''

Linnet thought there was an edge to the other's voice, and knew there was still something that wasn't being said, but she smiled. ''Yes, it will do.''

''Good. Now, can we discuss something else? Like the

betrothal ball, for instance? First, and most important of all, what are you going to wear?''

Linnet had to laugh. ''That's the most important item on your agenda?''

''My dear girl, the clothes one's rivals wear are of the utmost consequence. You'll be the belle of the ball, and rightly so, but I wish to shine just a little, too. So, what are you going to wear on the night?''

''I hadn't even begun to think.''

''Then think.''

Linnet pursed her lips, mentally going through her considerable wardrobe. A year of exile in Grasmere had meant she hadn't ordered any gowns for the new season, and since the ball was going to take place as quickly as possible, there wouldn't be time to have one made now. She'd have to wear something she already possessed.

Venetia waited impatiently. ''Have you got so many to choose from?''

''Stop bullying me,'' protested Linnet, smiling suddenly as she remembered a gown she had never worn, and which was perfect for the occasion. ''I believe I know the very thing,'' she said tantalizingly.

''Yes? What?'' Venetia sat forward intently.

''I don't know that I should tell you.''

''You beast! How am I to manage if I don't know how you're going to turn out? Tell me, or I'll throttle you!''

''Oh, all right. Just before I left London, Madame Leclerc made me a gray lace gown with a gray taffeta petticoat.''

Venetia looked pinched. ''A Leclerc? Plague take you, Linnet Carlisle. And I suppose you'll wear your disgustingly beautiful rubies with it?''

''Yes.''

''I think I hate you. I'll sink without trace.''

''You've never sunk without trace in your life,'' replied Linnet dryly.

Venetia gave a sleek smile. ''I do my modest best.''

''By the look in your eyes, you have the very thing to demolish me.''

"Well, I would not go so far as to say *that*, but I think I shall be able to hold my head up. Just."

"The primrose silk you boasted about a few months ago?"

"Yes. Now, then, on to other matters. We must pick a date, and do so with great care, for there's so much going on at the moment that we might clash awkwardly with something important. We don't want to forfeit some of the more prestigious guests, do we? I've consulted my diary at great length, and it seems to me that two weeks Friday is ideal."

"Isn't that cutting it a little fine? Invitation cards have to be printed, and sent out . . ."

"I've thought of all that. It may be rather imminent, but it's miraculously free. I heard a whisper last night that Lady Lydney will have to postpone her rout, which was scheduled for the same date, so we'll be sure of an excellent attendance. I took the liberty of calling at Higgs's, the printers in John Street, on my way to you this morning, and they can commence printing the cards straightaway. I told them we'd need at least four hundred and fifty."

Linnet was startled. "Venetia, this is a mere betrothal ball, not a state occasion!"

"It's not a *mere* betrothal ball, it's *the* betrothal ball, and as far as I'm concerned it's as important as any state occasion. I don't want to have fewer than four hundred guests, for any less would be considered thin for a prominent social occasion, and since there are bound to be refusals, and absences, we'll need extra invitation cards."

"Yes, but four hundred . . ."

"We're going to eclipse Lady Georgiana Cavendish's wishy-washy do at Devonshire House, and *they* had three hundred and fifty."

"Wishy-washy? I understood it was very lavish, and very successful."

"In my opinion it was eminently forgettable, but it still seems to be this year's yardstick."

Linnet smiled a little. "All I can say is that I'm glad I

don't have aspirations to be one of London's leading host-
esses.''

"My dear, you'd never find the stamina, tenacity, or
the sheer determination,'' retorted Venetia. "I'm going
to outshine Devonshire House, and that's the end of it.
The only thing they did well that night was to have Gunter's to provide the supper, the rest of the business was
atrocious. The floral decorations were meager and a
hodgepodge of colors, and as to the music, well, it was
a caterwauling cacophany to which it was impossible to
dance.''

Linnet had to laugh. "They do say that sarcasm is the
lowest form of wit.''

"Sarcasm? Darling, I thought I was being generous,''
replied Venetia wickedly. "So, it has to be Gunter's for
the ball supper, but I have some very novel ideas for the
floral decorations and the music. There's a new German
orchestra, Herr Heller's Ensemble, and they're really excellent. They haven't been long in England, and I heard
them when I was a guest at Althorp last month. They
were playing something grim by Bach, as I recall, but I
couldn't help thinking how excellent they'd be at a ball,
playing something more agreeable, like Mozart. If they
played at your ball, I know they'd soon become the rage,
and *I* would be credited with having discovered them.''

"Quite a feather in your hostess cap,'' remarked Linnet.

"Oh, *definitely*,'' purred Venetia, sleek with gloating
anticipation. "Another feather is going to be my sheer
brilliance with the floral decorations.''

"Your modesty amazes me,'' murmured Linnet, grinning.

"One has to have the courage of one's ambitions, my
dear, and when you hear my ideas, you'll know I'm jus-
tified in bragging. As I said, at Devonshire House they
had a few of every flower under the sun, but I plan to
have just red roses, thousands of them. The red rose is
the emblem of the Gresham family, did you know?''

"No, I have to confess that I didn't.''

"It's rather like a four-petaled Tudor rose, but since

I'm hardly likely to find the exact bloom, I'll settle for any red roses. I want them to be garlanded everywhere, and to hang from ceiling baskets, but most of all I want them to form an immense column in the center of the ballroom floor. At the top of the column, soaring out like the spokes of a horizontal wheel, there are to be silver unicorns.''

''Carlisle unicorns? But the viscountcy of Carlisle has been extinct for . . .''

''What does that signify? The unicorn is still associated with you. To continue, then, at the stroke of midnight, when Benedict places the ring on your finger, the unicorns will fly down on ribbons, releasing a flock of linnets from a cage hidden inside the column. There, what do you think?'' Venetia sat back, her eyes shining expectantly.

''It all sounds very dramatic.''

Venetia detected a note of reservation. ''What's wrong?''

''Well, I like everything, except the business with the linnets. I hate seeing birds caged.''

Venetia was silent for a moment, then she smiled. ''Well, think of it this way. The poor little things will have been caught and caged before we purchase them, but when they fly out into the ballroom, they will be gaining their freedom. We can have all the French windows open so that they can fly out into the garden, where the trees will all be hung with lanterns, and they can hide in the branches until daylight. How does that sound?''

''Persuasive.''

''Good. Do I have *carte blanche* to proceed with everything?''

''You do.''

''Excellent. Oh, I can hardly wait to begin. By the way, about the guest list . . .''

''Yes?''

''If you could give your side of it some thought, and then let me know? We can confer later this week.''

''All right.''

"There are bound to be some names we'll wish to exclude."

"One name, anyway," replied Linnet.

"Nicholas?"

"Who else?"

"Well, I suppose that's understandable." Venetia smiled, twirling her parasol again. "Right, I think that's the most we can discuss about the ball for the moment, so let's move on to the wedding itself."

Linnet was appalled. "One thing at a time, please. I really don't want to discuss the wedding before the ball is over and done with."

"Oh, but . . ."

"No! Let's just enjoy the rest of the drive."

"A drive is a drive, and it's only Hyde Park," protested Venetia.

"I happen to like Hyde Park, and this is the first time I've been here for more than a year."

Venetia gave a heavy sigh. "All that lakeland air has affected you, and not beneficially. The sooner you become reaccustomed to the crush of stuffy drawing rooms, the better." But she refrained from saying anything more about wedding arrangements, and the barouche bowled on around the park, turning to drive northward as it followed the wide track.

The Serpentine glittered to their right, and the walls of Kensington Palace rose to the left. The breeze stirred through the branches of a great oak tree as they passed, and the easy thud of hooves carried as a party of gentlemen rode across the drive ahead. Sunlight glinted on harness and carriage panels as the endless procession of elegant vehicles followed the time-honored route around the park, and everywhere there were riders, both male and female.

Ahead, on the shores of the Serpentine, there stood a little classical rotunda where one could sit in comfort to watch the water. A nurse was inside, with two small boys, one of whom was crying because his paper kite had become entangled in the overhanging branches of a nearby tree. There was nothing the nurse could do, for the kite was too high for her to reach, and the little boy was inconsolable, his sobs audible as the barouche approached.

The child's distress hadn't gone unnoticed, for one of the gentlemen who'd ridden by a moment before reined in and turned his mount, riding back toward the rotunda.

At first Linnet hardly noticed him, she was too intent upon the little boy, but then she glanced at the horseman. He rode a magnificent Arab horse, and was accompanied by two rust-colored greyhounds; it was Nicholas.

The barouche was slowing down, for there was a crush ahead, and came to a standstill right alongside the rotunda. Linnet watched as Nicholas stretched up in his stirrups to retrieve the kite. He looked immaculate, in a sage-green coat and cream kerseymere breeches. His face was in shadow from the brim of his top hat, and the breeze fluttered the loose folds of his unstarched neckcloth. There were golden spurs on the heels of his top boots, but they were purely decorative, for he had no need of such aids to improve his already superb horsemanship. He controlled the mettlesome horse with consummate ease, disentangling the kite and handing it down to the delighted child.

Venetia had noticed Nicholas as well. "Oh, dear, I do hope he doesn't see us."

But it was a vain hope, because he suddenly looked directly at the barouche. For a moment it seemed he would ride away without acknowledging them, but then he urged the horse toward them.

Linnet's heart sank, but quickened its beats at the same time. Her mouth seemed suddenly dry, and she strove to appear entirely unconcerned as he reined in beside her.

"Good morning, Miss Carlisle. Lady Hartley." He removed his hat.

Venetia inclined her head. "Lord Fane."

Linnet met his eyes. "Good morning, sir."

"I trust you enjoyed the theater last night?"

"I did indeed," she replied smoothly. "I don't think I've ever enjoyed the play more."

A faint smile touched his lips, and his gaze seemed to see right through her. "I'm glad to hear it."

Venetia sat forward suddenly. "There is something else you will no doubt be glad to hear, my lord. Miss Carlisle is soon to be betrothed to my brother. The news will be all over town after Almack's tonight."

His eyes hardened, the clear blue becoming chill as he continued to look at Linnet. "Indeed?" he murmured.

"Is it not excellent news?" declared Venetia, watching him closely.

"It's news, and that's about all I can say of it," he replied, his gaze not wavering from Linnet's face. "How reticent you were yesterday when I asked you a question on that very subject."

Venetia seemed determined to press the point. "Aren't you going to offer your congratulations, sir?"

His glance flickered toward her. "No, madam, I am not," he said coldly, turning his impatient horse and urging it swiftly away.

Linnet swallowed, aware of how she was trembling, and Venetia turned to watch him as he rode swiftly to rejoin his companions, who'd waited some distance away. Her eyes were thoughtful. "How gracious he was," she murmured.

Linnet didn't deign to give him a backward glance, for fear that he'd turn and see. "You surely didn't expect him to be otherwise, did you?"

"I was curious to see his reaction."

"I trust it was worth the effort," replied Linnet.

"Oh, it most certainly was."

Linnet leaned out, to try to see what was holding up the line of carriages, and when she saw the reason, her heart sank yet again.

A rather showy white landau, its hoods down, had negotiated a very difficult turn right in the middle of the drive, forcing everyone else to stop until it had completed the maneuver. The team of two creams had ostrich plumes springing from their heads, like the performing horses at Astley's Amphitheatre, and the coachman was clad in white livery, braided with gold. It was a vehicle that was very well known in London, for it belonged to Judith Jordan.

The Cyprian was seated inside on the sumptuous white velvet seat, and with her was her pet white poodle, wearing a jeweled collar. The theme of virginal white was a favorite with the Bird of Paradise, for she was well aware of how it infuriated the ladies and amused the gentlemen. It suited her, though, for with her cloud of golden curls, she looked quite angelic. Today she wore a full-length pelisse, with a very low neckline that revealed the flawlessness of her lovely throat and the alluring curve of her bosom. The impression given was that she didn't have a gown on underneath, which was probably quite true. The only splash of other color she wore apart from white was the brilliant fuchsia-pink of the plumes that streamed from her cheeky little hat.

Linnet watched her as the white landau progressed closer. Whatever else one thought of London's most notorious demimondaine, one had to concede that she had both beauty and style. Every eye was upon her as she drove by, and yet she glanced neither to the right or the left but sat facing the front, fondling the ears of the devoted poodle.

Venetia watched her rather sourly. "No doubt the creature imagines herself to look good," she murmured, "when the truth is that she is ridiculous."

"Is she? I vow that if *I* were such a famous demirep, I'd deck myself out like that," replied Linnet astutely.

Venetia glanced at her in surprise, but then said nothing more because the Cyprian had observed the barouche and its occupants, and leaned forward to order her coachman to draw up alongside.

Still stroking the poodle, the Bird of Paradise gave Venetia a cursory glance, but then looked directly at Linnet. "Good morning, Miss Carlisle. I understand betrothal congratulations will soon be in order?"

Linnet was nonplussed, not only that the Cyprian had the audacity to address her, but also that she somehow knew about the betrothal.

Judith smiled faintly, but her eyes were as cold as they'd

been at the theater the night before. "News travels, Miss Carlisle, and there is very little one can do about it."

"Your interest in my affairs is flattering, Miss Jordan, but of no consequence at all to me."

The carriages ahead were beginning to move again, and in a moment the barouche and landau would separate. The Cyprian's dark-blue eyes remained chill. "I will bid you farewell for the moment, Miss Carlisle, but I haven't done with you yet, believe me." She nodded at her waiting coachman, who urged the team of creams on.

The carriages drew apart, and Linnet had to turn to look back at the retreating landau. She was both stunned and angry. Why was Judith Jordan so very interested in her? And how had she found out about the betrothal?

10

The following morning, Linnet sat on her own at the breakfast table in the sun-filled conservatory. Exotic plants grew all around her, their leaves pressing against the glass, and the smell of citrus and damp earth hung in the air. The French windows stood open to the terrace at the rear of the house, and beyond the stone balustrade surrounding it she could see the lawns and trees of the garden, as well as the mews lane and the rear of the houses in adjacent Curzon Street. She could hear the servants attending to the lowering and polishing of the chandeliers in the ballroom next to the conservatory, and see them through the open doorway.

She sat back in her wrought iron chair, sipping a cup of coffee as she waited for her great-aunt. Her dark-red hair was brushed loose, and tied back with a pale-blue ribbon, and she wore a simple, long-sleeve white muslin gown. A blue cashmere shawl was draped over the back of the chair, and a journal rested unopened on her lap. Her thoughts were all of Benedict, and of how happy she'd been at Almack's the night before. Every moment spent with him served to reinforce her certainty that he was right for her. There was such strength and reassurance in his company, and no one else could make her smile as he did. He was amusing, adoring, attentive, and considerate; what other quality could she possibly seek in order to be assured of happiness?

In the ballroom, Sommers was a little tetchy, for one of the chandeliers was refusing to lower to the floor. He

raised his voice a little, sending two footmen scurrying
to steady the immensely tall stepladder, at the top of
which a third footman was endeavoring to free the chain
from which the chandelier was suspended, and which
should, under normal circumstances, have lowered quite
freely. Linnet replaced her cup on the table, smiling a
little as she watched the work in progress, then she
opened the journal to glance through it for a moment or
two until her great-aunt joined her.

Cadogan's Exhibition of Arts was a monthly periodical
dealing with furnishings and furniture, dress, carriages,
and all the trappings of superior living, and it was Linnet's favorite reading matter, offering hours of interesting
browsing. As she turned one of the pages, her gaze fell
upon a very inviting advertisement. It was by Messrs
Harding, Howell & Company, of Schomberg House, Pall
Mall, one of the most exclusive shops in London. Actually, it was many shops in one, with separate departments
dealings with haberdashery, gloves, fans, millinery, perfume, *objets d'art,* furniture, and fabrics, and there was
even a fine tea room on the second floor, with a magnificent view to the rear over St. James's Park. The advertisement announced a new delivery of fine woolen cloth
from the royal merino flock at Windsor, which was sold
only at Schomberg House. Linnet had purchased the cloth
before, and knew it to be excellent, and she immediately
resolved to call there that very morning to examine the
new delivery.

Her great-aunt came in at last, looking very cool and
fresh in a mint-green lawn gown. Her powdered hair was
pinned up beneath a starched white biggin, and there was
a white shawl over her shoulders. "Good morning, Linnet," she said crisply, moving to the side table set with
the domed silver breakfast dishes.

"Good morning, Great-Aunt," responded Linnet,
placing the journal to one side and getting up to select
her own breakfast. As she joined her great-aunt, she
wondered what sort of reception she was going to have
because of her continuing determination to be betrothed
to Benedict.

The old lady selected a plate of eggs, bacon, and tomatoes, and then went to sit down. Linnet contented herself with a poached egg and some toast, and then resumed her own place.

Her great-aunt eyed the poached egg. "One has to eat in order to keep body and soul together," she observed.

"I'm not terribly hungry."

"So it seems. May I inquire why?"

"I don't have a particularly hearty appetite."

"It seemed hearty enough at Ivystone House." Great-Aunt Minton applied herself to a sausage, and then looked at her again. "Too many late nights will not do you any good. You've been back here for three days, and already you've spent more time out than in. I suppose I have Mr. Gresham to blame?"

Linnet was determined not to be drawn. "If I'd wished to return to my bed, I was quite at liberty to do so," she replied truthfully.

"But you chose not to. May I remind you, my dear, that you've had a very difficult time of it for the last year, and that to immediately plunge into a whirl of socializing is hardly going to prove beneficial."

"Two nights hardly constitute a whirl of socializing," protested Linnet.

"Possibly. It's how you mean to go on that concerns me." Her great-aunt's head turned as she heard the activity in the ballroom. Seeing the work on the chandeliers, she frowned at Linnet. "And it seems that you mean to go on as you please, in spite of my advice that you delay."

Linnet put down her knife and fork. "Let us be frank with each other, Great-Aunt Minton. You don't want me just to delay, you're still determined to make me cancel it altogether."

"You know my opinion of the gentleman concerned, and I doubt if I'll ever have to eat humble pie on the subject. So, we'll have to agree to disagree, for although I have no time at all for Mr. Gresham, I have all the time in the world for you, my dear."

Linnet smiled, then. "I know."

"I mean well, Linnet. You do know that, don't you?"

"Of course."

"So, even if I oppose you on this one matter, you know that on every other front I will always offer you the love, comfort, and support that I have in the past?"

"I know you will." Linnet smiled, leaning across to put a quick hand on her great-aunt's arm.

"May I ask what arrangements have been agreed on so far concerning the, er, ball?" There was a very noticeable hesitation, and an eloquent omission of the word "betrothal."

Linnet ignored both, keeping her tone very amiable as she related all the things she and Venetia had discussed the day before.

On hearing the numbers being invited, Great-Aunt Minton was staggered. "Such extravagance!"

"One only becomes betrothed once, Great-Aunt."

"Indeed? I seem to recall that you used to entertain hopes of Lord Fane."

"Vain hopes."

Great-Aunt Minton surveyed her for a long moment. "Are you still in love with him?" she asked at last.

"No. Certainly not."

"No?"

"No!"

"Well, I tell you this, my dear. Flushed with apparent happiness you may be at the moment, but it's as nothing to the sheer joy and exhilaration that pervaded your entire being when you fell in love with Lord Fane. I visited you not long after you'd met him, if you remember."

"I remember."

"Can you look me in the eye and tell me you feel the same now?"

"I'm older and wiser now."

"Older, not wiser, and not in love. Nor is Mr. Gresham in love with you. He's a very personable, charming, and clever young man, with an eye to the main chance. You, my poor Linnet, are that main chance. He would like to be the nabob he claims to be, and with your fortune he can realize that ambition. Now, then, let us leave such a disagreeable topic, and speak of something more pleasing. Tell me, what are your plans this morning?''

Linnet quelled the resentment her great-aunt's words had aroused. It wasn't right or fair to continually speak so cruelly of Benedict!

Great-Aunt Minton applied herself once more to her breakfast. ''Does your silence signify that you're going to stay at home?''

''No. Actually, I thought I'd call at Schomberg House. They're advertising a new delivery of royal merino cloth.''

''Indeed? I must make a point of visiting them myself, but not this morning. I've received a message from my old friend, Lady Anne Stuart, who has heard I'm in town. She wishes me to call upon her, and that is what I intend to do.''

''I'm sure you'll enjoy it.''

''There's no doubt of that, for she and I go back a long way.'' The old lady looked at her. ''My dear, if you go to Schomberg House, you must be sure to take your maid with you. A lady must guard her reputation at all times, even when merely visiting a shop.''

''I know,'' replied Linnet wearily.

Her great-aunt smiled fondly. ''It isn't fair, is it? Gentlemen are free to do as they please, but we must always be looking back over our shoulder in case of a breath of scandal. Oh, scandal, what a bane it is to us all—yes, even to me.''

''To you?'' Linnet looked curiously at her. ''What do you mean?''

''My dear, just because I'm a withered spinster, it doesn't signify that I've never had experience of life. My heart was broken once, and had the story got out, it would have caused scandal.''

Linnet poured another cup of the thick, dark Turkish coffee. ''Did it involve Nicholas's grandfather?'' she asked quietly.

The old lady gave her an arch look. ''I'm not prepared to answer you.''

''Which is answer enough. It *did* involve him.''

"I would prefer you not to draw that conclusion, and certainly not to voice it to anyone else."

"You know me better than that," chided Linnet gently.

"My dear, when I see you being so completely gulled by Mr. Gresham, I begin to think I do not know you at all." Great-Aunt Minton suddenly put down her knife and fork, placing her napkin on the table. "I do believe I've eaten enough, and must prepare to call upon Lady Anne. No doubt she will insist that I take luncheon with her, which means that you and I will not meet again until this evening. Enjoy your visit to Schomberg House."

"Yes, Great-Aunt Minton." Linnet watched her leave. Both the conversation and the breakfast had been brought to a very abrupt close, and the reason was most definitely the suggestion that Nicholas's grandfather had played a significant part in the old lady's past.

An hour later, when Great-Aunt Minton had departed for Lady Anne Stuart's residence, Linnet and her maid set off for Pall Mall. Linnet was dressed perfectly for shopping in London, in a stylish buttermilk silk pelisse over a matching gown, with her hair swept up beneath a pale-pink jockey bonnet from the back of which trailed an almost floor-length gauze veil. Mary was at her neat best in a cream linen cape over a light-green chemise gown, and she was in buoyant spirits. The visit to Schomberg House had given her the opportunity to ask a favor of Linnet; the maid's cousin had a position at a nearby bookshop, and an invitation to his wedding that had hitherto been turned down because Mary had been in the Lake District could now be accepted after all.

Pall Mall was one of the finest shopping streets in London, and Schomberg House stood on the southern side, between the ducal residence of Marlborough House and the property once occupied by Nell Gwynne, a lady of far less than ducal antecedents. Messrs Harding, Howell & Company had occupied the handsome seventeenth-century house for a little over four years, and in that time had built up an enviable reputation for excellence. Once the residence of the Duke of Schomberg, it had subsequently been divided into several elegant apartments but now was one entity again. The four-story, red-brick, stone-faced facade looked grandly down onto the street, and the curb outside was cluttered with fine carriages.

Linnet's coachman had to maneuver the team to a place further along the street, and quickly alighted to open the carriage door and assist his mistress and her maid to alight. Linnet was just instructing him to wait when she saw a face she knew and liked approaching along the pavement. It was Freddy Grainger.

He was strolling along on his own, his cane swinging idly in his gloved hand. He wore a dark-orange coat and light-brown breeches, and his waistcoat was a particularly handsome shade of deep-peacock. His face, usually so good-natured and quick to smile, was withdrawn and almost sullen, and was such a contrast to his normal self that Linnet paused in surprise, her smile of greeting dying on her lips.

He saw her, she knew that he did, but he made no acknowledgment—indeed, it seemed to her that he quickened his step a little in order to pass her by.

"Freddy?" She made to engage him in conversation.

He glanced at her, or perhaps it would have been more correct to say that he looked straight through her, and he made no attempt to pause, walking on along the pavement without a single word.

"Freddy?" She spoke again, taken complete aback by the deliberate snub.

Still he walked on, and was soon lost among the crowds on the pavement. Linnet remained where she was, shaken at being so publicly cut by someone she'd always regarded as a good friend. Why had he behaved like that? What did he imagine she'd done to warrant it? For a moment she contemplated hurrying after him to demand an explanation, but then she thought better of it. In his present mood he was quite capable of delivering another snub, and that was a risk she wasn't prepared to take. No, it would be better to send him a note, asking in what way she'd offended, if, indeed, she'd offended at all. Try as she would, she couldn't think of anything she'd done that might have upset him.

Taking a deep breath, she smiled at Mary, who was waiting nearby. "You mentioned wishing to see your cousin?"

"Yes, Miss Linnet. He has a position in Mr. Mitchell's bookshop, just across the street."

"Well, I'm sure the new cloths will take me some time, and I'm equally sure that I shall linger over a dish of tea in the tearoom afterward, so you may take three quarters of an hour to see your cousin."

"Oh, thank you, Miss Linnet," cried the maid gratefully. "I'll come to you in the tearoom."

"Very well." Linnet turned to walk quickly into Schomberg House, escorted to the door by the coachman, and the maid hurried away in the other direction, dodging across the cobbled street when there was a convenient break in the almost continuous flow of traffic.

Freddy Grainger was still on Linnet's mind as she entered the building. She was both puzzled and hurt by his odd conduct, and a little concerned, for it just wasn't like Freddy to behave like that. Then she had to put him from her thoughts, for the premises of Messrs Harding, Howell & Company was a veritable bear garden of noise and excitement as a gaggle of elegant ladies squabbled over the desirable bolts of cloth.

Linnet had to push her way toward the relevant counter, passing the glass-partitioned departments displaying furs and fans, haberdashery, ornamental ormulu and French clocks, and then the millinery. It was impossible to even see the cloth counter, there was such a press of determined ladies around it. The young men endeavoring to serve were hard put to keep things in control, especially when three ladies seized the same bolt of emerald-green cloth and began tugging it in different directions.

Linnet halted, somewhat put off by such a battleground. Her glance moved to the staircase. Maybe if she took her tea first, and then returned to the cloth counter afterward, the battle would be over, and she could examine what was left of the coveted cloth. Yes, that was what she'd do, for to be sure there wasn't any point in trying to look at anything now, not when the ladies of Mayfair were in full acquisitive flow.

The floor above was mostly devoted to a magnificent display of fine furnishing fabrics, and was remarkably quiet and deserted after the mayhem on the ground floor. The tearoom was toward the rear of the building, looking out over the gardens of Carlton House and Marlborough House toward the green expanse of St. James's Park. There was a table laden with cakes and pastries, and the delicious smell of toasted currant buns, and a number of small tables, each one with a dainty lace-edged white cloth. The tables had four chairs each, and against the wall there were a number of fine crimson velvet sofas, but not a single place was occupied. It seemed that the delivery of royal merino cloth was the sole attraction of the day.

Linnet went to a table next to a window, teasing off her gloves as she sat down. As she ordered a dish of China tea from the waitress who hastened to serve her, her thoughts were again on Freddy Grainger.

She didn't hear anyone come up the staircase, nor did she hear the rich, seductive rustle of a corded-silk train. She didn't even hear the patter of a poodle's paws on the polished wood floor. She knew nothing until someone spoke.

"We meet again, Miss Carlisle."

She looked up into Judith Jordan's shining, feline eyes.

11

The Cyprian was dressed in a fitted, full-length pelisse made of a particularly fine mustard-colored corded silk, and a wide-brimmed brown hat from which sprang the inevitable plumes. They were spectacular plumes, mustard-colored to match the pelisse, but with their tips cleverly dyed brown to echo the hat. A brown feather boa was draped casually around her neck, with one long end trailing almost to her hem at the back, and there was an elegant lozenge-shaped brown velvet reticule hanging from her wrist. She toyed with the poodle's lead, pearl-studded brown leather today, and a vaguely taunting smile played about her lips.

"How agreeable that we should encounter each other again," she murmured.

"I have no wish to speak to you, Miss Jordan," replied Linnet stiffly.

"Oh, I'm sure that's so. However, we cannot always have what we wish, can we?" The Cyprian glanced across at the startled waitress, who hovered uncertainly nearby. "Another dish of China tea, if you please," she said, drawing out a chair at the same table and sitting down. The white poodle sat beside her, gazing at her with bright, adoring eyes.

Linnet looked coldly at her. "I would prefer it if you sat elsewhere, Miss Jordan."

"No other table offers the same fine view," replied the other, still smiling a little.

"Then I shall sit elsewhere," answered Linnet, beginning to get up.

The Cyprian put out a quick hand, restraining her. "I think we should talk, Miss Carlisle, and this is a miraculously deserted place today. Instinct told me you'd be lured by the royal merino, and, having gone to the trouble of searching you out, I don't intend to let you simply walk away."

"I have nothing to say to you, madam."

"No?" The incredible dark-blue eyes gleamed.

"No." What did the creature want? The battle had been fought and won over a year before, even though she, Linnet Carlisle, hadn't realized there had been a war until it was all over. But as she looked at the demimondaine, Linnet suddenly realized that Nicholas, Lord Fane, was still the bone of contention. Judith knew about his call at Carlisle House, and was jealous and angry. What other explanation could there be? It was a quaint thought, and an enlightening one, for it showed that London's most sought-after fashionable impure wasn't as sure of her hold over Lord Fane as she'd like the world to believe.

Linnet was suddenly intrigued. Perhaps it would be interesting to hear what the other had to say. She relaxed, sitting back. "Very well, Miss Jordan, what is it that you think we have to say to each other?"

The demimondaine removed her gloves, placing them on the table, then stroked the poodle. Her glance moved critically over Linnet's clothes. "Last year's togs, Miss Carlisle? How very remiss of you."

"Well, maybe it's better to be unfashionable and pure, than to be the opposite," replied Linnet coolly.

The blue eyes flickered. "Causticity is the weapon of sour-puss old maids, Miss Carlisle, and I doubt if you are yet in that category. Ah, but I was forgetting, you are soon to be betrothed, are you not? An old maid's cloak is not for you."

"Perhaps it is for you, Miss Jordan. Or is Lord Fane going to make an honest woman of you?"

"He didn't make an honest woman of you, my dear.

Or had you forgotten?'' Judith's eyes became even more feline.

"A fortunate escape.''

"Really? You do surprise me. Still, that is in the past, isn't it?''

Linnet didn't reply, but smiled in an equally feline way that was calculated to provoke. If jealousy was the reason for Judith's interest in her, then she, Linnet, was quite capable of ruffling her adversary's paradise plumes.

The Cyprian's gaze sharpened. "Now I am the one being remiss, for of course Lord Fane is history to you because it's Mr. Gresham who is now your love. I understand there is to be a grand betrothal ball?''

"You seem remarkably well informed, Miss Jordan.''

"I am, rather. By a strange coincidence, I am at present organizing a ball as well, a *bal masqué*.'' A sly note crept into Judith's voice. "No doubt our guest lists will be very similar—at least, they will as far as the gentlemen are concerned.''

Linnet forebore to reply, for it was only too true.

The Cyprian smiled a little. "Do I shock you, Miss Carlisle?''

"Do you wish to shock me?''

"I don't know. I'm curious about you, that's for sure.''

"Why?''

Judith glanced down at the poodle, fondling its head. "I have my reasons,'' she murmured.

The maid at last brought the dishes of tea, and as Linnet prepared to sip hers, Judith spoke again. "If you aren't exactly shocked by me, you're certainly disapproving, aren't you, Miss Carlisle?''

"What else do you expect?''

"Nothing, I suppose, but I ask you to explain why I am so frowned upon when an adulterous wife, whose marriage was entered into for convenience only, is accepted through society. I, at least, am honest about what I do.''

"Is it honest, then, to consort with other women's husbands, Miss Jordan?''

"A husband won't stray if his wife keeps him satisfied,

Miss Carlisle. That is a cardinal rule. Tell me, do you
intend to keep Mr. Gresham satisfied?''

"That isn't any of your business," replied Linnet
shortly.

The Cyprian's dark-blue eyes were veiled. "No, to be
sure, it isn't any of my business," she said softly.

"Why all this interest in me?" asked Linnet, holding
the other's gaze. "I would have thought that my impend-
ing marriage would have pleased you, for it signifies that
I am no longer interested in Lord Fane. That *is* what all
this is about, isn't it? I'm flattered to think you fear me
as a rival.''

A dull flush entered Judith's cheeks. "Is that what you
think?''

"You haven't offered another explanation.''

"Nor do I intend to." The Cyprian gathered the poodle's lead and rose from her chair, leaving her dish of tea
untouched. "I wished to get the measure of you, Miss
Carlisle, and I rather think I have. We will be meeting
again.''

"I sincerely hope not, for yours is the sort of society
I abhor.''

"Oh, I feel the same way about your society, Miss
Carlisle, but you have become something of a thorn in
my side of late, and I'm afraid I'm going to have to deal
with you. *A bientôt, ma chère,* you'll soon be hearing a
great deal more of me, and I don't think you'll like any
of it." With a cool nod, the demimondaine walked away
toward the staircase, the poodle pattering obediently at
her hem.

Linnet gazed after her, and then slowly exhaled. She
hadn't realized how tense she'd been throughout the interview, but was only too aware of it now. She lowered
her glance. Maybe it was gratifying to know that the Bird
of Paradise was vulnerably jealous, but what wasn't so
gratifying was the fact that Judith Jordan was also gloriously beautiful, fascinating, worldly, witty, and stylish.
No wonder such a creature had triumphed over dull little
Linnet Carlisle, who must have seemed boring in comparison.

* * *

Another disagreeable interview awaited Linnet when she returned to Carlisle House with her hard-won purchase of royal merino cloth, several yards of heather-colored wool that would make a handsome spencer. As she and Mary entered the house, Sommers informed her that Nicholas had called and had insisted on waiting until she returned.

The butler was more than a little uneasy about having admitted such an unwelcome visitor, but in the absence of both Linnet and her great-aunt, he'd felt ill-equipped to refuse the request of such an important gentleman, especially when that gentleman had been determined to have his own way.

"I'm so sorry to have allowed him to wait, madam, but it really was difficult to refuse."

She sighed, and glanced at the gloves, fawn beaver top hat, and ivory-handled cane on the table. What did Nicholas want of her now? "It's all right, Sommers, I quite understand. Where is he? In the drawing room?"

"No, madam. The ballroom. He said he could wait there as easily as anywhere else."

That sounded like one of Nicholas's remarks. "Very well." She took off her gloves and jockey bonnet, placing both on top of the brown paper parcel of cloth Mary was carrying. "I'll be with you directly, Mary."

"Yes, Miss Linnet." The maid bobbed a curtsy, and then hurried away up the staircase.

Sommers waited awkwardly. "Madam, would you prefer me to be present with you in the ballroom?"

"No, that won't be necessary."

"Madam." He bowed, and withdrew.

Linnet took a long breath to steady herself. Following so quickly upon her encounter with the Bird of Paradise, she was prepared for this second interview to be equally as unpleasant. She moved toward the ballroom, passing beneath the colonnade and then pausing at the top of the steps.

The servants had almost completed the cleaning and polishing of the chandeliers, and were just raising the final one into place. Nicholas had tossed back the white cloth covering one of the royal-blue velvet sofas and was lounging back, watching them. He wore a fawn coat and brown silk cravat, and his long, well-made legs, encased in cream cord breeches, were stretched out before him. His top boots were highly polished, and his long fingers drummed restlessly on the arm of the sofa. He seemed to be absorbed watching the lengthy progress of the chandelier from floor to ceiling, but there was something distant about his expression, telling her that his thoughts were elsewhere.

She descended the steps, pausing again at the bottom, her hand resting on one of the African prince candleholders. As she watched him, he ran his fingers through his dark tangle of hair, and then leaned his head back, closing his eyes for a moment.

"Too many late nights, my lord?" she asked, her voice carrying clearly across the ballroom.

The servants glanced quickly toward her, and then hastened to complete their task, raising the chandelier the final few inches and making it fast. Then the footman at the top of the stepladder quickly descended, and they all hurried away toward the French windows, carrying the stepladder carefully outside to the terrace and closing the window behind them.

Nicholas rose and walked toward her. "Good morning, Miss Carlisle."

"You wished to see me?" she asked without preamble. His mistress had toyed with her, and she didn't intend to allow him to do the same.

"That was the general purpose of my visit, yes."

"Then please be brief, for I have much to do."

He glanced around the ballroom. "Ah, yes, the famous betrothal ball. But what do *you* have to do? Isn't it all in Lady Hartley's ambitious hands?" He gave a low laugh. "Yes, of course it is, for she wouldn't pass up such an excellent opportunity to further her reputation as a hostess."

"You make that sound very insulting, my lord," she

replied coldly. "Will you come to the point of this unwelcome visit?"

"I merely wished to be certain that the equally unwelcome item of news that was imparted to me in Hyde Park yesterday was actually true, and judging by all the frantic polishing of the chandeliers, I fear that it is. You made a fool of yourself a year ago, Linnet, and I really didn't think you'd do it all over again."

She raised her chin angrily, specks of hot color staining her cheeks. "If you've come here merely to offer insults, my lord, I'd be obliged if you'd remove yourself immediately."

"How quick you are to want to eject me yet again. Do I make you feel uncomfortable?" His eyes, a much more icy blue than his mistress's, seemed to see right into her. "You know Gresham's gulling you, don't you?"

"The only one to ever gull me, sir, was you," she replied shortly.

"You're still wrong about that."

"Are you going to tell me you didn't trick my uncle out of Radleigh Hall? And you didn't deceive me with Judith Jordan?" Her gaze rested haughtily on him. "Go back to her, Nicholas, for to be sure you've already made her green with jealousy. A second call at this address will only provoke her into another attempt to impose her company upon me."

"I don't understand."

"Your fine feathered bird appears to regard me as a rival for your affections, and she's issuing threats that she intends to subject me to her unwelcome attention. I don't appreciate being approached by whores, Lord Fane, and so I ask you to instruct yours to keep away from me."

"She isn't my whore."

"No, she's everybody's."

"Now whose talons are showing?"

She looked angrily away, aware that she'd allowed herself to be provoked.

He watched her. "I didn't come here to discuss Judith, Linnet, I came here to try to persuade you out of this folly with Gresham."

"How dare you presume . . . !"

"I happen to think I'm well qualified to offer advice," he interrupted. "After all, I was your first choice."

"Yes, you were. And you cheated me most foully. Now, please go."

"Not until I'm sure you've paid proper attention to what I'm saying."

"I'm not a child that you can order about, sirrah!" she cried.

"Then please stop behaving like one. Gresham isn't the man for you, and to proceed with this betrothal will be utter madness."

"I happen to love him," she breathed, trembling with rage, and with a tumult of other conflicting emotions. How dared this man presume! How dared he attempt to interfere in her life after having so cruelly spurned her the year before!

"Love him? You don't love him, Linnet, you're just turning to him on the rebound."

She strove to keep her temper. "A year is hardly 'on the rebound,' my lord."

"Isn't it?" He laughed a little. It was a scornful laugh, calculated to goad, and it succeeded.

"Please leave, before I feel obliged to send for Sommers." Her voice trembled, and she was so angry that she had to clench her fists to keep herself under strict control.

He studied her, making no move to do as she asked. "If you really loved Gresham, nothing I said or did would disturb your serenity. But look at you, a few considered words from me and you're all emotion and rage. Perhaps you should take another year in lakeland to reflect upon what you really want from life."

"I know what I want."

"Gresham?" He laughed again. "Dear God above, your judgment slips from bad to appalling."

"Maybe it does, but one thing is certain, sirrah. My judgment was more than just appalling when I was unfortunate enough to fall in love with you."

His eyes had seldom been a more piercing blue. "That

wasn't when your judgment let you down, Linnet. It let you down when it allowed you to believe the lies you'd heard about me, and when it permitted you to actually accuse me to my face of having cheated both you and your uncle. I haven't forgotten a single moment of what happened a year ago, nor have I forgiven.''

Her eyes flashed. *"You* haven't forgiven?'' she gasped, unable to believe her ears.

He smiled. ''That's correct.'' His glance moved over her again. ''One thing I had forgotten, however, is how very beautiful you are when you're angry. I'm almost tempted to prove that Gresham means absolutely nothing to you.''

''Prove to me?''

''I wonder how long you'd protest if I chose to kiss you now,'' he mused softly.

Her fury exploded, and she struck him across the cheek. It was a stinging blow, leaving angry marks on his skin, and she was shaking so much she could hardly speak. ''Leave this house immediately, sir, and never call here again.''

He rubbed his cheek, but the smile still lingered on his lips. ''Well, I think my point is proved after all, don't you? In your heart of hearts you're not at all sure of your feelings for Gresham, nor are you sure you're over me.''

Turning, she gathered her skirts to hurry up the steps toward the hall, calling the butler as she did so.

Sommers materialized immediately. ''Madam?''

''Please show his lordship out, and if he calls again, he is not to be admitted, is that clear?''

''Yes, madam.'' The butler looked uneasily past her to where Nicholas was taking his time about ascending the steps.

Linnet paused at the foot of the staircase, a hand on the newel post. She was still trembling, but she didn't want to give him the satisfaction of seeing her flee to her room.

He accepted his hat, gloves, and cane from Sommers, and then turned to look at her again. ''Don't marry

Gresham, Linnet, for it would be the greatest mistake of your life.''

She didn't reply.

He said nothing more, but walked toward the front door, which Sommers was pointedly holding open for him. As the butler closed the door again, Linnet turned to go up the staircase.

Nicholas's words echoed inescapably in her head. *I wonder how long you'd protest if I chose to kiss you now?* She paused. How long *would* she have resisted? Guilt cut through her like a knife, and she felt as if, merely by doubting for a second, she'd betrayed Benedict; she also felt as vulnerable and full of pain as she had the year before, when she'd been the one who'd been betrayed.

12

Linnet's self-reproach increased rather than diminished over the next week. She plunged into the endless round of social diversion that London offered, and she entered wholeheartedly into the preparations for the ball. Every opportunity that presented itself for being with Benedict, she seized with an eagerness that Great-Aunt Minton viewed with increasing misgiving, for in that wise lady's opinion, one did not have to continually prove that one was in love, one simply knew it, and that was sufficient.

Linnet said nothing to anyone about Nicholas's second visit, and she instructed Sommers to remain silent about it as well. Nor did she say anything about the confrontation with Judith Jordan at Schomberg House, for she had no desire for anyone to learn that she'd been subjected to such a disagreeable interview with so immoral and abandoned a creature. She had no intention of encouraging unwelcome whispers, and certainly didn't wish to have her name connected anew with either Nicholas or the Bird of Paradise.

Venetia's enthusiasm for the betrothal ball helped a great deal, for it was easy to forget other matters when faced with such exuberance. It was almost as if the betrothal ball were Venetia's own, she devoted such attention to every detail. The guest list was very quickly compiled, and the invitations printed and sent out. Gunter's was engaged to provide both the ball supper and the large blocks of ice that would be placed at strategic points around the ballroom to cool the air on what would undoubtedly be a hot night. The German orchestra was booked, and news of this unexpected choice soon leaked out over town, causing much speculation, for any break with what was conventional or fashionable was always regarded with raised eyebrows.

Venetia also pursued her ideas where floral decorations were concerned, causing much panic in the market gardens of Chelsea by ordering vast numbers of red roses. She was determined to have the tour de force in the ballroom, approaching a man at Covent Garden to provide two wicker cages of linnets, and then a small business in Cheapside for papier-mâché unicorns, painted silver. Vast quantities of champagne were ordered, and various wines, and Venetia reveled in all the work involved. No one could have been happier than she about the betrothal, and no one could have made Linnet feel more welcome as a future sister-in-law.

There was one person, however, who went out of his way to make Linnet feel very alienated indeed, and that was Freddy Grainger. True to her decision outside Schomberg House, she sent him a note, but it was returned unanswered. Puzzled, and more than a little upset by his inexplicable hostility, she called at his residence in Berkeley Street, but suffered the humiliation of being turned away at the door. This last episode forced her to accept that her friendship with him was at an end, but she had no idea why. She wasn't destined to find out for the time being, either, for a day or so after that he suddenly left town to return to his home in Cornwall. He gave no notification to any of his friends, not even Venetia, and Linnet found it all rather distressing, for she'd always liked him, and had done her best to promote his suit where Venetia was concerned. Briefly, she wondered if there were any truth after all in Benedict's suspicions concerning Mr. Coleridge, and if Freddy had found out, but almost straightaway she discounted the thought, for it didn't explain why she, Linnet, had been singled out. She consulted Great-Aunt Minton on the matter, and was advised to leave things as they were for the time being, and then to write to Freddy again in Cornwall, when perhaps he would be more inclined to tell her what was wrong. It was sensible advice, and Linnet took it. She would write again in a month or so's time, when, as her great-aunt so eloquently put it, "any fur would probably have stopped flying."

Freddy or no Freddy, the social whirl of London went on, and Linnet was part of it. There was so much happening all the time, from an assembly at Chesterfield House and a formal dinner at Hampton Court to a charity ball at Carlton House and a delightful water party on the Thames at Syon House. Benedict was always her escort, with either Venetia or Great-Aunt Minton in attendance, and when she was with him, Nicholas didn't seem to matter so much. She found it hard to forgive herself for that moment of doubt when Nicholas had last called. Benedict adored her, and was flatteringly thoughtful and attentive at all times, whereas Nicholas was simply amusing himself by seeing how much he could still interfere in her life. Such arrogance was no more than she'd come to expect of him, for he was a monster of the first order, and she simply couldn't believe she'd even paused to reflect upon the length of her resistance to his kisses. It was Benedict she loved now, and there was no place in her heart for a callous lord like Nicholas. And yet sometimes still, when she first awoke in the morning, she knew Benedict hadn't been the one in her dreams, and the guilt settled over her until she was with him again.

She tried to put Nicholas entirely from her thoughts, as she did his equally odious mistress. A lady did not concern herself with the petty spites and jealousies of a demimondaine like the Bird of Paradise, at least that was what she told herself, but at an exhibition at the Hanover Square Rooms at the end of that week, she was forced to concede that Judith Jordan was a force to be reckoned with, and to accept that the Cyprian's threats hadn't been idly uttered.

The day of the exhibition began auspiciously enough, with bright sunshine, another gratifying delivery of invitations, and the arrival of a florist's cart with a basket of red roses from Benedict, who was to escort her to the Hanover Square Rooms.

Sommers opened the door, standing aside for the florist's boy to bring the beribboned basket inside. There was a note attached to it, and after giving the boy a coin, the butler brought the note to Linnet, who'd come down the staircase at that very moment, dressed to go out. The message was brief, but very tender. *The Gresham rose is at your feet, my darling. B.* Smiling she thought how fortunate it was that she'd elected to wear her crimson velvet spencer with her cream sprigged muslin, and the straw bonnet with the crimson ribbons, for they matched exactly the color of the roses.

She gave the card back to the butler. "Have the roses taken to my room, Sommers, and tell Mary I wish her to prepare a little posy of them to pin to the underbrim of my bonnet."

"Yes, madam."

"And tell her to be quick, for Mr. Gresham should be here at any moment. I'll be in the drawing room with my great-aunt."

"Madam."

He hurried away, and Linnet went into the drawing room. Her great-aunt was seated at a sofa with her embroidery frame, and looked rather crisp and prim in a high-necked oyster lawn gown. A dainty mobcap rested on her powdered hair, and a pair of spectacles adorned the end of her nose as she endeavored to thread a needle that had a particularly small eye.

Linnet smiled, going to assist. "Shall I do it for you, Great-Aunt?"

"If you would, my dear." The old lady sat back, inspecting her niece's appearance. The combination of cream sprigged-muslin gown and crimson velvet spencer evidently met with her approval, for she nodded. "You look very pretty this morning, Linnet."

"Thank you." Linnet returned the threaded needle to her.

"You're far too good for that fellow."

"Oh, please don't start that again," pleaded Linnet.

"Poor Benedict doesn't deserve your continuing opposition."

"That's just what he is, isn't he? *Poor* Benedict, the impoverished coxcomb with ambitions to live in the lap of someone else's luxury."

"You really do hold him in contempt, don't you?"

"On the contrary, my dear, I have a grudging admiration for him, for he really does carry it off very well. He has you believing his tales of woe, and he's gulled his half-sister as well. She's providing for him in every way, and he hasn't had to produce a single penny. Oh, he's very clever, and has acting talents that would make him the rage at Drury Lane."

"I love him, Great-Aunt Minton, and I know he loves me. He's sent me a beautiful basket of red roses this morning."

"No doubt they're from the very florist who is grateful for the immense order Lady Hartley has sent his way."

"What a horridly cynical thing to say."

"But the truth, I'll warrant," murmured the other, resuming her embroidery.

More than a little put out by her relative's relentless hostility toward the man she intended to marry, Linnet moved to the window, looking out over the courtyard toward the gates and Charles Street.

Her great-aunt glanced at her. "I think you will enjoy the exhibition, my dear, for from what Lady Anne Stuart told me of it, it sounds very interesting indeed."

Linnet sighed at the cordial tone, for it was always the same. Her great-aunt had an acid manner when Benedict was under discussion, but a warm and considerate one when speaking of anything else. She turned to look back at the seated figure. "Yes, I'm sure it will be most diverting."

"I'm sorry I cannot accompany you, but I did invite Lady Anne to call this morning. I take it that Lady Hartley will be with you?"

"No, I'm afraid not. She isn't satisfied with something concerning the silver unicorns, and she's descending upon

Cheapside to deal with it. Mary will be accompanying me, to see that all is proper.''

"I understand why you find the necessity of a chaperone irritating, my dear, but a lady's reputation *is* all-important, as I believe I've said before.''

"You have," murmured Linnet.

Her aunt shot her a sharp glance, and was about to remonstrate with her when there was a discreet tap at the door and Mary came in with the posy of roses for Linnet's bonnet. The old lady contented herself with jabbing the needle through the taut linen cloth stretched on the embroidery frame.

Linnet stood very still while the maid pinned the flowers to the underbrim of the bonnet, and then went to inspect the result in the mirror over the fireplace. The roses were the very same color as the bonnet ribbons and the spencer, and she was very pleased indeed with the way they looked.

A carriage sounded in the courtyard, and she turned quickly to see that Benedict was in Venetia's barouche. Venetia's barouche. In spite of herself, she glanced at her aunt, who met her eyes somewhat shrewdly. Not a word was said, but Linnet knew full well what her aunt was thinking. Here he is again, said the look, in his *sister's* carriage. Linnet sighed inwardly, returning her glance to her reflection in the mirror. Oh, how she wished Benedict would do something to prove her great-aunt wrong.

Sommers announced Benedict, who came in smiling. He wore a dark-blue coat with brass buttons, a fawn-and-white-striped valencia waistcoat, and fawn kerseymere breeches that vanished into handsome Hessian boots with golden tassels. He sketched a dashing bow. "Good morning, Miss Minton. Linnet.''

Great-Aunt Minton sniffed, continuing with her needlework. "In my day, sir, a gentleman did not address the young lady he was to marry by her first name, for it smacked of overfamiliarity.''

He glanced secretly at Linnet, rolling his eyes in a long-suffering way.

Great-Aunt Minton looked up from her embroidery.

"Tell me, sir, has Lady Hartley received any word from Mr. Grainger?"

"No, Miss Minton."

"I must say, I find his conduct somewhat strange, and totally out of character. I always thought him such a mild, considerate, charming young man. Your sister would have been wise to accept him when she had her chance, for I doubt if she'll do better."

"I've said the very same to her, Miss Minton."

The old lady's eyes flickered. "I'm sure you have, sir, for it is always good policy to pursue advantageous matches, is it not?"

Embarrassed, Linnet turned quickly to Mary. "Go put on your bonnet and cape, Mary, we'll be leaving directly."

"Miss Linnet." The maid gave a hurried curtsy, and went out.

Linnet had no intention of lingering, thus allowing her great-aunt to deliver any more thinly veiled barbs. "We'll go now, Great-Aunt," she said, going to slip her arm through Benedict's.

Great-Aunt Minton eyed him over her spectacles. "Look after my niece, sir, or you will have me to answer to."

"She's in safe hands, Miss Minton," he replied reassuringly.

"Hmm." The needle stabbed the linen cloth again.

Linnet drew him quickly toward the door, breathing out with relief as it closed again behind them. "I fear my aunt is in a venomous mood."

"She always is when I'm around," he said with feeling.

"Well, it doesn't make any difference to the way I feel about you," she said softly, reaching up to kiss him on the cheek.

He glanced quickly around to see that the entrance hall was empty, and then he swept her into his arms, kissing her passionately on the lips. He held her close, his heart beating against hers as he lingered over the stolen moment. He drew back at last, his face flushed with desire. "I love you so much, my darling."

"I know, and I love you, too."

He smiled, touching the posy of roses with his fingertips. "I was afraid that I would arrive before they did."

"They're beautiful, Benedict. I told Sommers to take them to my room."

The butler appeared in the entrance hall, ready to hand Benedict his hat, gloves, and cane, and they moved discreetly apart. Benedict turned to her, striking a classical pose. "Do I look very sculpture exhibition?" he asked, grinning.

She laughed. "Well, thinking of certain statues, perhaps you're a trifle overdressed . . ."

"Miss Carlisle, I'm shocked," he replied, pretending to look very taken aback. "Well, if I don't look particularly sculpture exhibition, perhaps I look messenger boy."

"Messenger boy?"

"I'm charged with my sister's invitation. She wishes, nay, *demands,* that you and your great-aunt come to dine a week on Thursday, that's the evening before the ball."

"Oh." Linnet lowered her eyes. She didn't want to go to Fane Crescent, not even for Venetia.

He took her hands. "Please come. There'll only be four of us, you, me, Venetia, and the dragon."

"Benedict . . ."

"It will be a big hurdle to put behind you. Just consider how many friends you have who now reside there. Are you going to turn down their invitations, too? There would soon be talk if you did, and I'd be in the unenviable position of hearing my future wife's name connected yet again with Lord Fane. I would find that somewhat hard to bear."

"I—I hadn't thought of that."

"Then think of it now. Will you accept?"

She knew she had to, and she managed a smile. "I'll come, and I'm sure my great-aunt will as well."

"Oh, I'm sure the old besom will; she won't miss a

chance like this to harp on and on about how much of my sister's hospitality I enjoy.''

Linnet hesitated, but the opening was there. ''Then don't give her the satisfaction. Move out of Venetia's house and set up somewhere on your own.''

''I'm about to do just that.''

''You are?''

''Yes. I've found the very property. It's in North Audley Street, and will suit me down to the ground. When it's ready, that is.''

''Ready?''

''I'm having it refurbished from cellar to attic, for it won't do at the moment. God knows who lived there before, but it's been done out in the most execrable taste. There's *brown* brocade on the drawing room walls, would you believe? A man could swiftly become suicidal with such a dismal color.'' He raised her hands to his lips, smiling into her eyes. ''When we've been to the exhibition, I'd like to take you to see it. It's modest by Carlisle House standards, but will do for me until we're married.'' He glanced around the impressive entrance hall. ''Of course, if the marriage takes place as quickly as I wish it to, North Audley Street may never be honored with my presence after all, for it goes without saying that when we are married, this will be our London *pied-à-terre*. It's unthinkable that the last Carlisle should reside anywhere else.''

Mary hurried down the stairs, still tying the string of her little blue cape, and Benedict went to take his hat, gloves, and cane from Sommers. A moment later they all three emerged from the house to enter the waiting barouche.

The Hanover Square Rooms stood in the southeast corner of the square. They were contained in a four-story red-brick building that had windows gazing over the octagonal garden in the center of one of Mayfair's loveliest areas.

The sculpture exhibition was being much patronized by society, and there were many carriages outside. With

Mary following at a discreet few paces behind, Benedict and Linnet entered the building. The exhibition took up all four floors, and there were sculptures of every description, from full-length statues and decorative panels from Ancient Greece to a number of busts by Mr. Nollekens, the most sought-after sculptor in England.

They'd only been looking at the exhibition for a short while when an attendant approached Benedict to tell him that two men wished to speak to him outside. Apologizing and leaving her to examine a statue of Zeus that had been found in the Tiber, Benedict went out to speak to the men.

Curious to see them, and conscious of a stirring of the unease she'd felt at the Theatre Royal, she slipped to a window to watch as he spoke urgently to the two men. They were of unsavory appearance, their faces in shadow from their hats, and they were most definitely not gentlemen. Benedict seemed to be a little agitated, but was agreeing with what they said for he nodded, and spread his hands, as if to say that something was beyond his control, then he came back into the building.

She saw how pale his face was again. "Who were they, Benedict?" she asked anxiously. "I—I looked out, and saw them."

"Oh, they were only workmen I've engaged to refurbish the house in North Audley Street. There was some problem with the new glass for the back windows, and they sought my permission before proceeding. It's nothing to worry about." He smiled, drawing her hand through his arm. "You shouldn't worry so about me."

"I love you, so of course I worry," she replied.

He paused, turning her to face him. "Do you still promise that we'll be married as swiftly as possible? I doubt if I can bear to be apart from you for much longer."

"I promise," she whispered, her voice almost lost in the mutter of genteel conversation around them.

He glanced at the crowded room. "Let's go up to the top of the building, for I'm sure it will be less of a press there."

On the top floor the exhibition amounted to little more

than a collection of marble fragments piled higgledy-
piggledy on trestle tables. One of the rooms was completely deserted, and Benedict saw that it presented an
ideal opportunity to be alone with Linnet for a while. He
took it upon himself to instruct Mary to wait outside,
and then ushered Linnet into the empty room.

So much old stone made the air dusty, and sunbeams
danced in the light streaming in through the windows.
There was an alcove containing a gray velvet sofa and a
very large potted fern and anyone seated there could remain unseen and very private. He led Linnet toward it,
drawing her into the shadows to kiss her on the lips.

As she slipped her arms around him to return the kiss,
two gentlemen suddenly entered the room, and she pulled
guiltily away. The gentlemen were talking loudly, and
both she and Benedict recognized their voices. One belonged to Lord Frederick Cavendish, whom they'd met
outside the theater, and the other to the equally elderly
Mr. Algernon Halliday, a leading light of every fashionable drawing room and the scourge of prim spinsters,
who all fled the moment he approached.

Under any other circumstances, Linnet and Benedict
would have discreetly slipped from the alcove to make as
if they'd been examining the exhibits on a nearby table,
but the subject of the gentlemen's conversation kept them
rooted where they were. A list of hilarious mishaps was
being gleefully discussed, and these mishaps were supposed to have befallen Linnet herself. What was more,
the stories had originated at a certain house in Portman
Street, the residence of none other than the Bird of Paradise.

13

The moment Benedict realized what the conversation was about, he made to step angrily into view, but Linnet quickly restrained him, for she wanted to know what the demimondaine was saying about her. Benedict gave in very reluctantly, but his eyes were bright with indignation that a creature like the Bird of Paradise should dare to spread untrue tales about the woman he loved, and he was equally furious with the two unwary gentlemen, who were so mirthfully spreading the calumnies.

Algernon Halliday was chuckling wheezily, for he was a very round person who needed to be tightly laced into the fashionable clothes he liked so much. In his youth he'd been handsome enough, but had now lost both his figure and his charm, although he apparently did not realize it, for he still pursued the ladies with a leering confidence that had the very opposite effect to the one he wished. "By gad, Fred," he said, controlling his laughter, "I'd like to have been there. I've always suspected that the little Carlisle has some of the neatest ankles in town, and I'd have seen for myself when that sofa of a horse somehow managed to throw her."

"She's a bit thin for my taste," replied Lord Frederick, busily examining a piece of marble with his quizzing glass. "I prefer 'em a trifle more well padded, like Mrs. Siddons or Miss Pope, or even the Bird of Paradise."

"You and your wretched Mrs. Siddons. I vow you've carried a torch for her ever since I've known you."

Algernon strolled to the nearest window, which was

mercifully well away from the alcove. He looked down into the square below. "I do wish I'd been there when the Carlisle wench took that tumble," he murmured wistfully. "No, better still, I wish I'd been there when she was walking her three dogs in The Mall, and they got their leads tangled around her legs when they saw that cat. To think I wasn't there when she went flying into that puddle and got so soaked that her muslin gown clung to every delicious portion of her anatomy."

Lord Frederick surveyed him. "Still too thin for me. I say, Algy, I didn't know you found the Carlisle so appealing."

"She, er, interests me, that's all. I never did quite understand that business last year, I didn't return from Ireland until after the dust had settled. Why on earth didn't Fane just marry her, and then visit the Bird of Paradise on the side?"

"There was more to it than just that. The Carlisle also got it into her head that Fane cheated her uncle out of Radleigh Hall, and said as much to his face."

"Did she, by gad? That would take pluck, for I vow I wouldn't care to accuse Fane of anything, he's too handy with sword and pistol."

Algernon turned to look at Lord Frederick. "*Did* Fane cheat?"

"No. He may not be a close personal friend, but I'd stake my life on his honesty. He deceived the Carlisle girl with Judith Jordan, but he didn't do a damned thing that wasn't above board when it came to acquiring Radleigh."

Algernon nodded. "If anyone could cheat, I'd say it would have been Joseph Carlisle himself. I went to school with him, and he had the sharpest pair of dealing hands I ever clapped eyes on."

"Yes, he did, rather."

In the alcove, Linnet was listening with stunned disbelief. They were intent upon whitewashing Nicholas and painting as black a picture as they could of her poor uncle.

Benedict slipped an arm around her waist, pulling her

closer to whisper in her ear. "We should stop them in their gossipmongering tracks before this goes any further."

"No. I must hear everything."

Lord Frederick joined his friend at the window. "Well, whatever the rights and wrongs of Fane's actions, it's Gresham who's going to enjoy the Carlisle now."

"Lucky dog."

"I saw them at the Theatre Royal recently. They seem very taken with each other."

"They're certainly in a rush to make the betrothal official. You don't think . . . ?" Algernon allowed his voice to die away suggestively.

"Eh? Oh, I see your meaning. Well, it's possible, I suppose, but then I doubt if they'd be making such a song and dance about the betrothal ball, do you? It would take a very cool head to do that, and know that the eyes of society were upon one."

"There've been any number of such cool heads in the past," reminded Algernon, chuckling.

"From the sound of it, you're leading up to a wager," observed the other.

"I am, but not on that particular subject," replied Algernon.

"What then?"

"On La Jordan's ability to infiltrate the betrothal ball, as she says she intends," answered Algernon.

Linnet froze, her lips parting on a silent gasp. Judith Jordan was actually intending to attend the ball? Her eyes fled to Benedict's. His face was very grim and still.

Lord Frederick drew a long breath. "D'you think she'll pull it off?"

"Have you ever known the Bird of Paradise fail in anything she sets out to do?"

"Well, no, I suppose not . . ." Lord Frederick considered for a moment. "But it's one thing to mingle with society's gentlemen, quite another to attempt to do so when their wives are around. Ladies don't like demireps."

"That, dear boy, is a classic case of stating the glaringly obvious," observed Algernon dryly. "I think La Jordan has nerve enough, and style enough, to carry it off. She only needs a demure dress, a wig, and a change of voice, and bingo." He snapped his fingers.

Lord Frederick considered the matter for a long moment. "All right, I grant you that she might conceivably gain admittance, but as to carrying out the second part of her plan . . ."

"To steal a suitable trophy of the occasion? If she's gone so far as to step over the threshold at Carlisle House, you can bet your last pair of boots she'll do the other, too."

Lord Frederick exhaled thoughtfully, then shook his head. "I don't think she will."

"Fane believes she'll have a shot at it, and if *he* thinks it, then so do I. I'm prepared to put a hundred guineas down." This last was said tauntingly.

Lord Frederick rose to the bait. "You're throwing a hundred guineas away, dear boy, but if that's the way you wish it, here's my hand on the wager."

Evidently they shook hands, for there was a brief silence, and then Algernon spoke again. "Mind you, although I'm prepared to bet upon the Bird of Paradise's spirit, I'm not so rash where the Carlisle is concerned."

"I don't follow."

"Well, La Jordan may be bold enough to sneak into the society ball, but I doubt very much if her own *bal masqué* will be similarly infiltrated by the chatelaine of Carlisle House."

"As I said earlier, the little Carlisle had spirit enough to accuse Fane to his face, so why should she not show a similar spirit by secretly attending the Cyprian's ball. I have a hundred guineas that say she will."

Algernon chuckled. "My dear fellow, you're getting quite carried away."

"I'm prepared to be public about it. Well, as public as White's betting book could ever be," qualified Lord Frederick.

"You're that sure of yourself?"

"Why not? I truly believe that Linnet Carlisle will, if

she finds out about La Jordan's activities, pay her back in kind.''

Algernon grunted. ''I look forward to seeing the out-come. Mind you, I wouldn't mind a timely peek at White's book, anyway, for it always makes illuminating reading. For instance, did you know that Poky Withing-ton fancies his chances with no less a paragon than Lady Hartley?''

Lord Frederick gave a guffaw of disbelief. ''Pull the other one!''

''It's true, I tell you. He's actually laying odds on his success.''

''But she can't stand the sight of him!''

Algernon chuckled. ''That's very true, but with Freddy Grainger so abruptly off the scene, who knows what might transpire?''

Lord Frederick sniffed. ''Who knows, indeed, but I'd rather put my money on a certain gentleman poet.''

''Coleridge? Never.''

Lord Frederick sniffed again. ''The ladies appear to find him to their taste.''

''Aye, but not Lady Hartley. You mark my words.'' Algernon was quite firm.

''You weren't at the Holland House ball. I tell you, she spent an *unconscionable* length of time in his company,'' insisted Lord Frederick.

''I'm also informed that she spent a considerable time with Fane. Are you going to tell me that *he* is assured of success with her?'' Algernon laughed. ''On reflection, maybe he would be so assured, *if* he wished to be, but it's my opinion he barely knows she exists. Anyway, we've supposed this and supposed that, so perhaps it's time we removed ourselves to the betting book and made it all official, so to speak.''

''Well, it'll be more entertaining than these dusty lumps of stone,'' agreed Lord Frederick.

Laughing together, they left the room, and at last Lin-net and Benedict could emerge from the alcove. Bene-dict's lips were a thin line of fury, and his eyes were cold and very bright. Linnet was trembling, for what she'd overheard had both infuriated and upset her. Judith Jordan's parting words suddenly returned to her, their meaning now clear. *You've become something of a thorn in my side of late, and I'm afraid I'm going to have to deal with you. A bientôt, ma chère, you'll soon be hearing a great deal more of me, and I don't think you'll like any of it.*

The demimondaine had embarked upon a campaign against her, intending to make her the laughingstock of society. And why? Because of jealousy over Nicholas. Try as she would, Linnet could think of no other explanation.

Benedict went to one of the trestles, crashing his fist down so furiously that the fragments of marble shook. "You shouldn't have kept me sitting there like that! I should have taken them by their damned throats for what they said!"

"I needed to know what she was up to."

He turned sharply. "You say that as if you half-expected something like this."

She lowered her eyes guiltily. "I didn't know what she intended to do, just that she threatened me with something of the sort."

He stared at her. "You've *spoken* to her?"

"Yes."

"When?"

She drew a long breath. "When I went to Schomberg House. She waylaid me in the tearoom."

"What did she say?" he demanded.

"Just that I was 'a thorn in her side' and that I'd soon hear more of her. She said I wouldn't like what I heard. She was right; I don't."

"What else did she say?"

"Nothing of consequence." She turned away.

"This is all because of Fane, isn't it?"

"It has to be. What else is there between Judith Jordan and me? She can't have liked it very much that he called on me on my return." Linnet sighed. "Oh, how amused he must be by this."

"He won't be amused when I call him out."

Linnet's eyes widened in horror as she turned quickly back to him. "Oh, no, Benedict, you mustn't!"

"You heard what they said, he *agreed* that that woman is capable of trying to attend our ball. He's in on all her spiteful activities, Linnet."

She lowered her glance, for that part of it all hurt her more than anything, but then she met his eyes again. "Promise me you won't be foolish enough to call Nicholas out. You heard what Mr. Halliday said a moment ago."

"That Fane is too handy with sword and pistol?"

"Yes."

"Linnet, my honor demands . . ."

"And my love demands that you remain safe," she interrupted quickly. "You've heard the old saying that sticks and stones will break one's bones, but names will never hurt one? I can endure Judith Jordan's spiteful stories; indeed, I intend to treat them with the contempt they deserve. Her barbs can only work if they're seen to find their target."

"Even so . . ."

"Please, Benedict. For me?"

He hesitated, and at last he smiled. "Very well, but only because you ask it of me."

"I know." She went to him, reaching up to kiss his cheek.

He held her close for a moment. "Why didn't you tell me that Judith Jordan had approached you?"

"Because I wished to forget all about it, just as I wish now to forget about her foolish stories." She drew away. "But I don't intend to forget her threat to attend the ball. That creature will not get in, that I can promise you."

"Do I see the glint of battle in your eye?"

"That demirep isn't going to set foot in my house, and she certainly isn't going to purloin a trophy to prove to society how artful and audacious she's been!"

He smiled a little, tilting her lips toward his. "Forget about the Bird of Paradise, my darling," he murmured, kissing her very softly, "and let us think of more agreeable matters instead. Our nuptials, for example. The wedding must be soon, sweetheart, before I expire of passion.''

"It *will* be soon," she whispered, closing her eyes as he kissed her again.

He drew gently away, then. "Perhaps we'd better rejoin the rest of the press, or I might feel obliged to give in to my base desires.''

He took her hand and they left the room, to find Mary still waiting patiently outside.

As they descended through the building, it seemed to Linnet that the atmosphere had changed. Was she being oversensitive because of the conversation she and Benedict had overheard, or were people glancing at her and whispering together? As she and Benedict examined the exhibition, however, she realized that she was indeed being subjected to a little more scrutiny than usual. She could see Algernon Halliday and Lord Frederick, who had yet to leave for White's, and knew they'd been spreading Judith Jordan's tales to whomever they met. How long had the Bird of Paradise's spiteful stories been circulating? A day? Two? Since the meeting at Schomberg House, or before? Just how much amusement was being had throughout society at her expense?

She held her chin high and pretended to be sublimely indifferent to anything that was going on around her, but the undercurrents infuriated her beyond belief. Just let that odious Cyprian attempt to enter Carlisle House on the night of the ball! Just *let* her!

14

For the next week Judith's scurrilous tales continued to circulate, and were generally so amusing that they kept society vastly entertained, the ladies as well as the gentlemen. If Linnet had indeed endured so many mishaps, then she would have been battered and bruised beyond belief, for she was variously described as having had a sash window close upon her while she was leaning out to admire a handsome guards officer riding by; having been doused with a bucket of water by a gentleman who thought she was a burglar; had the train of a gown ripped from hem to waistline by a nail, leaving only a petticoat to hide her modesty; and had her foot stepped upon by a horse so that she'd had to limp her way through an entire evening at Almack's.

The fact that all of these things were patently untrue didn't seem to make any difference, and, unbelievingly, even those who'd been at Almack's that particular night, and who'd actually spoken to her, still believed the story to be fact. It was quite incredible, and most frustrating, for it was bad enough to have to endure the general mirth, but totally insupportable that people should be foolish enough to give credence to the endless calumnies.

Other stories emanated from Portman Street as well, and Linnet found them even more intolerable, for they made her uncomfortably aware that the Bird of Paradise appeared to possess a great deal of detailed information concerning the arrangements for the betrothal ball. First of all, word got out that the Cyprian had engaged Herr

Heller's Ensemble for her masked ball, and then that she'd ordered every white rose in London's market gardens—*pure* white, of course—in order to fill her house with as many blooms as possible. Finally, there was the matter of poking fun at Venetia's idea of a column of red roses, with silver unicorns leaping out from the top; Judith let it be known that a similar column would spring up from *her* ballroom floor, only it would consist of virginal white plumes surmounted by golden poodles!

This, together with the fact that there was now considerable betting at White's on whether or not the demimondaine would manage to attend the Carlisle House ball and steal a memento of the occasion, made Linnet absolutely furious, and she was utterly determined that the circumstance didn't exist under which a creature like Judith Jordan would cock such an insufferable snook at her, Linnet's, expense. All possible safeguards were to be employed on the night, and Sommers was issued with minute instructions concerning the Cyprian's exclusion. If the Bird of Paradise was foolish enough to arrive at the door of Carlisle House, she'd have her elaborate wings severely clipped!

Linnet was equally determined that Judith wouldn't have the satisfaction of knowing the effect her odious campaign was having upon her victim, and so she endured it all with a smiling face, even finding the spirit to laugh in public at some of the stories. She took some unexpected pleasure in this last, for she knew it would annoy the Cyprian, but it was still difficult to do when in reality she was so upset about the whole thing. She was also hurt, for it became more and more and more clear that Nicholas was frequently present at the initial telling of each outrageous tale. How he must be basking in the knowledge that it was all on his account!

It was impossible to keep the stories from Great-Aunt Minton, who first heard them from her friend, Lady Anne. Much shocked and outraged that a vulgar and immoral creature like the Bird of Paradise should presume to take Linnet's name in vain, the old lady always spoke up in her great-niece's defense when the occasion arose, and woe betide anyone who had the lack of wisdom to laugh at one of the stories when she was present.

Great-Aunt Minton's opinion of Nicholas sank even further. She now considered him to be quite beyond redemption, and a blot upon the good name of the Fenton family. Linnet knew that it was of his grandfather that her great-aunt was thinking, for there was now no doubt in her mind that in her youth, Miss Edith Minton had been head-over-heels in love with the earlier Lord Fane. Linnet would dearly have liked to probe further into her great-aunt's past, but it was clearly a closed subject.

The old lady's regard for Benedict didn't show any improvement either. She wasn't impressed when told of the house in North Audley Street, for as she pointed out to Linnet, he wasn't actually going to live it yet, but had merely produced yet another delay. If he'd purchased it and moved in straightaway, then the old lady might have conceded a point or two, but as it was, he remained in her black books, so much so that she wasn't even impressed when she learned of his wish to call Nicholas out. In the old lady's opinion, he'd mentioned his angry intentions to Linnet in the firm knowledge that she'd plead with him to desist, and that if it had actually come to the point when he'd had to carry out his threat, he'd have run the proverbial mile! Linnet had merely sighed, and said nothing more, for there was no reasoning with her great-aunt where Benedict was concerned.

With so much happening, to say nothing of the continuing preparations for the ball itself, Linnet was quite weary by the Thursday that she and Great-Aunt Minton were expected to dine at Venetia's house in Fane Crescent. When the invitation had been relayed to her great-aunt, Linnet hadn't really expected her to accept, given her low opinion of both Venetia and Benedict, but to her surprise the old lady had agreed to attend.

As the town carriage drew up in the courtyard in readiness to drive them both to Fane Crescent, Linnet was almost relieved to be leaving the house. The ball was to take place the following evening, and preparations were in full swing. Venetia's silver unicorns had been delivered, and littered the entrance hall. Soon there would be more, for Venetia had had more new ideas for the decorations. The first score of rose baskets had also arrived, and the sound of hammering echoed throughout the building as alterations were made to the orchestra's apse in the ballroom. Mayhem reigned in Carlisle House, and the peace and quiet of one of Venetia's elegant little dinner parties seemed a positive utopia.

The perfect summer weather continued unabated, and it was another warm, sunny evening as they set off in the town carriage. The team's hooves clattered pleasantly on the courtyard cobbles as the coachman maneuvered the vehicle toward the gates, and out into the street.

Linnet wore her favorite apple-green silk gown, and with it her emerald necklace and earrings. Her dark-red hair was swept up into a delightful loose knot that seemed as if it must surely tumble down into a profusion of curls at any moment, and her eyes seemed very large, soft, and brown. She wore long white gloves, with satin slippers dyed to match the gown, and she toyed with the golden strings of her spangled reticule, for she was still very uneasy indeed about setting foot in what was most definitely Nicholas, Lord Fane's lair.

Opposite her, her great-aunt was splendid in damson taffeta, with aigrettes in her powdered hair. Her shawl and elbow-length fingerless mittens were made of fine beige lace, and she carried a black velvet reticule that was looped over her wrist by a silver chain.

The carriage drove north along John Street, and Linnet's heart began to beat more swiftly. Soon the lodge and gates of Fane Crescent and Fane House would appear ahead. How she wished Venetia had chosen another fashionable address, *any* other fashionable address, but there was no gainsaying that to be able to boast a residence there was the equivalent of a permanent voucher to Almack's.

Great-Aunt Minton observed Linnet's face for a long moment. "I must say that I'm curious as to what I will find at Lady Hartley's."

"Find? What do you mean?"

"I mean that I'm interested to discover any evidence that Mr. Gresham does indeed possess funds of his own."

"Is that the reason you've accepted tonight's invitation?"

"Yes."

"Well, at least you're honest about it," replied Linnet dryly.

"Which is more than can be said of Mr. Gresham," came the quick response.

"Oh, Great-Aunt . . ."

"Don't you 'oh, Great-Aunt' me. My intuition tells me that your intended husband is a fraud, and I shall not rest until I've exposed him. I told you that I'd do my utmost to prevent this match, and I meant it."

"Isn't it a little underhand to accept poor Venetia's invitation, simply so that you can work against her brother if you can?" inquired Linnet a little trenchantly.

"What nonsense, it's the only sensible thing to do," replied the other, without conscience.

Linnet fell silent, glancing ahead along John Street to see the gates and lodge of Fane Crescent and Fane House, but as the carriage drew closer, it became apparent that gaining actual access to the crescent was going to be impossible. The drive into Fane House was clear, but the drive into Fane Crescent was completely blocked by a landau that had shed a wheel. The rather restive team of four bays was being unharnessed, and several men were examining the almost overturned vehicle, deciding how best to remove it from the roadway. The lodgekeeper, who had been alerted to expect Linnet's carriage, was most apologetic, hastening to advise her that access to the crescent could be obtained by driving around through Fane House, joining the crescent at the other end, beyond the central garden. Great-Aunt Minton wouldn't countenance this. Actually drive past the frontage of Fane House? Never! No, she and Linnet would walk across the sunken garden and up the steps that were almost opposite Venetia's house, half-way along the crescent.

The lodgekeeper continued to apologize, hastening to open the carriage door for them to alight, and assuring them that the way would be clear by the time they wished to leave again. He escorted them past the broken-down vehicle, and into the sunken garden, where they told him they would prefer to go the rest of the short distance alone.

As they walked slowly across the garden, the paths of which radiated from the central area where the newly-erected equestrian statue of Nicholas's grandfather stood among the trees, Linnet couldn't help looking toward the windows of Fane House. Her gaze was drawn toward the drawing room, and with something of a jolt she found herself gazing into Nicholas's eyes as he chose that very moment to stand there to look out. She looked quickly away, walking on at her aunt's side without glancing again toward the house.

Reaching the central area, Great-Aunt Minton paused to look up at the likeness of the third Lord Fane. Linnet gazed up at it, too; it was like looking at a statue of Nicholas himself, the resemblance was so great. The sculpted face possessed the same handsomeness, was aesthetic and yet rugged, and the hair was as thick and curly, telling those who saw it that it had been the same shade of almost-black as that possessed by the present holder of the title. Even the eyes seemed to take on color, a pale, piercing blue.

She turned to her great-aunt. "You *did* love him, didn't you?" she asked softly.

Great-Aunt Minton's breath escaped on a long, wistful sigh. "Yes," she whispered. "Yes, I loved him with all my foolish, adoring heart."

"What happened?"

"Nothing."

"But . . ."

"He was married, my dear."

Linnet stared.

"Oh, don't misunderstand, for there was nothing illicit or underhanded about it. We didn't speak of our love for each other, and I never even knew what it would be like to kiss him. He was the most honorable of men, and he was ashamed of having lost his heart to me, just as I was ashamed of having fallen in love with another woman's husband. So, not a word was whispered, but we both knew. It was in our eyes when we looked at each other, and in our voices when we spoke.'' She lowered her eyes, which were suddenly misty with sweet memory. "I could have had my pick of husbands, I certainly didn't lack offers, but there was only one man for me, and he was beyond my reach. For a whole year I endured this loving torture, and then I knew I had to break away.''

"And that was when you left London?"

Her great-aunt nodded. "Yes. I wasn't a great heiress, but I had sufficient funds to purchase Ivystone House, and to live very adequately indeed in my self-inflicted exile.''

"But, when he died, why didn't you come back to live in London? Uncle Joseph importuned you to come back, didn't he?''

"Yes, my dear, he did. But, you see, London has never been the same for me, it's a hollow, empty place now, and it always will be. I've been to stay from time to time, and that is sufficient." The old lady smiled. "Perhaps now you understand why *I* understand so much where you're concerned. We both fled from London to escape the misery of loving a Lord Fane, but there is one signal difference between us. My Lord Fane was a paragon, a god of nobility and rectitude, whereas yours is a rapscallion of the meanest order, arrogant, heartless and totally without principle.''

Nicholas's voice suddenly spoke behind them. "Good evening, ladies. I trust the statue meets with your approval?''

Linnet froze. She'd been so engrossed in her great-aunt's story that she'd quite forgotten he'd observed them from Fane House. Slowly, and very reluctantly, she turned to face him, wondering as she did so if he'd heard her great-aunt's scathing description of him.

He was standing about ten feet away, leaning back against one of the tree trunks, his arms folded. He wore a dark-red coat and cream breeches, and he hadn't bothered to don a top hat before coming out. His dark hair was ruffled, and leafy shadows moved over him as a faint breeze stirred through the garden. The diamond pin in the folds of his starched neckcloth flashed as he straightened, coming toward them.

"The statue is an excellent likeness, don't you agree?" he said.

Great-Aunt Minton turned to look severely at him, a light passing momentarily through her eyes at the shock of seeing again how closely he did indeed resemble her old love, but then extinguishing with coldness as she reminded herself that this was the grandson, not the grandfather. "Sir, the statue may indeed outwardly resemble your grandfather, but there the similarity ends, for you aren't like him in the slightest."

Linnet looked anxiously at her, detecting a battlenote in her tone. "Great-Aunt . . ." she began.

"Hush, child. This fellow needs a lecture, and I am just the one to deliver it." The old lady surveyed Nicholas again. "You, sirrah, are not a gentleman, and you certainly do not deserve to hold an old and much revered title such as that of Lord Fane. Your conduct toward my great-niece has been both disgraceful and unforgiveable, and if I were a man I'd have called you out for your despicableness. Not content with having treated her abominably last year, and with having robbed her uncle of his estate, you now compound your sins by aiding and abetting your unscrupulous paramour in her vicious campaign of lies and spite. So, sir, the likeness to your grandfather begins and ends, you will agree, with your looks alone."

Nicholas heard her out without a flicker of reaction, and when she'd finished, he raised an eyebrow. "You are, of course, entitled to speak as you please. Believe me, if you were indeed a man, I'd have accepted your challenge."

"Sirrah, you have no honor to defend," she replied icily. "Come, Linnet." Without the courtesy of even a nod of her head, she turned and swept away in the direction of the steps leading up to the crescent in front of Venetia's house.

Linnet made to follow her, but Nicholas spoke to her. "I take it that you are still in full agreement with your great-aunt where I'm concerned? Yes, of course you are, for it's from you that she's acquired her information."

Linnet turned in her steps, looking into his eyes. "Nicholas, the information is freely available all over town. You did deceive me with Judith Jordan, you did acquire Radleigh Hall by means that you aren't prepared to explain, and you are in league with her now that she's setting about making me a laughingstock."

"You already know my response to the first two charges, but as to the third . . . Well, yes, I admit to having been present when the stories began their life, but I promise you this, they would have been much more venomous had I not interfered."

"Do you really expect me to believe that? Am I supposed to see you in the guise of a guardian angel?"

"Yes, as it happens."

She gave an incredulous laugh. "You really are beyond belief! After all you've done to me, you now expect my gratitude! Your vanity is quite extraordinary, I vow it's a wonder you can gaze at yourself in the mirror and see past the dazzle of your halo!"

He smiled a little. "What a quaint picture you paint, to be sure. Let me say this, Linnet, if you find me beyond belief, then I feel the same way about you. Every tiny whisper you hear, you believe, and every vile accusation about me, you dutifully repeat. As I've said before, I find your conduct reprehensible in the extreme. Your great-aunt has just seen fit to inform me that she'll never forgive me for what I've supposedly done to you, and now it's my turn to tell you that *I'll* never forgive *you*, Linnet, for all you've done to me."

She stared at him, words fighting for precedence on her angry lips. Then she turned to walk on to where her great-aunt was waiting impatiently by the steps.

"Linnet?" he called after her. "One of the things you've done, or omitted to do, is send me an invitation to your ball."

She was goaded, whirling about to face him again.

"You're the last person on earth I wish to see on that night. No, perhaps not the last, for that place is reserved for your malevolent *belle de nuit*. Please warn her not to attempt to gain admittance to Carlisle House tomorrow night, for if she does, she'll be ejected very ignominiously indeed."

"I'll pass the message on," he replied, sketching a mocking bow.

"I'm sure you will."

He held her angry eyes. "You may not believe this, Linnet, but I hope she doesn't succeed in her plan."

"Then prevent her from carrying it out, sir. You've already bragged once that your interference has been used to good effect, so, pray, attend to it again, but on her behalf this time."

"Judith is a law unto herself, and if she's set on attending your ball, there's precious little I can do about it. Unless you wish me to lock her up for the night."

"Oh, I'm quite sure you can find another way to keep her fully occupied," she replied acidly.

"Your faith in my prowess is very flattering," he murmured, coming closer to her again, and pausing in the shadow of his grandfather's statue. "I really do hope you succeed in keeping her out, Linnet, for to be sure the evening will be humiliating enough for you as it is."

"Humiliating?"

"What else would you call it when the highlight is the placing of that blackguard Gresham's ring upon your willful little finger? Witching hour indeed. I'm sure that that will be sufficient disgrace without Judith's humiliating triumph adding to your distress. It might prove too much for your delicate constitution."

"Your wit is as becoming as your modesty, sir."

He smiled, but then became serious again. "Don't marry him, for you don't love him." Then he turned to stroll away, beginning to whistle softly. The tune was "Greensleeves."

Alas, my love, you do me wrong, to cast me off discourteously. For I have loved you, oh, so long . . .

15

E vening shadows were lengthening, and it was almost
time to dress for the ball. Linnet stood impatiently
on the ballroom steps, watching Venetia supervising the
positioning of the six large blocks of ice that would serve
to cool the temperature when the ball was in full swing
and the room a tremendous crush. The ice had only just
been delivered from Gunter's cellars, and each block had
to be carefully placed on a silver stand that had a bowl
beneath to catch the water. The moment a stand was in
place, a group of maids hastened to border it with arrangements of ferns, so that the effect of coolness was
enhanced still more.

Venetia had been very busy all day, ordering the Carlisle House servants about their designated tasks and seeing that every one of her careful plans for the decorations
were attended to precisely. There were roses everywhere,
standing on the floor on either side of the blue velvet
sofas, twined around the pillars beneath the orchestra's
apse, where Herr Heller's Ensemble was tuning up, and
garlanded around the walls in delightful loops of crimson
flowers. But most especially there were the roses in the
great column rising from the center of the floor; it ascended in what seemed like a solid mass of crimson petals, and at the top there were the leaping silver unicorns,
arranged like the spokes of a huge horizontal wheel. Silver ribbons were tied around the unicorns' necks, ex-
tending to the corners of the ballroom ceiling, through
metal hoops fixed there, and then descending to metal

rings attached to the floor, where they were firmly tied in readiness for the climax of the evening. At the stroke of midnight, as Benedict placed his ring on Linnet's finger, footmen would untie these ribbons, the unicorns would slowly descend on wires hidden in the rose column, and as they descended, the linnets in their cages inside the column would be set free. After that, the guests would continue to dance the night away, not leaving until after dawn.

The notion of red roses and silver unicorns had quite carried Venetia away, and the firm in Cheapside that provided them had received order after order. Now there were unicorns in many places other than just the great column, they were also on the orchestra's apse, and at the foot of the steps where Linnet stood waiting. They lined the entrance hall and the staircase, they guarded the main entrance, and they stood proudly above the courtyard gates, their necks garlanded with roses, their silver horns studded with sequins that made them glitter constantly. The whole effect was breathtakingly lavish, and original, and Venetia was justifiably proud of her efforts.

The one item she didn't have to oversee personally was the ball supper, for Gunter's had sent their own staff to prepare and serve it. They were in the supper room across the entrance hall, hurrying to set everything out correctly on the white-clothed tables. It was an extravagant supper, one of Gunter's best, and there were dishes of chicken, ham, and beef, mousses of salmon and trout, salads of every description, desserts as spectacular and delicious as was expected of the famous confectioner, and an array of tasty tidbits guaranteed to tempt the most jaded of appetites. The champagne was in readiness, standing in huge buckets of ice, and a positive infantry of glasses was gathered in battalions upon more white-clothed tables.

Linnet paced nervously up and down at the top of the steps, the knotted ends of her white shawl dragging over the floor behind her. She wore a cream lawn day dress, and her hair was pinned up into the simplest of knots.

She glanced across the hall at the clock on the mantle-piece. Time was marching on, and still Venetia fussed around with the blocks of ice. Why couldn't she leave the footmen to finish without her, so that the business of dressing for the ball could commence?

Sommers appeared from the direction of the kitchens, and Linnet paused to look at him. "Is everything in order?" she asked.

"Yes, madam. I've carried out your instructions to the letter. All entrances will be guarded throughout the ball, and . . ."

"Especially the méws lane entrance?" she interrupted. "I'm sure that that is the way she'll choose, for it would normally be less well watched."

"Including the mews lane entrance," he confirmed reassuringly. "And every invitation will be checked as the guests arrive, so that no unauthorized, er, persons, will gain admittance."

"You will be certain to remind everyone again, won't you? There mustn't be a single slip."

"Everything that can possibly be done, will be done, madam."

"Very well. Thank you, Sommers."

"Madam." He bowed, and withdrew again.

As he did so, Great-Aunt Minton came down the staircase to join her. The old lady looked at Venetia, who was still ordering the somewhat harassed footmen around with the final block of ice. "Lady Hartley is a very demanding task mistress," she murmured.

"She wants everything to be as perfect as possible."

"So it seems. I wonder how much of it is for you and her half-brother, and how much simply for herself?"

"That's unfair, Great-Aunt," chided Linnet.

"Possibly. I'm still not quite sure about that lady. However, I *am* quite sure about Mr. Gresham." The old lady paused, evidently wanting to choose her next words very carefully indeed. "Linnet, my dear, I can't approve of this betrothal tonight, and so I feel I must ask you for a final time to reconsider. I know this is the eleventh hour, and that there would be a great deal of gossip and speculation were the betrothal to be broken off, but . . .''

"I will not change my plans, Great-Aunt," Linnet broke in quietly. "I love him, and I wish to be his wife, so please don't ask me to break matters off now."

The old lady nodded sadly. "I understand, my dear. I only trust that you understand why I felt obliged to ask you this one last time. I won't say anything more, for I now accept that the betrothal is absolutely inevitable, but I cannot promise not to do my best to deter you from marriage itself. Forgive me for being unable to accept Mr. Gresham as being the ideal husband for you, Linnet, but one cannot deny one's instincts and conscience. Well, it's nearly time now, and if I'm to be togged out in all my evening glory tonight, I'd best be getting on with it. I will see you in due course, my dear." She kissed Linnet lovingly on the cheek, and then walked back toward the staircase.

Linnet watched her, and then lowered her glance. Oh, how she wished her great-aunt had come around to the betrothal, and therefore to the marriage, but it seemed that that wasn't to be.

Venetia hurried up the ballroom steps in a flurry of white muslin. "There. What do you think of it?" she asked Linnet, pointing to the finished ballroom.

"It's truly wonderful."

Venetia looked sharply at her, detecting a strained note in her voice. "Is something wrong?"

"No, of course not."

"You seem a little . . ."

"I've been waiting an age for you to stop moving those wretched lumps of ice around," replied Linnet, smiling.

"I suppose I *have* been a long time," admitted Venetia ruefully, "but everything has to be perfect. Speaking of which, has Sommers attended to everything necessary to keep La Jordan at a distance?"

"I sincerely hope so."

"Oh, don't worry, for I'm sure she won't get in," reassured Venetia, linking her arm warmly. "Just think about how marvelous a night this is going to be. Oh, I can't *wait* for you to see the ring, for I know you're going to adore it.''

"From which I gather you've already seen it?''

"Yes, it was delivered to me yesterday.''

"To *you?*''

"Until Benedict's financial affairs are straightened out once and for all, I'm allowing him to use various accounts of mine, including the one at Loudon's of Bond Street.'' Venetia smiled. "Only the very best jeweler in town would do for your betrothal ring.''

Linnet returned the smile, but knew what her greataunt would have said had she heard. It would be seen by that lady as still further proof that Benedict's financial affairs weren't all they should be.

Venetia was looking around the ballroom again. "Oh, I *do* think it looks excellent. I confess I'm very pleased indeed. Lady Georgiana Cavendish's ball is about to be completely shipwrecked.''

"It will founder upon the rocks of your brilliance,'' Linnet answered her with a laugh.

"It will indeed. After this, I shall have to really excel on the night I at last . . .'' Venetia broke off suddenly, looking quickly away.

What had she almost said? Linnet studied her. "When you at last what?''

"Nothing. It's not important.''

"Were you thinking of Freddy?'' Linnet didn't know why his name came into her head, but it did.

"No, I certainly wasn't,'' replied Venetia firmly.

"Have you heard from him at all?''

"Not a word, and I don't really expect to.''

Linnet fell silent, for there was something very final in the other's tone.

Venetia glanced at her. "I'm sorry, I didn't mean to sound sharp.''

"It was my own fault for being ill-mannered enough to probe.''

"And before you ask yet again, no, I'm definitely *not* carrying a secret torch for Mr. Coleridge, even though White's betting book apparently believes that I do. I vow there's nothing the gentlemen of London wouldn't wager about, even upon Poky Withington's chances of succeeding with me! One thing's certain, they'll never guess who it is that I really . . .'' Again she broke off, this time coloring a little guiltily.

Linnet looked quizzically at her. "Do go on," she urged, "for the cat's out of the bag now, isn't it?"

"Only the tail, and that's about to be firmly pushed back in," replied Venetia, still blushing.

"Aren't you going to tell me his name?"

"No."

"Do you love him?"

Venetia paused, and then nodded. "Yes, and I have for a very long time."

Linnet was curious. "Does he love you?"

"He will, in the end. Goodness, is that the time? Benedict will soon be here!"

"And it's all your fault, yours and that horrid ice."

"I fling myself upon your mercy," replied Venetia, drawing her away from the ballroom toward the staircase.

"Venetia, I trust you'll forgive me for mentioning Freddy yet again, but he *is* a friend of mine; at least, he was."

Venetia ushered her up the staircase. "What do you want to say about him?"

"Just that I still intend to write to him soon, to see if he'll tell me what's wrong. I can't leave matters as they are, I like him too much for that."

Venetia looked at her. "My advice is to let sleeping dogs lie. If it pleases him to treat you abominably, I don't see that there's any onus upon you to make any effort with him."

"I just feel there's been a terrible misunderstanding of some sort."

"Just leave well alone, that's my advice," said Venetia.

Linnet didn't say anything more, but was still determined to write to Freddy. There had to be an explanation for his conduct, and she was sure that all could be put right in the end.

They parted at the top of the staircase. Venetia went to the room that had been set aside for her for that day and night, it having long since been decided that with all the effort she'd been putting into the ball, it was hardly right that she should drive back to Fane Crescent at the end of the day. Besides, she and Linnet were looking forward to breakfast, when they'd be able to talk *ad infinitum* about the night's events.

Linnet went to her own room, where Mary was waiting to attend her. The room smelled of roses from the basket Benedict had sent, and the perfume grew stronger as she went briefly to the window to look out. A small team of footmen was scattering ferns over the courtyard, and the silver unicorns on the gateway shone in the evening sunshine, their sequined horns glittering like diamonds.

Before darkness fell, the courtyard would be thronged with elegant vehicles: would one of them have conveyed the Bird of Paradise on her mission? Would the Cyprian successfully carry out her foray into her long-suffering victim's territory?

16

B enedict arrived just as Mary put the final touch to
Linnet's hair. The evening light was golden, and the
shadows very dark and long. Candles had been lit.

The gray lace gown by Madame Leclerc looked perfect
for the occasion, and not at all like a last-year's acquisi-
tion. The gray taffeta petticoat was sleeveless and clinging, and the overgown was made of the richest Brussels
lace available. It had a daring neckline, and long, tight
sleeves, and was set off exquisitely by a ruby necklace
and earrings.

Mary had taken great pains with Linnet's hair, leaving
some soft curls to frame her face, and twisting the rest
back into a smooth knot from which tumbled a cascade
of little ringlets, each one twined with a thin gray satin
ribbon. The ribbons fluttered a little as she rose to look
out at the arriving carriage.

Mary smiled. "Mr. Gresham will think you look lovely
tonight, Miss Linnet."

"I hope so." Linnet returned the smile.

The maid hurried to fetch the gray gauze shawl and
arranged it carefully over her mistress's arm. Then she
brought the carved ivory fan, and Linnet turned to examine her reflection in the cheval glass in the corner of
the room.

There was a tap at the door. "Madam?"

"Yes, Sommers? Come in."

The butler entered, looking very splendid in his best
dress livery, his hair hidden beneath a handsome new

bagwig. He bowed. "Mr. Gresham has arrived, madam. I've shown him into the library."

"Thank you, Sommers. Is Lady Hartley with him?"

"No, madam, she's still dressing in her room as is Miss Minton."

"Thank you, Sommers."

"Madam." He bowed again, and withdrew.

Linnet took a final look in the cheval glass, and then hurried out to go to Benedict in the library.

Joseph Carlisle had been very proud of his collection of books, housing them in a fine second floor room overlooking the garden. It was to one side of the ballroom, looking toward the mews lane and Curzon Street, and boasted a number of deep, comfortable armchairs upholstered in dark-brown leather. There was still a vague hint of tobacco smoke in the air, a reminder of the many hours Joseph had spent in his favorite chair by the fireplace. There was another reminder of the past in the painting that hung on the chimneypiece, for it was a view of Radleigh Hall, the family estate Joseph had forfeited to Nicholas's sleight of hand.

Benedict stood by the fireplace, one foot on the polished fender as he flicked through a book. He wore a black corded silk coat, white pantaloons, a white waistcoat, and a frilled shirt. There was a sapphire pin in his neckcloth, and his white gloves lay on the mantelpiece.

The moment she entered, he replaced the book on the shelf and came to meet her, taking both her hands and raising the palms to his lips.

"You look exquisite, my love," he murmured, looking deep into her eyes.

"I want to look my very best for you tonight."

"And so you do." He kissed her fingertips. "In a few hours you will be wearing my ring, and I vow that it will seem a lifetime before that ring is joined by a wedding band."

"It will not be all that long, I promise you," she whispered.

His fingers tightened, and then he released her, standing back to survey her more deliberately. "Poor Venetia,

I fancy her teeth will start to grind the moment she sets eyes on you.''

"She'll probably manage to put me in the shade.''

"Never.'' He went to the window, looking down into the gardens, where the footmen were beginning to light the lanterns in the trees. His glance moved to the far end of the garden, and the mews. "I see you have someone on guard down there.''

"Our feathered friend isn't going to get in.''

"I doubt if she'll even try. It's probably all been an exercise to send you into a tizzy.''

"If that was her purpose, she succeeded.'' Linnet joined him at the window. "She intends to come here tonight, I know she does.''

"Nothing is going to spoil our evening,'' he said softly, slipping an arm around her waist and pulling her close. "Tonight is ours, Linnet, and every second of every minute of every hour is going to add to our happiness.'' He kissed her warmly on the lips, enveloping her in his arms.

Almost immediately they had to pull guiltily apart, for a rather embarrassed footman knocked upon the door. "Begging your pardon, madam, but Mr. Sommers has sent me to say that the first carriages are arriving, and it is time for you and Mr. Gresham to go to the ballroom.''

There were spots of color on Linnet's cheeks as she nodded. "Very well.''

He bowed, and hurried thankfully away.

Benedict grinned at her. "Methinks we were observed in a moment of unseemly intimacy that will soon echo throughout the kitchens,'' he murmured. "Now, then, shall we adjourn post haste to the ballroom? It would hardly be the thing for the guests to be announced, and there to be no host and hostess there to welcome them.'' Taking her hand, he hurried her to the door.

Herr Heller's Ensemble was already playing softly as they descended the ballroom steps to take their places beside one of the African prince candleholders. The air was noticeably cooler because of the blocks of ice, and the French windows stood open to the terrace and gardens. The scent of roses was almost heady, and the column in the center of the sanded floor looked breath-takingly splendid, with the unicorns' sequinned horns glittering in the soft light of the chandeliers, which had been lit because the long summer evening was drawing to a close.

The guests' voices were in the entrance hall as Benedict glanced swiftly around at his sister's clever handiwork. "Venetia's pulled out all the stops, has she not?"

"She's done us proud."

"Perhaps I'll forgive her for throwing away her chance with Freddy," he said, grinning.

Sommers announced the guests' names just as Great-Aunt Minton, impressive in peacock blue taffeta and aigrettes, hastened down the steps to join Linnet and Benedict. "Her Grace, the Duchess of Devonshire, Lady Georgiana Cavendish, Lord Morpeth, and Mr. Peregrine Withington."

Linnet's heartbeats quickened, and a welcoming smile curved her lips. The evening had begun.

Over the next hour the guests arrived in increasing numbers. Very few invitations had been declined, and the courtyard was soon filled with carriages and chairs. More vehicles had to draw up in the street, causing inconvenience for other traffic needing to pass that way, and a small crowd of onlookers gathered at the gates to watch the guests in all their finery.

Darkness had fallen, but the first dance had yet to commence. There was much talking and laughter as the guests mingled, and Herr Heller's Ensemble played sweetly in the background, waiting for the signal that Linnet and Benedict were ready to start the ball.

Venetia had at last put in an appearance, having taken an unconscionable length of time over dressing. She looked very lovely in the primrose silk gown she'd decided upon, and her short, dark hair was completely concealed beneath a turban of cloth-of-gold. A shawl of the same cloth-of-gold was draped lightly over her arms, its long ends trailing prettily behind her, and the Hartley diamonds glittered at her throat and on her wrist. She bubbled with pleasure at the constant praise her decorations received, and the only blemish upon her horizon was the equally constant presence of a certain Poky Withington, who was determined to win his wager concerning his success with her.

Linnet watched him with some amusement, because it was obvious to everyone except Poky himself that Venetia abhorred him. Then Linnet's smile faded a little, for although it was obvious who Venetia *dis*liked, it wasn't as obvious who she did like. Was the mysterious gentleman she secretly loved here tonight? Linnet wondered again who he might be, and had to reluctantly draw the inevitable conclusion that the only reason Venetia didn't name him was that he was already married. She hoped the guess was wrong, but had the dismaying feeling that it wasn't.

Glancing around the crowded ballroom, she found herself wondering instead about the Bird of Paradise. There was a sea of faces, many of them made very different by the rage in some circles for wearing elaborate wigs. The Countess of Velborough, for instance, looked unrecognizable with a mass of white curls over her normally rather mouse straight hair. What if Judith Jordan was equally unrecognizable? What if she wore a prim gown and wig, and discarded her famous plumes, as Algernon Halliday had said at the exhibition? Without her famous trademarks, the Cyprian could become anonymous, and might at this very moment be secretly smiling at her.

It was a horrid thought, but one which had to be quickly set aside, for Benedict told her it was time to commence the first dance, and then beckoned to Sommers.

As the butler went to inform Herr Heller that the opening dance, the obligatory country dance, was about to be required, Benedict smiled at Linnet. "Whatever happens now, the evening is a success. You know that, don't you?"

She smiled, thoughts of Judith Jordan receding. "Yes, I know," she whispered, slipping her hand over the arm he offered.

A ripple of applause went around the gathering as the orchestra played the long opening chord, and the floor was cleared for the host and hostess to lead off the dancing. The jaunty country tune began, and Benedict and Linnet moved up and down before the column of roses. They accomplished several patterns of the dance before the other guests joined them, and soon two crowded but elegant rows of dancers moved on either side of the column of roses.

The country dance ended, and Herr Heller's musicians proceeded smoothly into a stately allemande. Benedict and Linnet danced this measure together as well, but then separated, as convention demanded, to dance with as many other partners as possible. And so Linnet enjoyed a minuet with the Marquess of Lorne, while Benedict accompanied Lady Georgiana Cavendish, whose own ball was being triumphantly eclipsed tonight. For the polonaise that followed Linnet took to the floor with handsome Lord Granville Leveson-Gower, and Benedict with Lady Georgiana's mother, the Duchess of Devonshire. Another country dance followed, and then a cotillion.

Soon the ball was in full swing, and the noise was considerable as everyone strove to be heard above the Herr Heller's musicians, who were now giving their all on this, their first important engagement. The temperature rose, and the blocks of ice began to slowly melt, dripping into their silver trays. Footmen circulated with champagne and iced water, and many guests strolled in the gardens, where the lanterns in the trees threw soft colors over the ground. In the ballroom, where the light was almost dazzling, the guests' reflections moved richly in the wall mirrors. Ostrich plumes trembled in the warm air, and just audible beyond the music and laughter was the endless hiss of hundreds of feet moving on the sanded floor.

It was just before the ball supper was served that Sommers had to announce a very startling late arrival. Great-Aunt Minton was in the supper room, dealing with a problem, Benedict was walking in the gardens with Venetia, and knew nothing about it, but Linnet was partnering none other than Mr. Algernon Halliday, whose gleeful enjoyment of Judith Jordan's stories had been overheard at the sculpture exhibition.

"Lord Fane," declared the butler, his voice carrying clearly in the sudden hush that had greeted Nicholas's appearance at the top of the steps.

Linnet's heart almost stopped, and she froze in her steps, staring at the elegant figure in the ballroom entrance.

He wore a black coat, unbuttoned to reveal a white waistcoat, which was itself only partly buttoned, so that the lace trimming on his shirt front could peep through. His neckcloth was lace-edged as well, and in it he wore a black pearl pin. His black pumps were absolutely plain, and he wore white silk stockings and breeches. A faint smile touched his lips as he handed the uneasy butler his invitation card, and then paused at the top of the steps, toying with the spill of lace protruding from his cuff.

Linnet couldn't move. It had never occurred to her that Nicholas would attend. Her gaze moved to the white card in Sommers's hand. How on earth had he acquired a card? His name had most definitely not been on the list . . . Oh, where was Benedict when she needed him?

There was a great deal of whispering. Herr Heller had stopped playing, and there was no dancing. All eyes moved from Nicholas to Linnet, and then back again. Fans were raised to sly lips, and quizzing glasses took full note of all that was going on.

It seemed that the guests standing around Linnet and Algernon Halliday somehow drew a little away, so that Nicholas couldn't help but see her. His blue eyes rested on her for a long moment, and then he slowly descended the steps. The guests parted as he reached the floor, and his path to her was left utterly clear.

Her first instinct was to open her fan, for her face was suddenly very hot, but she knew that such a gesture would reveal how very nervous and uneasy his arrival had made her. She strove to remain outwardly composed, but inside her heart was beating so swiftly she was sure its pounding was audible throughout the ballroom. She could almost feel Algernon Halliday's malicious delight as he remained firmly at her side.

Nicholas reached her at last, sketching an elegant bow. "Miss Carlisle. Halliday."

Algernon nodded. "Fane."

Linnet couldn't speak, for it was all she could do to retain her appearance of calm.

Another faint smile curved Nicholas's lips as he looked at her. "I must ask you to forgive my disgracefully late arrival."

Sommers was aware of the uneasy silence, and quickly gestured to Herr Heller to begin playing again. Within moments, the sweet notes of a ländler echoed across the ballroom, and the more considerate among the guests endeavored to smooth the awkwardness by beginning to dance. There were still whispers and intrigued glances, but Linnet and Nicholas were no longer the sole focus of attention.

Linnet was about to demand of him how he'd acquired an invitation when he caught her completely off guard by asking her to dance. "Will you do me the honor?" he murmured, taking her hand and leading her onto the floor before she had time to protest.

To have snatched her hand away and turned from him would have made a scene memorable enough to rattle teacups for weeks to come, so she didn't demur, but instead allowed him to whirl her slowly into the measure, his arms twined around hers. Her heart still thundered in her breast as he held her, his gloved fingers warm through the lace of her sleeves.

He smiled, noting how she averted her eyes, determined not to offer him any conversational opening. "Does this ländler take you back to our first meeting, Linnet? It was here, in this very ballroom, was it not?"

She had no intention of remembering such things. "Why have you come here tonight? If it's your intention to wreck the evening . . ."

"Credit me with more finesse than that. As to why I've come, well, you did send me an invitation, albeit a little tardily."

Her eyes flew to his face. "You weren't sent an invitation!"

"Nevertheless, one was delivered at my door this very morning."

"All the invitations went out two weeks ago."

"Then you evidently had a charming afterthought."

"No."

"Then someone else did. Ah, me, now I'm quite crushed, for I've been under the illusion that you'd decided to be pleasant to me after all."

A sudden terrible thought struck her. If Nicholas had somehow laid hands upon an invitation, then it was only too probable that his odious Cyprian had as well. "Have you brought that creature here tonight?" she demanded, her steps faltering.

"Remember your dancing lessons, Miss Carlisle, for it wouldn't do if we fell over in front of everyone, would it?"

"*Did* you bring her?" she demanded again.

"Please lower your tone, unless you wish the world and his wife to be in on it. No, I didn't bring her, and you do me yet another grave injustice by even thinking that I would."

"I wouldn't put anything past you, sir."

"No, I know," he replied dryly, "for you've made it tediously and ungraciously clear."

"Stop toying with me, Nicholas. I'm nothing to you now, and I wish to be left alone to live my life as I see fit."

"Left alone to make a complete mess of it, you mean," he said.

She didn't notice how he was maneuvering her to the edge of the floor, or that he was adjusting their progress now that the end of the dance was approaching. They were close to the conservatory, a place of sunlight during the day but now a haven of leafy shadows, lit only by the brightness from the ballroom.

The ländler was ending, and the conservatory door was right beside them. As the final chord sounded, he suddenly seized her hand, thrusting her out from the ballroom and through the doorway to the shadows beyond. It was done in a second, and no one else saw. As the quiet and seclusion of the conservatory closed over them both, she heard his low whisper.

"It's time to show you the error of your ways, madam, and I'm just the one to do it."

17

"How dare you!" she cried, at once furious and alarmed. Her heart was now pounding so much that she couldn't believe he didn't hear it. She glanced anxiously around, but there was no one else there. The leaves pressed close, and the scent of damp earth and citrus filled the still air.

"Oh, I dare, Linnet," he said softly, his eyes still a clear blue, even in such a shadowy place. He caught her wrist as she made to push past him toward the safety of the ballroom. "No, don't think of leaving just yet, for I haven't finished."

"Let me go!"

"If you wish to attract attention, then by all means do so, but I advise you to consider the consequences. What price your reputation if you were discovered in here with your former love? And on your betrothal night, too."

For a moment more she continued to try to wrench her wrist free, but then knew that it was futile. Besides, he was right, the last thing she wanted was to be found alone with him in such compromising circumstances.

As she ceased to struggle, he pulled her further into the shadows. The leaves folded over them, and anyone who entered the conservatory now wouldn't know they were there.

At last he released her, holding her gaze in the virtual darkness. "Right, madam, I suggest you explain to me exactly why you're persisting in this idiocy with Gresham."

"It's none of your business," she breathed, pressing back from him and finding herself trapped against the conservatory wall.

"I'm making it my business." He put his hand to her chin, making her look at him again. "I'm waiting for your explanation, Linnet."

"Very well. I'm marrying him because I love him."

"No, Linnet, you're doing it because you *want* to love him, which is an entirely different matter. He's a parasite who at present lives off his half-sister, but who has every intention of soon living off you. He looks at you and he sees a fortune, and that's all there is to it."

"Is there no end to your spite, Nicholas? You really can't bear it that I no longer feel anything for you, and you intend to destroy my love for Benedict if you can!"

"Believe it or not, I'm concerned about your welfare."

"As concerned as you were last year when you were unfaithful to me? And when you stole Radleigh Hall? Oh, yes, Nicholas, you're always *very* concerned about my welfare, aren't you?"

He was still for a moment, his eyes veiled, and then he spoke softly. "Very well, since you won't listen to reason, it's time to find out how strong your contempt really is."

Before she knew what was happening, he'd pulled her roughly into his arms, forcing his lips down upon hers. With a stifled cry, she tried to push him away, beating her fists futilely against his shoulders, but he was by far too strong for her. The kiss was relentlessly sensual, and allowed her no mercy. He pressed her close, his fingers caressing the nape of her neck. His lips were hard and yet soft, potent and yet gentle, and they laid inexorable and urgent siege to her resistance.

She continued to struggle to be free, but an inescapable warmth was beginning to seep through her, moving like a flame through her veins. It was a treacherous warmth, alluring and irresistible, and it stirred her unwilling senses like the opening of a window in a stifling and breathless room. She didn't want to respond, she wanted to remain immune, but her strength seemed to be deserting her. The warmth was invading her entire being, gathering power as it stole her will to resist. It was only with Nicholas that she felt this way, only with him that she knew such an intensity of desire, and with each passing second now she knew she was in danger of betraying Benedict by surrendering to the tumult of feelings that were being so forcibly aroused.

Her struggles were weaker, and the warmth drained the last of her resistance. With a moan, she gave in to the intoxicating desire that drove levelheadedness into oblivion, and left her completely at the mercy of this one man. There were no thoughts of Benedict now, only the overwhelming need to be dominated by Nicholas, to be loved by him, possessed by him.

But as she surrendered, he thrust her scornfully away, his eyes hard and his voice cold. "So, you love Gresham, do you? And you despise me as a dishonorable, double-crossing thief? How unfortunate for you that I also happen to be the one you still love. Oh, don't bother to deny it, for every word would be a lie, wouldn't it? You love me, not Benedict Gresham, and if you persist in marrying him, you can be assured of a lifetime of unhappiness."

Shaken and humiliated, she could only stare at him. Her composure was in tatters, and her pulse was still racing with confusion. His kiss burned on her lips, but his voice drove icicles into her heart. With a choked sob, she turned away, unable to face him.

"I trust that you now see the error of your ways, madam, for if you don't then I fear there's no hope for you. Good night." He turned, pushing his way through the leaves to rejoin the ball, where a minuet was playing.

She leaned wretchedly against the wall. The cold touch of reality reached out to her, and she had to fight the tears that rose hotly to her eyes. She mustn't cry, she *mustn't*. She had to face her guests again. And face Benedict. Shame swept through her. She'd betrayed his love, and on the very night he was to place his ring on her finger. And for what? A fleeting moment of passion, followed by yet another cruel rebuff. Oh, what a fool she'd been, what an utter fool . . .

She straightened, taking another steadying breath. Nicholas had done more than just point out the error of her ways, he'd concentrated her thoughts to devastating effect. She wouldn't allow one man's beguilingly persuasive kisses to cloud her judgment. Benedict was her future, and before another hour was out, she'd be wearing his ring.

Suddenly much more calm, she crept secretly out of the cloak of leaves, hurrying not toward the ballroom, but to the French windows that stood open to the terrace. If someone had noticed Nicholas thrusting her into the conservatory, she wasn't going to make the mistake of being seen leaving it shortly after he had. No, she'd return to the ballroom as if she'd been walking in the gardens, which was what she was going to say she'd been doing.

There were quite a few guests on the lantern-lit terrace, but no one glanced toward her as she slipped stealthily out. Snapping open her fan, she strolled casually along the terrace toward the ballroom, pausing to speak to the first group of guests.

"I'm sure you'll think me the end in fools," she said with a light laugh, "but I'm rather afraid that I've mislaid both Mr. Gresham and Lady Hartley. They were walking in the gardens, but although I've trailed around and around looking for them, they appear to have vanished."

Algernon Halliday was one of the group, and his clever eyes appraised her for a long moment, then he smiled. "Why, my dear Miss Carlisle, they returned to the ballroom several minutes ago. I believe, from their urgent manner, that someone had informed them of Lord Fane's arrival."

Yes, she thought frostily, and I'll warrant you were that someone. She met his rather sly gaze, disliking him even more than she had after overhearing him at the exhibition, and a bland smile curved her lips. "Thank you so much, I'll look for them inside."

She could almost feel his disappointment as he

sketched her a bow. Walking toward the ballroom, she encountered a rather anxious Great-Aunt Minton, who drew her discreetly aside for a moment. "Are you all right, my dear?"

"Yes, Great-Aunt, quite all right."

"It's just that Lord Fane's presence seems to have caused such a stir, and I was afraid that it would have upset you."

"I'm quite all right," said Linnet again, meeting the other's gaze with commendable equanimity, so that no one could have known she was anything but cool, calm, and collected.

Great-Aunt Minton nodded, somewhat reassured. "I'm relieved to hear it, but tell me, how did he acquire an invitation?"

"I only wish I knew. Still, the ball has continued in spite of his appearance on the scene. Now, if you'll excuse me, I think I should find Benedict and Venetia, for they'll be wondering as much as you."

The old lady patted her arm. "Yes, of course, my dear."

Smiling, Linnet kissed her, and then hurried into the ballroom, where she saw Benedict and Venetia almost immediately. They were talking seriously together, and Benedict glanced around anxiously from time to time. She'd almost reached them when Benedict turned suddenly and looked directly at her. She saw the moment of hesitation, of doubt, and guilt lanced through her anew.

Forcing a bright smile to her lips, she hurried up to link her arm warmly through his. "I've been looking for you all over the garden. Where on earth did you get to?"

Venetia returned the smile, but a little uneasily. "We were just walking. I can't think how you didn't see us."

"Well, it is rather dark out there, in spite of the lanterns," replied Linnet lightly. Then she leaned conspiratorially closer. "I suppose you know that Nicholas has somehow acquired an invitation, and has actually had the gall to attend?"

Benedict glanced at Venetia, and then cleared his

throat, giving Linnet a somewhat awkward smile. "Well, yes, we did know. I-I understand he danced with you."

"Yes, he did. I vow I'll never dance another ländler! I didn't want to accompany him, but to have refused would have caused a scene, and that was the last thing I wanted. I did do the right thing, didn't I?" She was all innocence as she looked into his eyes.

Venetia opened her fan, wafting it gently to and fro. "Linnet, I have to be honest with you. Benedict and I are afraid . . ."

"Yes?"

"Afraid that Nicholas may mean too much to you after all, and that you might wish to cancel the betrothal." She glanced at the clock on the wall. It was five minutes to midnight.

"Nothing could be further from my wishes," replied Linnet softly, squeezing Benedict's arm and smiling at him. "Unless, of course, *you* wish to withdraw?"

Benedict's hand moved swiftly over hers, and a relieved smile warmed his lips. "Never would I change my mind where you're concerned, my darling."

Venetia was smiling, too. The fan snapped closed again, and there was new light in her eyes. "Oh, Linnet, I'm so glad. I was truly alarmed when I heard about Nicholas, and your dance with him. And then when we came inside and there was no sign of you, or of him . . ."

Linnet glanced around. "Isn't he here, then?"

"Not that we've seen. Oh, wait a moment, isn't that him over there by that sofa? Yes, he's with that lady in . . ." Her voice broke off suddenly, and she gave a horrified gasp. "Oh, surely it isn't *her!*"

Linnet whirled about, her anxious gaze seeking out Nicholas and his partner. She saw them at last. The woman had her back to them, but was tall, with a tumble of bright red curls and a subdued gray-green silk gown that gave the impression of having been chosen because it was nondescript. Linnet's heart almost stopped. Was it Judith Jordan? Had the creature gained admittance after

all, and was she displaying the supreme audacity of talking to Nicholas right in front of everyone?

Fury bubbled up inside her, and she made to approach
them, but Benedict's hand tightened over hers. "Leave
it, Linnet. I'll tell Sommers, and have her discreetly
ejected."

Linnet looked at him torn between a desire to deal with
the Cyprian herself and a need to observe discretion.
When she looked toward the sofa again, Nicholas was
alone. The mysterious red-headed woman had vanished.

Venetia looked at the clock. "It's almost midnight. I'll
go to see Sommers, while you two get on with the betrothal ceremony. I'll be back to see my *pièce de résis-
tance.*" She gestured toward the rose column in the center
of the floor.

Linnet was trembling a little, shaken yet again, this
time by the thought that the Cyprian had somehow managed to penetrate the Carlisle House defenses; she was
also forced to the inevitable conclusion that in spite of
his protestations of innocence, Nicholas had after all assisted his mistress in her plan.

Benedict was leading her toward the center of the ballroom floor, and Herr Heller had stopped his orchestra in
the middle of a polonaise. Great-Aunt Minton took up a
prominent position nearby, making it clear that the betrothal was about to take place, and the guests drew back,
leaving a wide area around the column of roses.

Venetia was speaking in an undertone to Sommers, who
looked dismayed and startled, hurrying away with several
of the footmen to see if the lady with the bright red hair
and gray-green gown could be found. Then Venetia beckoned some other footmen, sending them to their ap-
pointed places in the corners of the ballroom, ready to
untie the silver ribbons and release the unicorns.

An expectant hush fell on the glittering gathering, and
with a tender smile, Benedict took the ring from his
pocket. It was a magnificent ring, gold with three large
diamonds, and it flashed in the light of the chandeliers
when he slipped it on to the fourth finger of her left hand.
A great cheer went up as he kissed her on the lips, and

then there were cries of wonder as the silver ribbons were released, and the shining unicorns began their slow descent. As they reached the floor, there was a fluttering sound from within the column, and suddenly the linnets were released, fluttering into freedom and flying above the guests. As Venetia had so confidently predicted, the little birds soon escaped through the open French windows, fleeing to the lantern-hung trees in the dark garden. At dawn they would fly away forever. Benedict held Linnet close for a long moment. "I love you, my darling," he whispered.

She hugged him tightly, but somehow couldn't say the same words to him. Another sliver of guilt passed through her, and she was relieved when Sommers at last announced that supper was being served.

Herr Heller's musicians began to play again, an allemande this time, and those guests who did not immediately move to the supper room began to dance.

Great-Aunt Minton was the first to congratulate the newly betrothed couple and she hid her sadness so well that only Linnet could detect it. Then Venetia appeared at their side, hugging them both, and then looking at Linnet's ring. "Did I not say that it was exquisite?"

"You did indeed. It's the most beautiful ring in the world."

"Well, now you're halfway to being my sister-in-law," replied Venetia, smiling.

Linnet glanced at Sommers, who stood by the top of the ballroom steps. "Venetia, did they find that woman?"

"Yes, actually. It was a certain Mrs. Horatia Ponsonby, and she wasn't at all pleased to be pounced upon by a party of footmen. She left in exceeding high dudgeon, and said that she would never again set foot in this house."

"Oh, dear," murmured Linnet. "Mrs. Ponsonboy? I don't know a Mrs. Ponsonby, do you? I don't remember her being on the list."

"She wasn't. She accompanied Lord Dymchester, whose invitation stated he could bring a partner. Anyway, she isn't important, nor is Lord Dymchester, who will, no doubt, soon be in equally high dudgeon. All that matters is that you and Benedict are safely betrothed, and there still isn't any sign of the Bird of Paradise. Now, if I don't have some refreshment, I vow I shall fade away. Oh, lord, here comes Poky Withington again!''

''Linnet and I will defend you,'' declared Benedict gallantly. ''If we all adjourn to the supper room together, he'll give up for the moment. Shall we go?'' He offered them both an arm, and they laughingly accepted.

He escorted them toward the steps leading out of the ballroom, but then the brief laughter died on Linnet's lips as she saw Nicholas ascending the steps before them. He paused at the top, turning to look directly at her. Another of those mocking smiles that taunted her so much played fleetingly upon his lips, and then he sketched a disdainful bow before walking out into the entrance hall.

She knew he was leaving the house.

18

It was an hour after dawn when the final guests drove away across the misty courtyard. A few street calls could already be heard in the distance, and there was a luminosity in the air that told of yet another fine August day to come. Sommers supervised the extinguishing of all lights, and Venetia's carriage was driven in readiness for Benedict to the steps of the house, for he alone remained to take his leave.

Great-Aunt Minton had retired to her room, and Venetia waited discreetly at the foot of the staircase in the entrance hall while Benedict said a tender farewell to Linnet. The cool morning air breathed damply in through the open doors, and the jingle of harness could be heard as the waiting horses tossed their heads.

He held Linnet close, his lips moving against her hair. "To leave you now is unbelievable torture, my darling," he whispered.

She closed her eyes, the wretchedness of guilt lingering in her heart. How could she have betrayed him? How could she have been so weak as to allow Nicholas to pierce her armor again? Tears stung her eyes, and she drew back.

He misinterpreted, taking her ring hand and kissing the fourth finger. "It will not be long now, my love," he murmured. "Soon we will be man and wife, and I will never again have to leave you like this."

The horses in the courtyard tossed their heads again, straining to be off, and the coachman spoke sharply to them. Benedict glanced toward the open doors. "I must go. Until tomorrow night, then."

She managed a smile. "Tonight, you mean."

He smiled, too. "Yes, I suppose I do. Until tonight, then."

"Yes."

He hesitated, and then kissed her again before hurrying out into the dawn. She heard the whip crack, and then the carriage was driving away toward the main gates. She listened until all sound had died away, and then turned to walk toward the patiently waiting Venetia.

With a smile, Venetia took her hands. "He's right, it won't be long before you're man and wife. You and I must begin planning straightaway, for I cannot wait to begin arranging it all." Her smile became a little sheepish. "I fear the bit is well and truly between my teeth after tonight's success. Oh, how my vanity was flattered by all that praise."

Linnet laughed a little as they began to ascend the staircase. "I think I should be a little jealous, for you certainly stole my thunder being so very brilliant with your decorations."

"You don't really feel like that about it, do you?" asked Venetia, pausing in sudden anxiety.

"No, of course not. I'm delighted that your efforts were such a triumph."

"I shall do your wedding even more splendidly."

"I've no doubt of it, for you certainly have a flair for such things."

"Devonshire House is extinct," Venetia observed with feline relish.

"Poor Lady Georgiana."

They reached the top of the staircase, and Venetia turned to face her.

"Wasn't Herr Heller a stroke of genius? I've never heard such music, and the guests were all much impressed, too. I vow I've started a new rage, just as I planned. There was one plan that didn't go off, though, wasn't there?"

"Was there?"

"Of course, you ninny. La Jordan didn't get in."

"Oh." Linnet smiled. "I was on tenterhooks all the time that she'd somehow manage to slip in."

"Instead, it was Nicholas who slipped in. Linnet, how do you think he got that invitation?"

"I have no idea. He insists that it was sent to him, but I don't believe him."

"It must have been an awful moment for you when he suddenly arrived."

"It was," replied Linnet candidly.

"I'm so sorry Benedict and I chose that of all times to take our stroll in the gardens."

"It was hardly your fault."

"I think it bad enough of Nicholas to attend at all, let alone to single you out so publicly for the ländler."

"I suppose the ballroom was buzzing about it when you returned?"

"Yes, it was, rather." Venetia paused, looking at her. "Where did you and he get to?"

"Get to?" Linnet trusted she sounded natural. "I don't understand."

"Well, I gather the dance ended, and you and he seem to have vanished from the floor."

"I promise you I left him as quickly as I could," replied Linnet, neither telling the truth nor lying. She drew a long breath. "I wonder how many of my guests are now under the impression that I deliberately invited him?"

"Too many for comfort, I fancy."

Linnet sighed. "No doubt that was his sole purpose—well, almost his sole purpose."

"What do you mean?"

Linnet sighed, and decided to confide a little. "He seems intent upon advising me against marrying Benedict."

Venetia stared at her. "He's what?"

"He's trying to prevent the marriage." Linnet glanced past her, for the door to the back staircase had opened and Mary emerged with Venetia's maid. They were hastening to their respective mistress's rooms with candlesticks, for the windows would remain shuttered for them to sleep. Linnet smiled at Mary. "I will be along in a moment."

"Yes, Miss Linnet." The maid bobbed a quick curtsy, and then hurried on.

Venetia waited until both maids were out of earshot, and then spoke again. "If he's trying to stop the match, does that signify he's had second thoughts and now wants you back?"

Linnet gave a wry laugh. "No, he doesn't want me. I just think he's being a dog in the manger."

"Are you sure it's just that?"

"Oh, quite sure."

Venetia smiled after a moment. "Well, what does he matter? You have Benedict now."

"Yes."

They didn't say anything more, for at that moment Mary's rather tremulous voice carried along the passage. "M-Miss Linnet? I th-think you'd better come."

Linnet turned, puzzled. The maid was standing by the bedroom door, the candlestick still in her hand. "What is it, Mary?"

"S-Someone's been here. Your ribbon stand has been tampered with, and the ribbons are all over the floor."

Followed by Venetia, Linnet hurried along to the doorway. The maid stepped inside, holding the candlestick aloft for them to see. The wavering light fell over the room, illuminating the dressing table. The ribbons had been tossed in confusion over the floor, but some remained on the stand, tied neatly into bows. Those that remained like this were the special ribbons, woven with linnets.

Taking the candlestick from the maid, Linnet went to see more closely. Venetia and Mary came too, and they trod carefully over the profusion on the floor in order to examine the rather odd bows on the stand itself.

Linnet ran her fingertips over them. Someone had gone to immense trouble to single out these particular ribbons, tying them in very neat, even bows. Why? Who would bother?

Mary's breath caught suddenly. "Miss Linnet, one of the special ribbons is missing!"

"Which one?"

"The cream one with the golden edging. It was there when I dressed your hair earlier, I know it was."

Linnet stared at the ribbon stand again. Yes, that ribbon *had* been there earlier. She drew a long, shuddering breath, for it was suddenly all quite clear. "Judith Jordan was here. Somehow she got in after all," she said quietly.

"Oh, Miss Linnet." Mary looked at her in dismay.

Venetia put a quick hand on Linnet's arm. "You can't be sure of that."

"Oh, yes I can. She swore she'd acquire a trophy, and she has. I'm the only person who wears those ribbons, and the only way she could purloin one would be to get into this house and take it. She's been here, not only in this house, but in this very room." Linnet held the candlestick up again, turning to look around at the moving shadows.

"Oh, Miss Linnet! Your lovely roses!" With a cry, Mary hurried to the basket. It had been roughly overturned, and its contents spilled over the floor.

As the maid set the basket upright again and began to rescue the roses, Linnet noticed some little fragments of white paper scattered on the carpet nearby. Bending, she retrieved one. It was a portion of the card Benedict had sent with the roses.

"What is it?" asked Venetia curiously.

"The card that came with the basket."

Venetia stared at her. "But, why on earth would Judith Jordan bother to do anything to the roses?"

"I don't know. Petty amusement, no doubt. Or to show me how utterly she holds me in contempt." As she spoke, a silent thought whirled bitterly around in her head; Nicholas had lied yet again, for contrary to his denials, he *had* aided and abetted his mistress in her spiteful purpose. What else was there to believe? His arrival had been intended as a diversion, for no doubt Judith had been with him as he entered the house, and while Sommers's attention had been distracted by the sudden appearance of a gentleman who was supposed to have been banned from the premises but who had somehow acquired an invitation, she had slipped upstairs to this room to carry out her plan. Yes, that was how it had been done; like most clever plans, its simplicity had made it successful.

Venetia put a gentle hand on her arm. "It might not have been her, Linnet. There are a number of disappointed ladies who envy you your match with Benedict. Any one of them could have come up here and . . ."

"If it had just been a matter of spilling the roses, I might have wondered, but what possible reason could such a lady have for stealing a ribbon, or for making so certain that the theft was discovered? No, it was Judith, make no mistake about it."

Venetia fell silent, and there was no sound in the room except for the rustle of the roses as Mary rearranged them in the basket.

Venetia glanced at Linnet. "Shall you pick up the gauntlet?"

"Gauntlet?"

"By attending the Cyprian's ball next Wednesday?"

Linnet gave a rather taut smile. "My first instinct is to say yes, but common sense tells me to stay well away. She may have slipped in and out of here without detection, but I might not be so lucky, and she has no reputation to forfeit, whereas I most definitely have."

Venetia nodded. "You're probably very wise, but I marvel at your restraint."

"You, I suppose, would enter the fray?"

"Well, hers *is* a masked ball, which does, you will admit, rather lengthen the odds in your favor. Still, I am a wicked, worldly widow, and you are a demure young lady who is only just betrothed, so perhaps I shouldn't seem to be encouraging you to do anything scandalous. Your great-aunt would nail my hide to the wall if she could hear me."

"I would indeed, Lady Hartley," said a rather frosty voice from the doorway behind them.

Great-Aunt Minton stood there in her voluminous white nightgown, her gray hair falling in two plaits from beneath her night bonnet. She advanced into the room, her glance resting angrily upon Venetia. "I find your so-called advice somewhat questionable, my lady."

Linnet spoke up quickly. "It wasn't as it may have sounded, Great-Aunt."

"No?" The old lady's glance took in the ribbons and the roses. "What has been going on?"

Linnet inhaled slowly. "I'm rather afraid that Judith Jordan was successful in her plan. She came in here and took one of my ribbons."

"I see. Well, there was always the possibility that she'd carry it off, I suppose. But I see no reason whatsoever for you, Lady Hartley, to urge Linnet to pursue a foolish tit-for-tat response."

Venetia lowered her eyes a little guiltily. "I'm sorry, Miss Minton, I didn't mean to speak out of turn. Perhaps it's time I went to my room. Good night, Linnet." With a quick, apologetic smile, she hurried out.

Great-Aunt Minton glanced at Mary. "Please wait outside, for I wish to speak privately with your mistress."

"Yes, madam." Mary hurried out, closing the door softly behind her.

Linnet faced her great-aunt. "It really wasn't necessary to speak to Venetia like that."

"On the contrary, it was very necessary indeed. I don't care for the influence she has over you, for she is somewhat lacking in principle."

The old lady paused, eyeing her. "Do we know yet how Lord Fane acquired his invitation?"

"Ho."

"So much for your detailed arrangements for keeping undesirables out."

"If *only* I knew who sent it to him."

"Was it a *genuine* invitation?"

"Apparently. Sommers believed it to be so."

"Then it must be so," murmured her great-aunt.

"I don't know how Nicholas obtained it, but I do know why he did so."

"Pray tell."

"It was a ploy to help Judith Jordan to get in."

"Did he admit that to you?"

"No," conceded Linnet, "but then I've long since given up expecting him to tell the truth about anything." She looked away, for she suddenly remembered the kiss in the conservatory. He'd shown her the truth about herself in those few seconds, and it was a truth she despised.

"Is something wrong, my dear?" inquired her great-aunt, noting her manner.

"No, of course not."

Great-Aunt Minton glanced at her ring. "He won't make you happy, you know, and you certainly won't come to love him as you think you will."

Linnet felt the color touching her cheeks, and was glad of the dim light from the candlestick. "Don't let's quarrel again, Great-Aunt."

The old lady smiled sadly. "We'll never agree on this particular subject, I fear. Very well, I'll leave you to rest. Oh, by the way . . ."

"Yes?"

"You are on no account to even contemplate Lady Hartley's disreputable advice concerning that masked ball. It simply would not do at all, is that clear?"

"Yes, Great-Aunt."

"Good. Good night, my dear."

"Good night."

As the door closed on the old lady, Linnet turned to look at the chinks of light piercing the shutters. The sun was up now, and the street calls were echoing all over Mayfair. She knew her great-aunt's counsel was wise, but, oh, the temptation to go against it!

19

Sleep proved virtually impossible, even though she was exhausted. After tossing restlessly for an hour, Linnet lay there awake, thinking about what had happened. Anger and resentment welled within her that Judith Jordan had carried out her threat after all, and there was an intense hurt that Nicholas had once again proved himself to be all that was low and despicable.

A confusion of emotions swirled through her. She didn't want to think about events in the conservatory, but she knew she had to. Briefly, oh, so briefly, she'd given in to feelings she'd hoped had been extinguished forever, feelings that had again lifted her to heights of desire she hadn't experienced for the past year. Benedict's kisses were tender and warm, but Nicholas's were an irresistible invitation to passionate fulfillment. She loathed her weakness, and was bitterly ashamed at having failed Benedict on the night of their betrothal.

She felt sick at heart as she gazed up at the shadowy hangings of the bed. Sunlight found its way into the room around the shutters, and the sounds of Mayfair drifted in quite clearly. Carriages drove along Charles Street, and once she thought she heard one in the courtyard, but then a church bell began to ring out and she heard no more.

There was no hope of falling asleep again, and at last she gave up trying. Sitting up, she rang for Mary, and within a few minutes the maid came in with a light breakfast tray. On the tray was a brief note from Venetia, and Linnet soon realized that she had indeed heard a carriage in the courtyard, for Venetia had returned to Fane Crescent.

The note had been hastily scribbled. *I think it prudent to remove myself from your great-aunt's vicinity, but promise to call upon you very shortly, as not even an outraged Miss Minton can keep me from early discussion of wedding plans. Venetia.*

Linnet sighed, and supposed that such a hasty departure was only to be expected after the sharp confrontation with the somewhat irate old lady.

Daylight flooded into the room as Mary opened the shutters, and Linnet sipped a cup of tea but left the breakfast, as she had no appetite at all. Today should have been so happy, but instead, thanks to Nicholas and his loathsome Bird of Paradise, it was very depressing indeed. She was betrothed to Benedict because she'd told herself that in time she would love him as fully as she should, but now, in the cold light of day, she knew it wasn't going to be easy. Just how many insults and hurts did Nicholas have to deal her before she could be over him once and for all? He'd been unfaithful, he'd lied and cheated, and he'd treated her more shabbily than she'd ever dreamed possible, but still she was fool enough to yearn for him. Was ever there a greater or more gullible fool than she?

A little later, she sat before the dressing table for Mary to brush and pin her hair. She wore a pink-and-white-checkered muslin gown, and her plain white shawl lay in readiness over the back of a nearby chair.

All traces of Judith's intrusion into the room had been removed. The ribbons were back on their stand, and the roses had been carefully rearranged in their basket, but, to Linnet, the Cyprian's presence was still almost tangible. That a woman like the Bird of Paradise had had the effrontery to come into the house after all, was too much to stomach, and Linnet found herself again contemplating paying the demimondaine back in kind. *Would* it be possible to attend the Portman Street masked ball, and remove a retaliatory memento? It would be sweet revenge, and no mistake.

She was so deep in thought that she didn't hear Mary address her.

"Miss Linnet?" said the maid again.

"Mm?" Linnet aroused herself, looking at the maid in the mirror. "I'm sorry, Mary. Did you say something?"

"I was wondering if there were any particular clothes you wished me to put out for you today?"

"No, I don't think so. A quiet day would appear to be wise, so I won't be going out at all."

"Yes, Miss Linnet."

"Is my great-aunt at home?"

"No, Miss Linnet. She breakfasted at the usual time, and then went out with Lady Anne to drive in Hyde Park. I believe they intend to call upon Mrs. Jeffreys in Kensington afterward."

Linnet nodded. Mrs. Jeffreys was another old friend, and no doubt there would be a great deal of talking and sipping of tea, which meant that her great-aunt wouldn't return before the early evening.

Mary finished pinning her hair into a soft knot at the back of her head, and then brought the shawl. Linnet rose from the dressing table, shaking out the skirts of her gown. "I shall be in the library if I'm needed, Mary."

"Yes, Miss Linnet." The maid glanced at the untouched breakfast on the tray. "Shall I bring some coffee a little later, miss?"

"Yes, that would be most agreeable."

"And some almond wafers?" ventured the maid.

Linnet smiled. "Yes. Thank you."

She sat in her late uncle's favorite armchair in the library, a book open on her lap. In the gardens she could see the servants taking down the many lanterns that had been hung in the branches. She wondered if the linnets had all flown safely away. There was no reason why they shouldn't, but she hated to think of even one of them coming to harm.

She glanced down at the book, turning another page. It was a collection of poems, light and easy to read, and the diamonds in her ring sparkled as she toyed with the leather bookmark. Her thoughts wandered on to the evening, and her next meeting with Benedict. Would he be able to see the guilt in her eyes? Would he know that her love for him wasn't as strong as his was for her? Tears stung her eyes, and she blinked them savagely away. He didn't deserve to take second place to a two-faced, heartless fiend like Nicholas, for he'd always been so loving, loyal, protective, and supportive. How *could* she have been so misguided as to hesitate for even a second? There wasn't a contest, for Benedict was worth a thousand Nicholases.

Sommers came suddenly to the library door. "Begging your pardon, madam, but Lady Hartley has returned. She wishes to speak urgently with you."

Urgently? Linnet looked at him in surprise. "Please show her in."

"Madam."

"Oh, and Sommers?"

"Madam?"

"Mary was to bring coffee to me in a while, would you have it served now? For two?"

"Yes, madam."

He withdrew, and a moment later she heard Venetia's skirts rustling as she hurried toward the library. Then she was there, looking very stylish in a light-blue velvet spencer and matching hat, and a gray taffeta gown that was so pale it seemed almost silver. But if she looked stylish, she also looked very flustered and agitated.

Linnet rose, a little startled. "Whatever is it? Is something wrong?"

"Wrong? Well, it isn't right, and that's a fact."

Linnet went to her, ushering her to an armchair. "Sit down and tell me what's happened. Some coffee will be brought in a moment."

"Coffee? I could do with something a little more potent," replied Venetia wryly, sitting down. She sighed, then. "Oh, that woman! If I could exterminate her, I vow I would."

"What woman?"

"The Vulture of Paradise, who else?"

"Oh." Linnet resumed her own seat. "I take it you've encountered her somewhere?"

"No, I've just been enlightened as to what she's been up to since leaving here." Venetia paused. "She's making a positive *feast* of her success, and it's already all over town."

Linnet leaned her head back. She'd been so engrossed in other things that she'd completely forgotten that the Cyprian would be bound to make as much capital as she could from her triumph.

Venetia looked at her. "The fortitude of many of your gentlemen guests last night is quite amazing, for they went on from here to a little breakfast party in Portman Street, where the highlight of the proceedings was the appearance of La Jordan's pet poodle—the four-legged canine one—with your ribbon tied very conspicuously to its tail. I gather that there was huge mirth at the spectacle, and the gentlemen eventually returned to their homes to gleefully spread this latest tale at your expense. I'm so sorry, Linnet, but I *had* to tell you. I didn't want you to hear from anyone else."

The anger that had bubbled inside Linnet since finding out about Judith's visit now rose hotly to the surface. "Oh, how I *loathe* her," she breathed. "Why on earth is it so important to her that she makes me look as foolish as possible? Surely she can't really be *that* unsure of her hold upon Nicholas?"

"It seems she must be." Venetia sat forward. "There were a great many successful wagers on her chances, for she more than came up to male expectations."

"She's had a good deal of practice in that particular art," murmured Linnet acidly.

Venetia smiled. "There's no disputing that. Well, now it appears to be your turn."

"My turn for what?"

"For coming up to male expectations—where the placing of wagers is concerned, that is. White's betting book is now rapidly filling up with gambles as to whether or not you'll rise to the challenge next Wednesday."

"By creeping into *her* ball to remove a souvenir?"

"Yes." Venetia glanced uneasily at the door. "I trust your great-aunt isn't likely to pounce upon me at any moment?"

"She's out."

"I'm relieved to hear it, for I'd hate her to think I was bent upon persuading you to throw your reputation to the winds."

"Actually, I *have* been thinking about somehow attending the masked ball," admitted Linnet slowly.

Venetia was startled. "Not because of anything *I've* said, I hope!"

Linnet drew a long breath, coming to a sudden and irrevocable decision. "In fact, I've gone beyond just thinking about it, now I'm actually determined to do it. I'm so furious about last night that I simply *can't* let her get away with it." She was surprised to hear herself saying the words, for she really hadn't realized how close she was to such a shocking decision; but the placing of her ribbon on the poodle's tail was simply the last straw.

Venetia was uneasy. "Linnet, you have to let her get away with it. It's far too risky for you to try to go there . . ."

"She managed the reverse."

"Well, as I think you said yourself after the ball, when we realized she'd been in your bedroom, she hasn't got anything to lose. I doubt if she can remember when she was last respectable, but it's very different for you."

"I know, but it's all too much to endure now. She's been blithely ridiculing my name throughout society, then she attended the ball *and* entered my room, and now she's tied my ribbon to her wretched dog's tail!"

Venetia looked shrewdly at her. "That isn't all, is it? She is also the one your lover played you false with."

Linnet looked away.

Venetia sighed. "You're in earnest about this, aren't you?"

"Yes."

There was a tap at the door, and Sommers escorted a maid in with the tray of coffee and almond wafers.

As the tray was set on a table before her, Linnet waved them both away. "I'll serve, Sommers, so you may go."

"Madam." He bowed, ushered the maid out again, and then closed the door behind them.

Not a word was uttered as Linnet sat forward to pour the coffee from the elegant silver pot into the dainty gold-and-white porcelain cups. She handed one to Venetia. "Would you care for a wafer?" she asked.

Venetia was exasperated. "How on earth can you ask something so mundane after just telling me you seriously intend to secretly gatecrash a demirep's masked ball?"

"Bold plans shouldn't come before politeness."

"Bold, *ill-advised* plans," said Venetia. "Have you really considered the implications? Let's presume that you do succeed, and that you steal a trophy, what will happen then? Do you imagine it won't get out over town? She's bound to see that it does, for she obviously wishes to harm your reputation."

"Whatever she says will merely be seen as another of her fanciful tales about me," answered Linnet. "I don't intend to give her any proof that she can use in public. Whatever I take, I'll send back with a verbal message, not a written one. All I'm concerned with is that *she* knows I've dealt her blow-for-blow, and I really couldn't care less about the rest of society, or about the contents of White's betting book."

Venetia studied her. "You *have* been thinking about this, haven't you?"

"I couldn't sleep, and I just found myself considering the matter. Then, before you came, I was doing the same, but it wasn't until you told me about my ribbon gracing the poodle's tail that I realized how carefully I'd been mulling it all over."

Venetia sighed. "And how do you imagine you're going to do all this without people knowing what you're up to? Benedict, for instance? Have you thought about his reaction? He won't like it at all, for no gentleman of honor could possibly accept his future wife's risking her entire reputation in such a place of ill repute."

"I don't intend to tell him. The masked ball is next Wednesday, which also happens to be the night of his reunion dinner at East India House."

"Reunion dinner? What reunion dinner?"

"Didn't you know? It's something to do with his time in Madras, but I'm not exactly sure of the details. Suffice it that he's otherwise occupied on that particular night. So is my great-aunt."

"With Lady Anne Stuart?"

"Yes." Linnet smiled conspiratorily. "It also so happens that I, like you, have been sent an invitation to Lady Lydney's postponed rout, an invitation that I intend to accept, and which I will let it be know I've accepted. I'll tell my aunt that Mary will be my chaperone, as she was when I went to the exhibition with Benedict, except that I won't be going to Lady Lydney's rout at all. When my aunt has left for Lady Anne's, my carriage will depart as well, its blinds down so that no one will know it's empty. I'm sure La Jordan will have someone watching this house that evening, she's bound to want to be sure of my movements after all the noise she's been making. She'll be vastly reassured if my carriage is seen leaving, apparently for the rout. Anyway, after my aunt has gone, and my carriage, I will actually depart from the mews lane, in a hackney coach hired for the occasion. It will take me to Portman Street."

Venetia drew an unhappy breath. "Linnet, I know that what happened last night has upset you a great deal, but I can't help wondering what *exactly* it is that's driven you to want to retaliate. Is is the Bird of Paradise herself? Or is it more to do with Nicholas?"

"He has nothing to do with it," replied Linnet quickly.

Too quickly. Venetia studied her closely. "I thought last night that a change had come over you after he'd arrived. You seemed a little, er, reserved."

"You imagined it."

"No, I didn't." Venetia continued to look at her. "Linnet, I know I asked you if Nicholas had had second thoughts about you, but I didn't ask *you* if you'd had second thoughts about *him*."

Linnet wasn't actress enough to hide the truth, and could only look guiltily back at her.

Venetia was dismayed. "Oh, *Linnet . . .*"

"I still intend to marry Benedict, and I mean to make him happy."

"Trusting to providence all the while?"

"Nicholas has no place in my life now, no matter what my feelings may or not be, and I *know* Benedict and I can be happy together."

"Linnet . . ."

"No, Venetia, I don't wish to discuss it anymore, just as you do not wish to discuss your mysterious gentleman love."

Venetia lowered her eyes at that. *"Touché,"* she murmured.

Linnet looked anxiously at her. "Do—Do you intend to tell Benedict?"

"That you still love Nicholas? Of course not! Whatever do you take me for? I love Benedict, but I also love you, and I still want to see you both happily married. I happen to agree with you, you see. You *will* make him happy, and your marriage will be the closest thing possible to a real love match. Now then, shall we forget your feelings for Nicholas and concentrate upon your plans concerning a certain *bal masqué?"*

Linnet managed a weak smile.

Venetia smiled, too. "So, at the moment we have your great-aunt obligingly removing herself to Lady Anne's and we have Benedict out of the way at East India House. What we don't have is your disguise, and the way you intend to get in to the house in Portman Street. Since you've been thinking so long and so deep upon the first items, I've no doubt you've done the same concerning the latter."

"Yes. I thought your dressmaker might be approached to alter one of my gowns."

"My dressmaker?"

"She's infinitely more discreet than Madame Leclerc, who positively trumpets gossip over town. I thought that you and I could decide upon a suitable gown, and then keep it at your house. I could then call upon you, and your dressmaker could take measurements and so on."

"And no one here in Carlisle House would be any the wiser?"

"Yes."

"All right, my dressmaker it is." Venetia hesitated. "I take it that this gown is going to be *à la Cyprian?*"

"Within reason. I don't intend to look completely abandoned."

"Just a little abandoned," murmured Venetia, smiling.

"Just a fraction."

They both smiled, but then Venetia became serious again. "Oh, Linnet, I'm filled with misgivings about this . . ." she began unhappily.

"I'm set upon doing it," interrupted Linnet. "Now, where were we? Ah, yes, the gown. Next I'll need a wig to hide my hair."

"I have one."

"Do you?" asked Linnet in surprise.

Venetia looked a little embarrassed. "When I had my hair cut short like this, I wasn't sure if I was doing the right thing, so I purchased a wig in order to hide the devastation, if necessary. As it happened, I rather liked my hair short, and so I've never used the wig. It's yours, if you wish."

"What's it like?"

"Like my hair used to be, long, curly, and very dark-brown."

Linnet smiled. "It sounds the very thing. All I need now is a mask, and I think I have one somewhere. I haven't been to a masked ball for a few years now, and the mask hasn't been used in all that time, but I'm sure it will be lying in a drawer or cupboard somewhere in my room. It's one of those masks that conceals the top of the face to just below the eyes, and has a veil below that."

Venetia sat back. "Right, so we now have everything sorted out except how you intend to gain entry to the house."

"All I've come up with so far is to try to get in through the mews lane at the back, and then through the gardens and kitchens. I don't think she'll have the lane entrance guarded. All the guests will be masked, and any guards would have to ask them to show their faces. That wouldn't be the thing.''

"She said blithely," murmured Venetia dryly. "Linnet, there's many a slip 'twixt cup and lip, so don't take any of this lightly. You have so much to lose if it all goes wrong."

"I'm not taking anything lightly, you may be sure of that," replied Linnet softly.

Venetia smiled a little. "I'm relieved to hear it. By the way, there's one thing you haven't mentioned. The small matter of the trophy you'll have to steal if you're to equal her exploits. Have you thought about it?"

"Oh, yes, it's quite simple. I intend to find the Bird of Paradise's bedroom and take one of her gaudiest plumes.''

20

There were only four days to Judith's ball, and many plans to lay in that short time. At Carlisle House, only Mary was told what was going on, for she had to accompany Linnet to and from Venetia's house for fittings of the gown that was being altered. The maid was horrified to learn of her mistress's intentions, and did her utmost to dissuade her, but it was to no avail, for Linnet was firmly set upon exacting her full revenge, and wasn't open to any persuasion to the contrary.

A trustworthy hackney coachman was engaged to wait in the mews lane behind Carlisle House on the evening of the Cyprian's ball. Mary's soon-to-be-married cousin lived next door to just such a coachman, and Linnet was assured that he could be relied upon to carry out his task with the utmost discretion. Apart from this man, and Venetia's circumspect dressmaker, only Linnet herself, Venetia and Mary knew anything about what was being planned, and that was the way Linnet intended to keep it.

Strangely enough, it didn't prove too difficult to find a suitable gown in Linnet's wardrobe but it had to be made *more* respectable, rather than less! Two summers previously she'd worn a dark-green tunic dress and citrus-yellow undergown combination that at the time had pleased her very much, but her taste had changed since then, and the item had hung forgotten for more than a year. The undergown had never been intended to be worn on its own, and the bodice was consequently somewhat skimpy, in order that the wearer of both undergown and tunic dress together would not feel uncomfortably hot at a crowded function. It was little more than a petticoat, barely respectable over the bosom, and no doubt the Judith Jordans of the world wouldn't have hesitated to wear it as it was, but for Linnet it was just unthinkable. She was prepared to be a Cyprian for an evening, but not that much of a Cyprian! The dressmaker was therefore instructed to provide the gown with lacy puffed sleeves, and to fill the neckline in with lace frills, as well as decorate the bodice with beaded embroidery. Even with these adjustments, the gown would still be improperly bold, but she comforted herself with the thought that her true identity would be safe behind a mask and a wig. She also convinced herself that it would all be worthwhile in the end, for even though society would never know what she'd done, Judith Jordan most definitely would. She did have another reservation about the gown, however, and that was that it was yellow, the color in which Nicholas liked her most of all.

Her determination was kept at boiling point over those four days because Judith's campaign against her hadn't ended with the betrothal ball. Foolish stories continued to emanate from Portman Street, and Linnet remained the butt of much sly amusement. She endured it all stoically, and gave no hint at all that anything was afoot. Great-Aunt Minton was angrily disapproving of Judith and never for a moment suspected any retaliation from Linnet, who gave every appearance of preparing for Lady Lydney's rout.

Benedict was reduced to a state of simmering anger, finding it virtually impossible to remain composed when he heard so much laughter at Linnet's expense, but he knew that she was right when she pointed out that any display of resentment would merely serve to gratify the Cyprian.

Of Nicholas nothing was heard at all, except that he had been seen at Judith's house on a number of occasions, but on the Wednesday of the masked ball, as Linnet and Mary were leaving Venetia's house with the finished gown wrapped up in a brown paper parcel, they found him waiting by the carriage.

He wore a dark-gray coat, cream breeches, and top boots, and his waistcoat was of a particularly rich wine-red brocade. A cane swung impatiently to and fro in his gloved hand, and his top hat was tipped back on his head. He gave every impression of having been waiting for some time, and turned quickly the moment the door opened. Removing his top hat, he bowed a little, his quick glance taking in the jaunty angle of Linnet's peach velvet hat, and the elegantly embroidered hem of her matching full-length pelisse.

Her steps faltered the moment she saw him, but it was too late to turn and go back inside. Besides, Venetia's footman had already hurried out to open the carriage door for her. A telltale flush leapt to her cheeks. Memories of the conservatory were all around her, and her lips seemed to tingle as if he'd kissed her only a few moments before. She felt foolish and embarrassed, and made to walk past him without speaking.

"Good afternoon, Miss Carlisle," he said, deliberately closing the carriage door with the end of his cane.

The footman looked at him in surprise, not knowing quite what to do. Nicholas gave him a thin smile. "That will be all, you may return to your duties."

Discretion proved the better part of valor, and the footman hastened back into the house.

Nicholas looked at Linnet again. "I said, good afternoon."

"I don't wish to speak to you, sir."

"How unfortunate, because *I* wish to speak to you."

The end of his cane still rested firmly against the carriage door, and she glanced coldly at him. "Please allow me to enter my carriage."

"Only if you consent to hear me out."

"We have nothing to say to each other," she said stiffly.

"I'm very much afraid that we do. Now, then, I'd be obliged if you'd politely invite me to travel to Charles

Street with you, so that we may talk in relative privacy,'' he glanced at Mary, ''but I'm quite prepared to stand here in the full gaze of the crescent, and insist upon saying what I have to say anyway. The choice is yours, but I think it would be prudent for you to agree to my request.'' He gave a slight smile. ''This is all so much more open than your conservatory, is it not? If I'm seen to pester you, Gresham might feel compelled to call me out on account of it, and I doubt very much if he'd emerge unscathed from the exercise.''

She drew a long breath. ''Very well,'' she said in a tight voice, ''but I do this under duress.''

''Naturally.'' He lowered the cane, and opened the door for her, seeming vaguely amused as she deliberately ignored his helping hand and climbed in on her own. He relieved Mary of the brown paper parcel containing the gown, assisted her into the carriage, and then placed the parcel on the seat.

He looked up at the waiting coachman. ''Walking pace will do, I'm not in any hurry.''

''My lord.''

Nicholas climbed in, sitting opposite Linnet, and a moment later the carriage drew away from the curb. Linnet averted her face, looking stonily out of the window. All she could think of was her foolish surrender in the conservatory, and the way he'd so cruelly humiliated her.

He watched her for a moment, and then turned his attention to Mary. ''Are you discreet?''

''Yes, my lord.''

''Good, for it wouldn't do for what I'm about to say to get out.'' He looked at Linnet again. ''You cannot be unaware that Judith attended your ball after all.''

''It would be rather difficult for me to remain in ignorance when she parades her poodle and my ribbon at every opportunity.'' She gave him a cold glance. ''But you've known all along, haven't you? You knew even when you denied it at the ball.''

''No.''

''Come now, surely you aren't *still* pretending you didn't assist her!''

"It isn't pretense, for I didn't help her in the slightest."

"No, of *course* you didn't. How unreasonable of me to doubt your word," she murmured sweetly.

"It's immaterial to me whether you believe me or not, for your ball is over and done with, and nothing can change what happened. However, Judith's ball is imminent, and I'm more than a little concerned that you may be contemplating something rather foolish."

"I'm touched that you're concerned about me."

He ignored the sarcasm. "You've let it be known that you're going to Lady Lydney's rout, but I'm not convinced. It could all be a stratagem, and your real intention could be to go to Portman Street."

"How telling that you should credit me with your devious ability to say you'll do one thing, when all the time you'll be doing quite another."

"I've never lied to you."

"Oh, come now . . ."

"Linnet, you're beginning to be tiresome."

She drew a quick breath. She mustn't let him provoke her. She managed a cool smile. "So, you think I'm on the point of beating your tawdry *belle de nuit* at her own game, do you?"

"It had crossed my mind, yes. Linnet, if you go to that ball tonight, you may find yourself playing her game in more ways than one."

"I don't know what you mean."

"Are you so naive? What do you imagine it's going to be like there? Do you think it's going to be similar to your own ball, but maybe slightly more rowdy? If you do, then you're greatly mistaken, for when the upper floors are opened later in the night . . ." He didn't finish.

She looked away. She hadn't considered it in depth because she hadn't wanted to.

"Look at me, Linnet."

Unwillingly, she obeyed.

He held her gaze. "Any woman who presents herself at that ball will be regarded as ready, willing, and able to oblige a gentleman's wish. Do I make myself clear?"

"Perfectly. No doubt you speak from considerable experience of such events."

"Now you're not only being naive, but childish as well!" he snapped, his blue eyes brightening with quick anger. "I may be a man of the world, but you, Linnet Carlisle, are *not* a woman of the world. You wouldn't know how to fend for yourself in an environment like that ball, and if you *are* plotting to get in there tonight, I cannot advise you strongly enough to forget all about it. Judith's taunts and barbs simply aren't worth the price you might find yourself paying."

Mary's eyes were huge, and she toyed nervously with the strings on the parcel.

Linnet said nothing, her thoughts a little confused. Why was he apparently so concerned about her? Was this just another ploy to deceive her? Maybe a glance in White's betting book would reveal he'd placed a large sum upon her *not* attending the ball!

"Linnet?" He was still holding her gaze. "Are you planning to go there tonight?"

Her eyes were unfathomable. "No," she replied coolly.

"I hope you're telling the truth."

"How many times in the past have *I* wished *you* were telling the truth? When you told me you loved me, I hoped with all my heart that you meant it."

The carriage had reached the corner of Charles Street, and the gates of Carlisle House were just visible. She got up to lower the window glass, calling out to the coachman, "Draw up at the curb, if you please."

"Madam."

The team was maneuvered to a halt, and Linnet opened the door pointedly, looking at Nicholas. "I believe our conversation is at an end, sir."

"So it is," he murmured, taking his hat and cane and climbing out, but he turned to look at her again before closing the door. His gaze was intense, and his tone very serious. "Don't go there tonight, Linnet. Believe me, I do have your best interest at heart." Without another word, he closed the carriage door, strolling away along the pavement in the direction of Berkeley Square.

As the coachman urged the team on once more, turning them beneath the gateway and into the courtyard of Carlisle House, Mary looked urgently at her mistress. "You mustn't go tonight, Miss Linnet, you really mustn't."

"I'm going, Mary, and that's the end of it."

"But Lord Fane . . ."

"No doubt has a multitude of sly reasons for so advising me."

The maid looked helplessly at her. "Miss Linnet, you heard what he said about the ball. If such things will be going on, you cannot possibly think of continuing with your plan."

"That's enough, Mary."

"But . . ."

"I said that's enough!"

The maid lowered her eyes. "Yes, Miss Linnet."

"I'm going there tonight, and nothing someone like Lord Fane says is going to change my mind."

"No, Miss Linnet."

The carriage swayed to a standstill, and Sommers came out to open the door. Linnet glanced again at the maid. "Not another word, is that clear?"

"Yes, Miss Linnet."

Linnet alighted and went into the house.

21

The weather changed abruptly by the evening. From being clear and bright, the skies became overcast, and it began to rain heavily. A breath of noticeably cooler air crept in through the slightly open window of Linnet's bedroom, carrying with it the dismal sound of the steady downpour. The evening had drawn in prematurely, and already a lighted candle had been placed on the dressing table, so that Mary could see clearly as she pinned and combed the dark-brown wig Linnet was to wear as a disguise.

The wig consisted of a mass of frothy curls, and when it had been fixed firmly over Linnet's chestnut hair, Mary took the mask, easing it carefully into place, and then fluffing out the veil that concealed the lower half of Linnet's face.

The candle flame swayed in the draft from the window, and it seemed to Mary that there was something ominous about such a complete change in the weather. She was anxious for her mistress. "Miss Linnet, I do wish you'd reconsider. This is all so very risky . . ."

"I'm going to Portman Street, Mary, and that's the end of it."

"Yes, miss." Mary fell silent, continuing to comb the wig at the back of Linnet's head. Then she put the comb down. "What necklace shall you wear, miss?"

"The diamonds, I think. I've hardly ever worn them in society, so no one will recognize them as belonging to me."

The maid brought the little leather box, and attended to the necklace. When it was fastened, and arranged satisfactorily, Mary looked at Linnet in the mirror. "There, miss, it's all finished."

Linnet studied her reflection, and sighed uneasily, for the gown's bodice was still very skimpy indeed, but at least it was impossible to see Linnet Carlisle in the dark-haired, masked woman gazing back at her. She rose to her feet, shaking out the gown's filmy skirts. The diamond necklace sparkled in the candlelight, and the scent of lily-of-the-valley surrounded her from the essence she'd put on earlier.

Another draft of cool air made her shiver, and she went to look out of the window. The rain was tamping into the puddles in the courtyard, and in Charles Street the lamplighter and his boy were already at work. It was all a far cry from the beautiful August evenings of recent weeks.

She smiled a little. "Well, it may be gloomy out there, but at least it's to my advantage."

"Is it, miss?"

"Yes, because if Sommers should happen to be in the entrance hall, which he shouldn't, since he's been told he won't be required this evening, he won't think it odd if I go down in a hooded cloak."

"Oh, I see, miss. Yes, I suppose that is a good thing." But the maid's voice was anything but enthusiastic.

Linnet glanced at her. "I suppose that hackney coachman of your cousin's *is* reliable, isn't he?"

"My cousin swears he is, miss. He says he'll be waiting in the mews lane as agreed."

"And what of my own coachman? Can he be depended upon to say nothing of driving around with an empty carriage?"

"Tom Carter has an eye for what he calls 'bits of muslin,' miss, and that eye happens to be on me at the moment. He'll do as we wish, because he wants to be in favor with me."

Wheels sounded in the courtyard, and Linnet looked out again to see her carriage. It pulled up by the door of the house, its blinds down in readiness.

Mary brought Linnet's cloak, placing it carefully around her, and raising the hood over the wig. The hood was particularly roomy, and could be pulled well forward so that no one could see the mask and veil over her face. Sommers was indeed the only hazard she was likely to encounter, for her great-aunt had already departed for Lady Anne's. Linnet was conscious of a pang of remorse where her great-aunt was concerned, for that lady had set off quite content that her niece wasn't contemplating anything improper. Linnet didn't like deceiving her elderly relative like this, but felt too goaded by Judith Jordan's activities to refrain from carrying out her admittedly outrageous plan. Linnet kept telling herself that her activities wouldn't be found out, that only Judith would ever know what had been done this night, and that Great-Aunt Minton would therefore never find out. Lady Lydney's rout was bound to be such a crush that it was quite possible for her to be absent without anyone realizing. All this was still wrong, however, and Linnet knew it; but pride dictated that she carried on with her plan.

She turned to Mary. "Will you see if the coast is clear?"

"Yes, miss." The maid hurried away, and returned a moment later to say that the entrance hall was deserted.

Taking up her reticule, and looping it over her arm beneath the cloak, Linnet left the room. She went down the staircase, pausing at the bottom while Mary went out to indicate to Tom Carter that he could now drive off with the empty carriage, then she returned to Linnet, and the two women slipped toward the ballroom. At the top of the steps leading down to the dance floor, the maid tried for a last time to dissuade her mistress.

"Please don't go, miss, for that woman really isn't worth all this. Lord Fane is right, all sorts of things will go on there later on, and if you should be caught up in it all . . ."

"I won't be," replied Linnet firmly, determined not even to contemplate such a dread possibility. "Now remember, if my great-aunt should happen to return early from Lady Anne's, you are to wait for me in the conservatory with your cloak. We must appear to have returned together from the rout, and if we should be seen entering the house from the rear, I think I can explain it away somehow. Just be prepared.''

''Yes, miss.''

The maid watched unhappily as Linnet slipped down the steps and across the shadowy ballroom, where white dust cloths again covered the sofas. As the cloaked figure vanished into the conservatory, Mary turned and walked quietly back toward the staircase, slipping stealthily up it to return to Linnet's room, where she would somehow have to while away the coming hours. Oh, no good was going to come of all this; it was going to be one of those times when the impetuous side of her mistress's nature was going to cause her trouble.

Linnet moved quietly through the darkened conservatory, where memories of Nicholas seemed to reach out tangibly to touch her, then she pushed open the French windows onto the terrace. The sound of the rain was loud as she hesitated just inside, and the chill of the damp air made her shiver.

The light was fading fast now, and there was no break in the low clouds. Gathering her skirts, she stepped out, hurrying across the terrace and down the stone steps into the garden. A light breeze stirred through the wet leaves, and the scent of flowers was fresh and clear. She could hear the rain beating noisily on the coach-house roof and gurgling down the drains.

She opened the wicket gate, stepping into the narrow lane, which was lined with coach houses, stables, and the dwelling of the many grooms and coachmen employed by the residences of Charles Street and adjacent Curzon Street. It was a cobbled lane, with deep gutters that ran with rainwater, and there was no longer the scent of flowers, but of horses.

The hackney coach was waiting by one of the stables, drawn up discreetly in the shadows, its single horse hanging its head in the downpour. The coachman was huddled on his seat, a heavy cloak wrapped around his shoulders.

He heard the wicket gate squeak on its hinges, and turned to see her cloaked figure hurrying toward his old coach.

"Miss C?" he asked tactfully, raising his voice a little to be heard above the rain.

"Yes," she replied, reaching out thankfully to grasp the wet door handle. "You know where to take me?"

"A certain address in Portman Street? Yes, miss, I know."

She climbed inside, and a moment later the horse was urged into action, drawing the somewhat rickety vehicle away along the lane. Linnet sat back on the uncomfortable seat, glancing around. Just as tonight's weather was a far cry from recent sunshine, so this old coach was a far cry from the luxury and comfort of her private carriage. The seats were threadbare and unevenly stuffed with horsehair, and the floor was strewn with straw to absorb the wet carried in by passengers.

The coach emerged from the entrance of the mews lane, and she glanced out of the rain-washed window, staring along Charles Street toward the gates of Carlisle House. She could see the lights in the house, and knew that Mary would be watching from one of the windows. Then the coachman brought his horse up to a trot, driving north along John Street toward Fane House and Fane Crescent.

She averted her gaze as she passed the lodge and gates, and found herself breathing out with relief as they faded away behind her. Grosvenor Square and North Audley Street were almost deserted, and the house that Benedict had purchased was shuttered and dark. The coach had to halt at the crossroads into Oxford Street, for there was a great deal of traffic, in spite of the weather. At last the coachman's whip cracked, and the horse moved forward again, crossing Oxford Street and entering Orchard Street, which led northward directly into Portman Square.

Linnet's pulse had quickened now, for she was close to her destination. Her nerve was beginning to fail her. She shouldn't be doing this, she should be heeding all the advice she'd been given . . .

The lamps of Portman Square shone dismally against

the endless rain, and several carriages rattled and splashed in the opposite direction. Linnet clutched at the seat as the hackney coach lurched suddenly, turning sharply right into Portman Street, and then right again almost immediately into the mews lane running behind the terraces of large town houses.

The mews was, if anything, even more narrow than the one behind Carlisle House, and its surface was rutted by the countless vehicles that came and went from the stables and coach houses. The hackney coach maneuvered its way along the lane, weaving between the various stationary vehicles drawn up prudently in this secluded place, for not all Judith's admirers wished to be overt about their association with her. There was no sign of a guard.

At last the coachman reined in, turning to tap a hand upon the roof of the vehicle. Linnet slowly opened the door, stepping carefully down into the rain. She turned to the coachman. "You must wait here for me."

He touched his dripping hat. "I will, Miss C." Then he pointed with his whip toward one of the nearby coach houses. "That's the one belonging to the house in question. Have a care, miss, for it's no place for a lady."

Slowly she picked her way across the lane, glancing cautiously around for any sign of a guard, but the coachhouse door was open, and no one seemed to be there. Taking a long breath, she moved closer to it, listening for a moment. The only sound was that of the rain. At last she took her courage in both hands and stepped through the doorway and into the shadows.

The coach house was silent, except for the drumming of the rain on the roof. There was straw underfoot, and a solitary ghostly carriage loomed to the right; it was Judith's white landau, and its presence told her once and for all that she was on the point of entering a world where no virtuous lady should ever set foot. She could hear her heartbeats as she hurried quickly across the coach house to the door opening into the garden beyond.

Her hand was on the latch when she thought there was a sound behind her. With a stifled gasp, she whirled about, her alarmed eyes searching the shadows, but all was still. She listened, her heartbeats quickening still more, and after a moment, she turned to the door again, carefully raising the latch and opening it.

The door swung slowly on its hinges, and the hiss of the rain was loud again. She could see along the garden toward the house, every window of which was brilliant with lights. Lanterns had been hung in the trees, but no one was out strolling in such weather. Some of the windows must have been open, for she could hear the sound of laughter, and several times she heard rather riotous squeals which told of ribaldry and horseplay.

Apprehension seized her. There was still time to turn around and forget all this. But then she remembered all the slights and insults she'd endured at Judith's spiteful hands, and the humiliation of having her ribbon tied to the poodle's tail. With sudden resolve, she removed her cloak, hiding it behind the landau, and then stepped from the coach house into the garden, hurrying toward the house.

22

The door into the candlelit basement kitchen stood open, and there didn't seem to be anyone around. The sounds of merriment and music continued from the open windows above, but the kitchens were strangely silent. Strangely indeed, for with so many guests one would have expected to see servants hurrying about their tasks.

Slowly she went inside. The candlelight moved gently, casting shadows over the dressers and cupboards lining the walls, and the fire in the hearth shifted a little so that a shower of sparks swept slowly up the chimney, but all else remained quiet and deserted.

She crossed the stone-flagged floor to the far door, pushing it stealthily open and peering up the wooden staircase leading to the rear of the entrance hall. The noise of the ball was noticeably louder from here, and she could hear a woman giggling flirtatiously just the other side of the door at the top. The giggling continued for a moment, then a man said something and there was silence. Linnet waited, listening carefully, but there no longer seemed to be anyone there. Gathering her skirts, she went quickly up the steps. Her hand trembled as she pushed the door open just an inch or so.

The noise of the ball swept in through the crack, a mixture of voices and Mozart, for Herr Heller's Ensemble was playing a minuet. Dazzling chandeliers lit the entrance hall, the walls of which were hung with pink brocade and garlands of white roses, and there was an elegant pink velvet sofa against the wall next to the door.

The scent of roses was strong, for baskets of them stood against the walls. Opening the door a little more, Linnet peeped cautiously out, afraid that at any moment she'd find herself confronted by someone. She inched out of her hiding place so that she could look along the hall, for her view was blocked by the main staircase, which ascended the wall directly above the doorway into the kitchens.

A rose-decked archway marked the way into the reception rooms, and there were other doors, all of them closed, and all of them hung with white roses and pink velvet curtains that were drawn back and tied with golden ropes and tassels. She could hear the ball beyond the archway, but there was no sign of anyone in the entrance hall itself, which was as oddly deserted as the kitchens.

Was it possible that fate was going to play so neatly into her hands that she'd not only gained entry without being detected, but would be able to creep up to the floor above, find Judith's bedroom, steal one of the plumes, and then leave again without anyone being any the wiser? She had to seize the moment, for a golden opportunity such as this might not present itself again. At any minute some of the guests might emerge into the entrance hall, and she'd be seen, but as things were at this precise second . . . Without any more hesitation, she slipped along the hall, but as she came within six feet of the foot of the staircase, her heart almost stopped, for standing silently on guard, their arms akimbo, were two tall black footmen in golden livery. They were guarding the stairs until the upper floors were opened later on, and they gazed steadfastly ahead toward the front door, giving no sign of having detected her presence.

Dismayed, she drew back toward the kitchen door again, her plans suddenly in confusion. How could she possibly gain access to the bedrooms now? Panic overtook her, then, and she decided to abandon the whole plan, but as she reached the kitchen door and was about to step back into safety, she heard voices from the basement stairs. Two maids and a footman were coming up toward her! She cast her eyes desperately around, but a party of guests was emerging from the ball as well, spilling noisily into the entrance hall. Her glance fell upon the sofa, and she sat down quickly. She lounged back in what she hoped was a natural way, for all the world as if the hectic pace of the ball had exhausted her and she'd come to rest for a while.

The maids and footman came out of the kitchen doorway, not giving her more than a cursory glance, and the guests chattered and laughed further along the hall. They were all masked, but she recognized several of the gentlemen, either by their voices or by their shapes. Poky Withington was easily discernible, for he had a rasping voice that would have been impossible to disguise. He was intent upon the charms of a rather voluptuous Cyprian in a clinging white muslin gown that barely kept her full bosom in check, and he made no attempt to be subtle as he leered at her, trying to pull her into his arms. She was very much the tease, seeming to spurn him but all the time slyly encouraging his unpleasant advances. The disagreeable Algernon Halliday stood nearby, and with him, almost inevitably, was Lord Frederick Cavendish. The ladies, though such they most definitely were not, were all clad in revealing gowns, and were all evidently well versed in the art of coquetting. They didn't flinch at the sort of advances that a real lady would have cut short in no mild manner, and they showed no modesty whatsoever in the way they stood or moved.

Appalled at such openly licentious conduct, Linnet glanced again at the kitchen door. Was it safe to go back down? But even as she wondered, the door opened again and another maid emerged. Were the kitchens suddenly filled to overflowing with servants?

There was a great deal of squealing suddenly as Poky Withington made a much more determined assault upon the nonexistent virtue of the demirep in clinging white. He strove to give her a passionate kiss, and she squealed playfully as she pretended to struggle, then she gathered her transparent skirts and hastened along the hall toward Linnet.

Alarmed, Linnet moved quickly from her place, just

as Poky launched himself at his prey, sending her head-long on to the sofa. Linnet edged away from them, in-tending to risk the kitchen door, but again it opened, this time to allow a maid and a butler to emerge with trays of empty champagne glasses. Linnet's dismay knew no bounds as the butler halted, took a key from his pocket, and locked the door behind him, replacing the key in his pocket. Then he walked past her toward the front door, balancing his tray in one hand as he locked the front door as well, placing its key in the same pocket. Linnet stared at him. She was trapped!

An elderly gentleman emerged somewhat unsteadily into the hall from the archway. A black velvet mask con-cealed most of his face, but his figure was elegant enough, and he had a remarkable thatch of thick gray hair that was swept back from his face. She knew him immediately, for only Sir Mortimer Critchley, the distin-guished physician, had such a head of hair. Seeing him startled her more than anything else so far, for he was a pillar of society, a model of church-going rectitude, and yet here he was, swaying drunkenly at a Cyprian's ball! She stared at him from behind her mask.

As she watched, he suddenly espied her. A lopsided smile broke on his lips, and he made his way unevenly toward her. She was rooted to the spot with horror, pressing back against the staircase as he leaned a hand on either side of her, his face only inches away.

" 'Pon me soul," he declared thickly, the words run-ning together because he was in drink, "how is it that I haven't seen you before? Who are you, fair incognita? Mm?"

She glanced frantically from side to side, hoping to be rescued, but she soon realized that Nicholas's words of warning had been only too true, and that as far as the gentlemen here were concerned, every woman was ready, willing, and able to pleasure them.

Sir Mortimer was too much in his cups to know or care that his advances weren't welcomed. He grinned at her, his breath reeking of brandy. "A kiss, my sweet beauty." He bent closer to raise her veil, but it was too much for her to endure, and with sudden revulsion she brought her knee up sharply, at the same time ducking beneath one of his arms and making good her escape toward the main part of the ball beyond the archway.

Behind her, Sir Mortimer doubled up with a grunt of pain, cursing roundly beneath his breath. It was a curse that would have shocked his church-going friends, she thought. Or would it? Maybe *they* were all here tonight as well!

She reached the archway, and then paused in astonishment to stare at the scene that greeted her. The room was noisy, colorful, and brilliant, and the conduct of the gathering was as open and demonstrative as that of the guests in the entrance hall behind her. There were roses everywhere, as at her own ball, and her gaze was drawn inexorably toward the center of the floor, where a poodle-crowned column of white ostrich plumes stretched up to the ceiling.

She heard a heavy step behind her, and turned to see Sir Mortimer approaching determinedly. With a gasp, she hurried into the press of people, swiftly vanishing from his sight. She edged around the floor, making for some tall windows which she hoped might offer her some access into the gardens, but when she reached them, she saw that they were well above ground level.

She glanced out at the night, where the rain was still falling heavily, then she turned to look at the seething gathering, where the minuet had given way to an enthusiastic country dance. She watched the dancers. There was little restraint, and certainly none of the polite, proper sort of flirting that would have gone on at a more decorous occasion, such as her own ball. Here, if a gentleman had an eye for his demimondaine partner, he made his interest quite plain, and if the demimondaine was receptive, then she made the fact equally as plain.

Linnet was in a quandary. What was she to do? No doubt Sir Mortimer would soon forget all about her, and she'd be able to go back into the entrance hall. But what could she do then? She couldn't return the way she'd come, because the door was locked, and she couldn't leave the front way for the same reason. She couldn't even slip upstairs to steal one of Judith's famous plumes, because of the black footmen guarding the staircase.

All her fine plans were suddenly a shambles. What a fool she'd been to embark on this in the first place, for now she was trapped. She should have paid heed to Nicholas's warnings. Nicholas! Her breath caught as she suddenly remembered him, and she glanced around again at the sea of people. Was he here? She found herself hoping he wasn't, for although she knew him to be a toad of the first order, and knew he'd long been Judith's admirer, she didn't like to think of him behaving with the same profligacy as most of the gentlemen present.

Sir Mortimer was approaching her again, and quickly she left her position, weaving away through the press of people. Her path took her toward a slightly quieter corner of the room, and suddenly she found herself looking at a sofa occupied by a woman in a simple but revealing gown made of cloth-of-silver. There were tall black plumes in her intricately dressed golden hair, and she wore a dainty silver mask, but her face was instantly recognizable; it was Judith.

The Cyprian looked magnificent, and the black plumes were surely her most spectacular ever. They were taller than usual, and sprinkled with brilliants that flashed and sparkled with even the tiniest movement, and they were the demirep's only adornment, for she wore no jewelry. Her voluptuous figure was shown off to superb advantage by the gown's simplicity, especially her curving bosom. A fan moved gently to and fro before her face, and she didn't glance toward Linnet, for at that moment a rather elderly Russian gentleman, his formal evening clothes bright with orders and decorations from St. Petersburg, came up to the sofa, asking her if she would honor him with a dance. He was far from agreeable to look upon, having a stooped figure and a thin, down-turned mouth that told of a harsh disposition, but the Cyprian appeared to find him very much to her liking. She bestowed a gracious smile upon him, quickly giving him her hand, and the plumes in her hair glittered brilliantly as she rose to her feet to accompany him onto the crowded floor.

Linnet was so intent upon Judith that she didn't notice the stout gentleman in plum-colored velvet sidling up next to her. Before she knew it, he'd seized her arm and whisked her boisterously onto the floor to join the country dance. He grinned eagerly at her as she strove to keep her veil down in place. "I have a taste for dark-haired wenches," he shouted above the noise and the music, "and I intend to make you mine before the evening's out, m'dear!"

Unutterable horror filled her, and she was relieved when the dance ended, but then the horror filled her again, for her unwanted admirer had no intention of relinquishing his hold upon her, and kept her where she was until the next dance, a ländler, commenced. Taking her almost in a bearhug, he swept her around the floor, murmuring in her ear that she was undoubtedly the tastiest little tidbit in the whole of London, and that he had every intention of sampling her charms to the full before very long. He importuned her to remove her mask so that he could see her face, but she declined, hoping that she'd soon find a way of escaping from his odious clutches. Oh, how she wished she'd never come to this disreputable and dangerous place.

Meanwhile, a carriage drove swiftly through the rain into the courtyard at Carlisle House, and a gentleman in formal evening clothes alighted, rapping urgently on the door with his cane. It was Nicholas, and he was in no mood to hear anything but the truth from whoever answered.

Sommers hastened to open the door, fearful that such rapping would damage the costly paintwork. He stepped back in astonishment as Nicholas brushed past him into the entrance hall. "L-Lord Fane? May I-I be of any assistance?"

"Is Miss Carlisle at home?"

"No, my lord, she left earlier for Lady Lydney's rout." The butler was then mindful of his instructions where this gentleman was concerned. "My lord, I'm afraid I must ask you to leave."

Nicholas ignored the request. "Did you actually see her leave?"

Sommers was a little taken aback. "Why, no, my lord, for I was told that I would not be required this evening. But I know that the coachman left to attend to his duties, and I heard the carriage in the courtyard so I know that she left."

"All you know is that the carriage left," replied Nicholas tersely. "I happened to see the vehicle a short while ago, and it wasn't driving toward Lady Lydney's residence, indeed it was proceeding in a very dilatory manner in any direction but that. Now then, if Miss Carlisle had indeed gone to the rout, wouldn't the carriage be expected to wait there for her, in order to bring her home afterward?"

Sommers was staring at him. "Yes, my lord, it would."

"Is Miss Carlisle's maid here?"

"No, my lord, she accompanied Miss Carlisle to the . . ." The butler's voice died away unhappily for he, too was beginning to wonder if his mistress was at the rout. "She isn't in the kitchen with the other servants, my lord," he said.

"Then I suggest you go to Miss Carlisle's room and see if she's there." Nicholas didn't somehow think Linnet would take her maid with her on the hare-brained escapade he strongly feared she'd embarked upon tonight.

Without a word, the butler hurried up the staircase, and Nicholas waited impatiently for him to return. He glanced around the entrance hall, catching a glimpse of his reflection in the mirror above the mantelpiece. He was dressed for Lady Lydney's, in an indigo corded-silk coat, white pantaloons and stockings, and black shoes. If he hadn't just happened to see Linnet's carriage, he'd have been enjoying himself at the rout now, not scurrying around London because Miss Linnet Carlisle was possessed of a stubborn streak that verged on idiocy!

His thoughts broke off, for Sommers was returning, and with him was a rather wide-eyed, frightened Mary. The butler appeared to be both mortified that such deception had gone on under his watchful nose, and appalled that his mistress may have set out on a very hazardous course. He virtually dragged Mary before Nicholas. "Miss Carlisle's maid, my lord. It seems you are right, Miss Carlisle has not gone to the rout, but has set out on quite another purpose."

Nicholas drew a heavy breath, fixing the terrified Mary with a bright gaze. "Has your mistress gone to Portman Street tonight?"

"Yes, my lord," she whispered.

"Tell me her exact plan."

"When her carriage left with its blinds down, she went out through the mews in a hackney coach. She meant to enter Miss Jordan's house from the garden if she could, to take a plume from the bedroom."

Sommers looked faint.

Nicholas kept his gaze upon the maid. "What was she wearing? If I'm to stand any chance of rescuing her from this unbelievable folly, I need to know exactly what to look for."

"She has a mask with a veil that covers the lower part of her face, a dark brown wig that's very curly and quite long, and her gown is yellow."

Nicholas saw the irony of it. Yellow? The very color that became her most. "How long ago did she leave?"

"About an hour, my lord."

He didn't say anything more, but snatched up his hat and gloves and strode from the house. He instructed his coachman to drive post haste to Portman Street mews, and then climbed into the carriage, slamming the door behind him.

The whip cracked, and the team's hooves struck sparks from the wet cobbles. The wheels splashed through the puddles in the courtyard, and the lamps carved an arc of light through the rain-soaked darkness as the coachman maneuvered the vehicle out beneath the gateway.

* * *

At the ball, Linnet had at last succeeded in escaping from her persistent admirer. Under the pretext of being in dire need of a glass of champagne, she'd languished on a sofa and looked appealingly at him from behind her mask, and he'd hurried away to grant her her wish. The moment he'd disappeared, she left the sofa, mingling again in the crush. She fended off several other hopeful gentlemen by telling them she was already "spoken for," and gradually managed to make her way toward the archway into the entrance hall. As she reached it, she realized with a start that the black footmen had left their places by the foot of the staircase; the way up to the bedrooms was suddenly clear. She glanced back at the ball, and saw that no one was as yet showing an interest in the bedrooms. On impulse, she decided to carry out her original plan, and remove one of Judith's plumes after all. Surely she'd somehow manage to leave the house afterward? The doors couldn't remain locked forever. Gathering her yellow skirts, she slipped swiftly up the staircase to the shadowy floor above, where very few candles indeed had been lit.

Behind her, a tall figure in cloth-of-silver emerged from the archway. The black plumes in Judith's hair glittered, and her fan still moved gently to and fro, like the slow swishing of a cat's tail. A cool smile touched her lips as she watched her quarry fleeing unknowingly up toward the bedrooms. Turning toward the kitchen door, she snapped her fingers, and the two footmen came to resume their positions at the foot of the staircase.

"Keep her up there until I'm quite ready to deal with her," said the Cyprian softly, then she turned and went back into the ball.

23

Nicholas's carriage turned into the mews lane behind Judith's house, negotiating the narrow confines and drawing up behind the hackney coach that Linnet had traveled in. Nicholas stepped down into the rain, turning up his collar and adjusting his top hat before going to speak to the hackney coachman.

"Are you waiting for a certain lady from Charles Street?" he asked.

The man was caught off guard, looking down suspiciously, his glance taking in Nicholas's elegant evening clothes. What did this fancy cove want? "And if I am?" he replied warily.

"You need wait no more, for the lady will return with me."

"My instructions . . ."

"No longer apply." Nicholas took some coins from his pocket and held them up to the man. "This should more than recompense you for your trouble."

"The lady requested me to wait for her, sir, and I intend to do just that."

"Your devotion to duty does you credit, but, believe me, the lady will not be requiring your services. Take the money, and go."

The man hesitated.

"Take it!" snapped Nicholas.

Reaching down, the man took the coins, then stirred his horse into action. The little coach bounced away along the lane, vanishing from sight around the corner at the far end.

Nicholas watched it with growing unease. He sensed that Judith had laid a careful trap, and that Linnet had stepped right into it. With a heavy sigh, he returned to his own coachman. "You know Miss Carlisle, do you not, James?"

"Yes, my lord."

"Well, I'm given to understand that tonight she is wearing a yellow gown and a dark brown wig. You are to detain her if she comes out before I return, is that clear?"

"Detain her?" The man's eyes widened. *Detain* a lady?

"I'll take full responsibility."

"Yes, my lord."

Nicholas turned, hurrying across the dark, wet lane toward the coach house. He hardly glanced at the ghostly white landau as he moved through the shadowy interior toward the door into the garden. The sounds of the ball drifted toward him as he walked up the path, and he could see people moving in the brilliantly lit drawing room. Leaving the path, he went quickly to a door that was almost concealed by shrubs. He tried to open it, but it was locked. He could only hope that the key was on the inside. Pursing his lips thoughtfully, he walked on toward the kitchen door, going down the basement steps only to find that that door was also locked.

There were servants inside busily washing trays of champagne glasses, and he also recognized a number of waiters from Gunter's. No one noticed him, and he tapped the glass to attract their attention.

The maid who was nearest to the door heard him immediately. She was a pretty fair-haired girl, and had long had a very soft spot for him. She came to unlock the door straightaway. "Oh, please come inside, my lord. I'm sorry the door was locked, but we have instructions to keep it so until further notice."

I'm sure you have, he thought wryly, for it's all part of Judith's machination. He smiled at the maid. "Surely you haven't been locked in like this all evening? I'll warrant a goodly number of guests preferred to arrive this discreet way.''

"Oh, the door was open until a short while ago, my lord. I really don't know why it is to be kept locked now.''

The butler suddenly realized that the maid was speaking unguardedly, and he came quickly over. "May I be of assistance, my lord?'' he inquired, giving the unfortunate maid a dark glance and waving her back to her tasks.

"Assistance?'' murmured Nicholas, removing his top hat and handing it to him. "Well, unless the remaining doors between here and the main house are also locked . . .''

"I will unlock them immediately, my lord.''

"I'd be most obliged.''

The man bowed, preceding him up the steps to the entrance hall door, unlocking it as well, and standing deferentially aside for Nicholas to pass.

As Nicholas entered the hallway beyond, the butler closed the door and locked it again. Nicholas toyed with his lacy cuff, glancing back at the door. So, Linnet had been allowed complete freedom to enter, had she? It was all as he suspected, for he now knew beyond a doubt that she'd walked right into a trap.

The entrance hall was still relatively deserted, and the black footmen were still in their positions at the foot of the staircase. He was still debating what action to take when Judith herself suddenly emerged from the archway, her skirts swishing as she went to speak to the footmen. She didn't see him.

"Is she still safely up there?'' she asked, her voice carrying because at that moment Herr Heller's Ensemble finished playing and there was a lull in the noise of the ball.

"Yes, Miss Jordan,'' one of the footmen replied.

"Good. It's taking a little longer than I'd planned, but I expect him to arrive at any moment. You are to remain here until further instructions.''

"Yes, Miss Jordan.''

Still without seeing Nicholas standing at the far end of the hall, she turned and went back through the archway.

Nicholas glanced thoughtfully up at the staircase. It could only be Linnet to whom Judith had been referring. A disagreeable denouement was evidently lying in store for the mistress of Carlisle House, and while it wouldn't entail physical harm coming to her, for not even the Bird of Paradise would sink so low in order to defeat a rival, it would most definitely not be pleasant. He had a very good idea what the Cyprian's purpose was, and knew that if he rescued Linnet in time he could spare her from one half of the denouement, but he also knew that he could only postpone the other half, for there were certain very painful facts that Miss Linnet Carlisle was going to have to face sooner or later. If he had any say in the matter, however, those painful facts would certainly be faced later, for she had to be removed from this place without delay. But how? That was indeed the question. Judith had chosen her guards well, for those particular two footmen were known to always stick rigidly to their orders, and tricking them into leaving their posts would require considerable cunning. Oh, perdition take Linnet Carlisle and her fighting spirit. Why couldn't she have been a meek, spineless nonentity who'd no more have thought of entering such a house than she'd have dreamed of flying to the moon?

In the meantime, Linnet remained totally unaware of the danger she was in. On reaching the top of the staircase, she'd glanced back down, and, thinking herself safe, had moved out of sight into the passage that ran from the front to the back of the house. She didn't see the footmen silently resuming their positions, cutting off her escape.

Very few candles had been lit where she now was, and those that were had been placed beneath special stands supporting open pot-pourri jars. The flames warmed the flower petals within, releasing perfume into the still air. She hesitated, glancing along the passage in both directions, and then decided to see if Judith's room was at the front of the house, which seemed the obvious choice.

The carpet beneath her feet was soft and almost sensuous as she moved silently away from the vicinity of the staircase. There were a number of doors opening off the passage, and each one had an ornately carved architrave. Pausing for a moment, she saw that the carvings were of a decidedly voluptuous nature, with numerous cupids and depictions of naked lovers. Her eyes widened a little, for some of the carvings were very explicit, and she hurried on toward the white-and-gold double doors at the end of the passage.

Opening them carefully, she slipped into the dimly lit room beyond. It was an elegant chamber, its walls hung with white silk and its floor covered with yet another deep, soft carpet, but although it was exquisitely furnished, her instinct told her that it wasn't Judith's room.

With a disappointed sigh, she turned to look back along the passage. There was nothing for it but to examine what lay behind every door. Gathering her skirts, she moved back the way she'd come, opening the first door and looking inside. It was another candlelit bedroom, as luxuriously furnished as the first, but still quite obviously not that of the Bird of Paradise herself.

The same applied to each chamber she peeped cautiously into, and soon there was only one door left, a double door like that at the front of the house, but opening into a room at the rear, overlooking the garden.

As she was approaching it, however, she thought she heard a sound on the staircase. She froze, but no one came up. Her heartbeats had quickened with alarm, and she wasted no more time, but hurried the final few steps to the remaining double doors, opening them quickly and stepping safely inside out of sight.

Glancing around, she knew immediately that she'd found what she was looking for. Judith's room was sumptuously furnished in pink and gold, with exquisitely ruched pink silk draped against the walls. The tall windows were hung with gold-tasseled rose velvet, and an immense four-poster bed occupied pride of place in the very center of the floor. It was the largest bed Linnet had ever seen, and the strangest, for although it was a four-poster, it had no canopy, so that whoever occupied it could gaze right up to the ceiling and see themselves in the mirror that was fixed there. There were other mirrors, so that Linnet's reflection moved on all sides as she went further into the room, determined to find one of the Cyprian's famous plumes. The carpet was woven with cherubs, and more cherubs were carved on the bedposts and around the door behind her. Several pot-pourri jars were on elegant tables against the wall, the candles beneath them casting a soft, dim light over everything. The air was warm, and sweet with the scent of flowers. She removed her mask, to see more easily. A sudden movement on the bed startled her so much that she dropped the mask, but then she saw that it was only Judith's white poodle. The dog's eyes shone in the semi-darkness, and it whined a little, sitting up with its tail wagging. Linnet glanced around again, forgetting to pick up the fallen mask as with something of a start she found herself looking at a painting on the wall. It was of Judith, naked and reclining on a sofa, and the eyes seemed to be looking directly at her. Uncomfortably conscious of the painted gaze, Linnet continued to look around. There was a door leading off the room, and she went quickly over to it and found that it opened into a dressing room beyond. A solitary candle stood on the frilled pink muslin dressing table, throwing a faint, moving light over the line of huge wardrobes built against the wall. The dressing table was laden with jars, phials, combs, pin dishes, brushes, and numerous jewelry boxes, but there was something else lying on it, too; one of the black plumes that Judith was wearing tonight.

With a triumphant gasp, Linnet hurried over to pick it up. The sequins shimmered and winked as the candle-flame swayed, and the vane brushed softly against her fingers. She saw immediately why it had been left behind, for the shaft was broken halfway along. Linnet gazed at it for a moment, and then bent to raise her skirt in order to tuck the plume neatly into her garter, so that it would lie concealed against her leg. But as she lowered her skirt again, she heard a soft step behind her.

Her breath caught, and she began to whirl about, but a hand was clamped roughly over her mouth, stopping her from making any sound. At the same time another viselike hand grabbed her around the waist, and she was hopeless to defend herself.

A harsh voice whispered urgently in her ear. "Be still now, or believe me, things will be unpleasant for you!"

Nicholas? She was frightened and confused, but could still recognize his voice. Helpless against her assailant's strength, she tried to turn her head to see his face.

"Not a sound, Linnet," he breathed. "I've sent those footmen on a wild goose chase, by telling them Judith needed them urgently. They believed me because I've always been her friend, but they'll soon realize I'm not here as her friend tonight."

Slowly he removed his hand from her mouth, and at last she could twist her head to look at him. "Nicholas? Why . . . ?"

He put on finger to her lips. "Just do everything I tell you if you wish to escape with your reputation and virtue intact." Taking her hand, he pulled her toward the furthest of the wardrobes and opened the door. It was the wardrobe where Judith stored her many famous plumes, and was large enough to step inside.

Linnet resisted a little. "But, why go in there?"

"Goddamm it, woman, just do as I bid you!" he breathed sharply, forcibly dragging her into the plume-filled darkness.

The door didn't fully close behind them, and Linnet turned to look back, for Nicholas was occupied searching for something at the rear of the wardrobe. She could see across the dressing room into the bedroom beyond, and heard the poodle give a sudden glad bark. The door from the landing passage opened, and the little dog jumped down from the bed, pattering past the mask lying on the floor where Linnet had dropped it.

But Linnet hardly saw the dog or the mask, for she was too intent upon the two persons who entered the bedroom. One was Judith, and the other was a masked gentleman who seemed uncomfortably familiar. The Cyprian glanced swiftly around the bedroom, as if hoping to see someone. Finding the room apparently deserted, her expression became displeased, but then she saw the mask on the floor and a cool smile touched her full lips.

She turned to her gentleman friend, and he immediately removed his mask as he drew her into his arms to kiss her on the lips. The moment his face was revealed Linnet's heart almost stopped with shock, for it was Benedict. He crushed the Cyprian in a passionate embrace, and it was obvious that this was far from being the first time he'd made love to London's most famous demimondaine.

Linnet felt numb as she watched from the secrecy of the wardrobe. It was like looking at a stranger, for he wasn't the Benedict she knew and thought so well of. His face was flushed with desire, but in a way that told her he believed that that desire was about to be satisfied, and his hands moved over the Cyprian in a knowing, practiced manner.

Judith pulled suddenly back from the kiss, glancing around the dimly lit room again. "I know you're in here, Miss Carlisle, so there's no point in hiding. It's all up with you and with your fine betrothal! He's mine, and he's going to stay mine."

Benedict leapt away from her as if scalded the moment she uttered Linnet's name, and his eyes were almost haunted as he whirled around, expecting to see Linnet looking accusingly at him. But there were only shadows and emptiness.

Neither of them looked toward the dressing room, and at that moment Nicholas found what he was urgently seeking at the rear of the wardrobe, a hidden catch that released a secret door. Snatching Linnet's hand, he pulled her through into the narrow staircase beyond, quietly closing the secret door again.

It was very dark in the confined space which Judith's more circumspect and important admirers were accustomed to using for their visits. Still stunned by what she now knew, Linnet stumbled a little on the steep steps, and Nicholas paused, steadying her. "Are you all right?" he asked in a low whisper that echoed eerily.

"I—I think so."

"The steps lead down to the garden, and the door at the bottom is usually kept locked from the inside, unless Judith is expecting someone in particular. It was locked when I tried it earlier." Still holding her hand he led her on down toward the door. There, he paused, listening carefully. The muffled sound of the ball was just audible through the thick walls, but from beyond the door all seemed quiet. He'd hardly dared hope to find the key in the lock, but to his relief it was. He turned it, and opened the door. It was still raining outside, and there was a strong smell of wet grass and earth.

A light suddenly appeared at the top of the steps behind them, and with a cry Linnet turned to see one of the footmen standing there with a lighted candle. Their search for Judith had ended when a guest informed them she'd been seen going up the staircase, and now they knew Nicholas had tricked them.

Nicholas needed no prompting, but stepped quickly out into the rain-soaked darkness, dragging her with him. They ran across the grass, Linnet's flimsy slippers slithering unsteadily. Tears were blinding her. She'd been cruelly deceived again. Benedict was Judith's lover, just as Nicholas had been before him, and for the second time, she, poor fool, had guessed nothing! A sob caught in her throat, and she almost lost her footing.

The coach house loomed ahead now, torrents of rain spilling from its roof and gushing down the drainpipes. A deep puddle had formed before the door, and her skirt dragged through it as Nicholas pulled her inside, closing the door firmly behind them.

He didn't pause to see if she was all right, but continued to drag her toward the mews lane. In a moment they were out in the rain again, and he was bundling her roughly into the waiting carriage. The startled coachman prepared to drive off, cracking the whip the moment Nicholas ordered him to drive to Carlisle House and then jumped swiftly inside himself.

Judith's footmen emerged into the lane just as the whip cracked, and they made to block the vehicle's way, but the coachman knew what was expected of him and urged the team to greater effort. The footmen fell back in alarm as the carriage swept past, and had to content themselves with shouting after it, brandishing their fists.

Linnet was so distraught that she hardly knew where she was. She only knew that Nicholas was putting his arms around her, murmuring her name. She hid her face against the damp cloth of his shoulder, the hot tears stinging her eyes.

24

As the carriage sped away from Portman Street, in Judith's room all was strained and quiet. The merriment of the ball continued unabated downstairs, but Benedict hardly heard it as he stood dazedly with his hand resting on a table. His head was bowed, and he could scarce believe what had happened.

Judith was by one of the windows, holding the curtain aside as she watched her unsuccessful footmen hurrying back through the rain. Her reflection shone back at her in the glass, and in spite of Linnet's escape a faint smile played about her lips. Maybe she'd been denied the ultimate satisfaction of seeing her rival's stricken face, and of ruining her reputation by exposing her presence in the house, but she'd come close enough. The smile faded a little as she pondered how Linnet had been so neatly whisked from her grasp. Nicholas's timely intervention hadn't been anticipated, and Judith was angry now that she hadn't suspected anything when the butler had mentioned to her that he'd arrived unexpectedly via the mews lane. It seemed Lord Fane still felt something for his former love, although what that something was remained a mystery.

Behind her, Benedict struggled to remain calm as he at last turned to look at her. "Why?" he asked in a choked voice. "Why did you do it? Do you suddenly hate me? Do you now want to see me completely ruined?"

"You know that I love you with all my heart. You are

the only man for whom I would gladly give up everything.''

''And yet you would see me in debtor's jail!'' He was bewildered by the seemingly wanton destruction of the match he'd needed so much. ''Another few weeks would have seen my debts settled and the Carlisle fortune completely in my hands . . .''

''Aye, and the Carlisle wench completely in your bed. I'm not a fool, Benedict, and I know full well that she had become more to you than just a conveniently wealthy wife. I've always been prepared to stand by you, but I draw the line at watching you fall in love with someone else.''

''I'm not falling in love with her.''

''No?'' She left the window. ''In the beginning I agreed to keep our affair a secret because you had such high hopes of inheriting a fortune from your prudish maiden aunt, and when that fell through I reluctantly agreed to your seeking a suitable dull heiress. I even consented to your haste to get her to the altar when the duns descended upon you at the theater, and then again at that exhibition. I agreed with you that Linnet Carlisle was ideal for your purpose, for although she's attractive enough on the surface, beneath it all she's a fool.'' Her fan moved softly to and fro as she halted in front of him. ''Who but a fool would have thrown a man like Fane away? I was content that she was far too shallow a creature to ever steal you from me, but when you came back from the Lake District that last time, I could sense the way the wind was beginning to blow.''

''You're wrong. I feel nothing for her.''

''Don't lie, Benedict, for it isn't becoming. The moment I knew what was happening, I determined not to permit that simpering little Miss Purity to supplant me in your affections. It gave me a great satisfaction to mount a campaign against her, and even more pleasure to know that there was precious little you dared to do about it.''

Angry color marked his cheeks. ''Damn you,'' he breathed.

''No, it's damn *you*, sirrah! How *dare* you want her,

and then warm yourself in my bed!" Her eyes flashed, and the plumes trembled. "You're mine, Benedict Gresham, and I'm not going to relinquish you to her."

"And so you'll relinquish me to His Majesty's justice instead?" He ran his fingers agitatedly through his hair. "Plague take you, Judith, for you say that you love me, but your actions prove that the very opposite is the case. To go to all these lengths . . . You actually lured me here tonight in order to expose me in front of her." He paused suddenly as something occurred to him. "And you could only do that if you knew what her plans were. You did know them, didn't you?"

"Of course." She turned, for the poodle whined a little, and as she bent to stroke its head, she smiled again. "I knew her every move. I knew how she meant to enter the house, and so I saw to it that her way was left conveniently clear. I knew what gown and wig she would be wearing, and I warned the servants to remain hidden, but to report to me the moment she'd arrived. Once she was in the house, all I had to do was keep her here until you were due to arrive, and then allow her to come up here, which she had to do if she was to steal one of my plumes." Her glance moved to the dressing table, where the black plume had lain so invitingly. "I didn't mean her to succeed, however, for it was my intention to expose her so that the fashionable world would know that little Miss Purity had so discarded her morals that she'd willingly entered this establishment. I meant to prove that although she may have shown a little spirit in attempting to pull it off, she'd failed miserably, and ruined herself as a consequence. Who would want a bride who had such scant regard for her reputation?"

He stared at her. "Who told you what she was planning? Did you bribe her maid?"

"No."

"Then who told you?" he demanded again.

"That would be telling."

"I want to know, damn it!"

"What does it matter now? Suffice it that I knew what she was up to, and I used it to my own advantage. Your

match with her is at an end, Benedict, and I think you
should face the fact. No amount of explanation will disguise what she saw here in this room. You were supposed
to be at a stuffy East India House dinner, but instead you
were here, making love to me.''

"You've thrown me to the duns, Judith, and I'll never
forgive you for that.''

"Oh, I think you'll forgive me everything, my darling,
because you're the most unscrupulously mercenary and
calculating soul I know, which is saying something, given
the souls I happen to be acquainted with.'' She turned
her head, smiling at him. "I still love you, though, heaven
help me, and I've done all this because I mean to have
you.''

He gave an ironic laugh. "Do you mean to keep me,
like your poodle?''

"Something of the sort,'' she murmured, going to the
dressing table and picking up a slim leather box, which
she brought to him. "Here, take this, for it is yours to
do with as you please.''

Puzzled, he took the box, but before he could open it,
she spoke again.

"Perhaps I should warn you that there is much, much
more where that came from.''

Slowly he undid the little catch, opening the box to see
a magnificent diamond necklace reposing within on a bed
of purple satin. His lips parted, and he looked askance
at her. "But, this has to be worth . . .''

"A small fortune? Yes, it is.''

He took it out, holding it up so that the diamonds
caught the candlelight. "How did you come by it?''

"How do you imagine? How does a creature like me
usually receive presents? My admirers are legion, my
darling, and some of them I have been keeping at arm's
length because of my love for you. But my love for you
has made me swallow my pride and a certain doddering
old Russian archduke, who has recently arrived in town,
and who has more money and estate than sense, has suddenly found his advances welcomed. In his gratitude, he
intends to lavish gifts upon me, and those gifts, my dar-

ling, I will gladly give to you. There is, however, one very important condition.''

He gazed at the diamonds. ''Name it,'' he said softly.

''When your debts are settled and all is well again, you are to make me your wife.''

His eyes swung to meet hers, and after a moment he nodded. ''If that is truly what you wish.''

She slipped her arms around his waist. ''I want you, Benedict Gresham, and nothing less than complete possession will do from now on.''

He pulled her close and kissed her on the lips. She closed her eyes, her body melting against his as she surrendered to the fierce passion he'd aroused from the first moment she'd met him. His eyes didn't close, though, they remained very much open, and there was a calculating glint in them as he looked again at the necklace in his hand.

Judith's breath escaped in a sigh. ''Linnet Carlisle need not mean anything to you from now on,'' she whispered.

''She has ceased to exist,'' he replied, his fingers closing tightly over the diamonds.

In the carriage speeding back toward Carlisle House, Linnet was at last managing to overcome her emotion, and she drew back in the darkness, her face illuminated now and then by street lamps. So much was now only too clear to her. Judith Jordan's enmity was suddenly explained, and it was all on account of Benedict, not Nicholas. The campaign of ridicule, the overturned basket of roses, the torn note that had accompanied them, and the warning about being a thorn in the side that would have to be dealt with, all could be traced back to bitter jealousy over a man, but not the man she, Linnet, had believed it to be. Oh, what a gull she'd been, falling for Benedict's lies, and suffering pangs of conscience because she'd given in to Nicholas's seductive influence.

Blinking back the new tears that immediately sprang to her eyes, she suddenly pulled off her wig and tossed it onto the seat opposite. Her chestnut hair tumbled down from its pins, falling warmly about her bare shoulders.

The citrus-yellow gown, already so immodest, was now damp and clinging from the rain, outlining every curve of her figure.

Nicholas took a handkerchief from his pocket. "You appear to have wept an ocean into your own handkerchief, so perhaps it is time to employ mine."

Still struggling to hold back the tears, she accepted the proffered square of white linen, then she took a deep breath and looked at him. "How did you know where I was?"

"A chance sighting of your somewhat aimless carriage, a little unfair pressure on your maid, and a certain amount of guesswork. You took a very foolish chance going there, Linnet, I trust you realize that now?"

"How could I not realize it?" She twisted the handkerchief nervously in her hands. "She knew all along, didn't she?"

"It appears so. You were allowed suspiciously easy entry, and then found the exits all mysteriously closed to you. Someone obviously warned her."

She nodded. "But who? No one knew except Venetia and my maid."

"Well, I can't imagine that Lady Hartley would wish to destroy a match she so obviously promoted from the outset, which, incidentally, also leads me to the conclusion that she doesn't know the truth about her brother."

"I'm sure she doesn't."

"And as to whether your maid would betray you, well, I can't think that she would, can you?"

Linnet thought of Mary, and then shook her head. "No."

"So, that means someone else must know."

"There isn't anyone else."

He raised an eyebrow. "Can you be sure? What of the hackney coachman who was waiting in the lane for you?"

"Well, I suppose he knew a little. And so did my maid's cousin, for he arranged the hackney coach. And I suppose my own coachman knew a little as well."

"The net widens, does it not?" he murmured dryly.

"Only Venetia and my maid knew everything, and I'm sure they're innocent."

"You're always so easily and completely sure about everything, aren't you? Look how *sure* you've been about what I may or may not have done. I can tell you that you've been wrong about me, so why can you not equally be wrong about them?"

"I'm certain Venetia and Mary wouldn't betray me," she repeated.

"I'll warrant that only this morning you would have staunchly defended Gresham's name, too."

She lowered her eyes.

"I tried to warn you about him."

She looked accusingly at him. "You knew he was Judith's lover, didn't you?"

"Yes, although he had no idea his secret was known to anyone except Judith, because they'd been at such pains to keep it hidden in order to keep sweet his prim aunt, who wouldn't have left him her fortune had she known about a liaison with a demimondaine. As it happened, the aunt wisely left her fortune elsewhere, and so the liaison still had to be kept secret while he searched for a suitably wealthy wife. I found out completely by accident, and at the same time discovered his monumental debts. Being a frequent visitor to her house, I was there when the pair of them had a rather indiscreet conversation. Oh, they thought themselves safe from prying ears, but the door was ajar and I heard enough."

"Why didn't you tell me all this? Why did you let me make a fool of myself?"

"With hindsight, I realize that I handled it all very badly, but I wanted to spare you the humiliation, and anyway I really didn't think you'd believe me. You haven't believed anything I've told you since all that happened a year ago, and I doubt if you'd have made a sensible exception for my tale-telling on Gresham. I thought it best to attempt to steer you away from him, for I'd disapproved of him even before I overheard that secret conversation. There was something about him that from the outset marked him as a fortune hunter, liar, and opportunist, although I could not have told you why I felt it so strongly.'' He paused. ''Perhaps now is the time to tell you once and for all that Judith and I have never been lovers. She's long been a friend of mine, but a platonic one. Oh, it *is* possible, you know. She's witty, amusing, good company, and an excellent hostess, and that is why I've always enjoyed her society. And if you think I must be lying, because I am so intimate with the layout of her bedroom, let me tell you that it is well known in certain circles that there is a secret way from the garden to her chamber, and not every gentleman who has used it is discreet enough to remain silent about his good fortune.''

Linnet searched his face, and knew that he was telling her the truth.

He leaned his head back against the upholstery. ''I know who told you that I was Judith's lover, but I doubt very much if even yet you're ready to hear the whole truth about a year ago.''

''What do you mean?''

He suddenly put his hand to her cheek. ''My judgment has been at fault throughout all this, and I've left unsaid things which I now realize should have been said. Soon I will tell you absolutely everything, but I think that tonight is perhaps not the moment, not when you've already endured so much.''

''I know how much I owe you tonight.''

''Consider your gratitude properly expressed.''

She glanced down at the ring on her finger, and slowly removed it, putting it in her reticule. ''I really believed he loved me.''

''So did Judith, which is where the trouble began,'' he observed.

She looked out of the carriage window. They were driving down John Street past the gates of Fane House and the crescent. Nicholas looked out as well, and could just make out the statue of his grandfather in the sunken garden. ''Linnet, I trust my actions tonight have restored a little of my apparently lost honor as far as you're concerned." He was remembering hearing her great-aunt's scathing condemnation in that very garden.

"What you did tonight was very gallant," she said slowly.

"But?" He caught the slight note of qualification in her response.

"Well, maybe you're going to explain it to me sometime, but until you do I still have no reason to think you acquired Radleigh Hall honestly a year ago. It seems to me that you stole it from my uncle, and that is what I must believe."

The reply caught him on the raw, and he gave a bitter laugh. "After all this, you *still* refuse to give me the benefit of the doubt about that? There was nothing dishonest about the way I acquired that estate, nothing illegal or underhand, and at this very moment, when I've just told you I intend to explain everything, I bitterly resent your repeated accusation!"

"My uncle said . . ."

"Joseph Carlisle said a great many things, God rot his pernicious soul! If ever a man deserved to be called out, he did, but his demise spared me the trouble."

She flinched, and then stiffened. How dared he speak so disparagingly of her uncle! "How easy it is to lay the blame on the dead, my lord," she said coldly.

His eyes were steel-bright in the light of a street lamp. "And how easy it always is for you always to attach blame to me! I'm not the devil on your shoulder, Linnet Carlisle, for you're your own devil! I begin to wish I'd left you to stew tonight, for you damn well deserve it!"

The carriage was slowing to negotiate the corner into Charles Street, and then slowed still more to turn beneath the gateway into the courtyard of Carlisle House.

Linnet was more distressed than ever. The humiliation of what had happened at Portman Street, and the uncertainty of her own feelings toward this man who was with her now, were added to now by the fierce resentment aroused by his uncalled-for insinuations about Joseph Carlisle.

The carriage swayed to a standstill before the house,

and she made to alight before him, but he forestalled her, climbing down into the rain first and then holding out his hand to assist her.

Unwillingly, she accepted the hand, and as she did so his fingers closed harshly over hers, pulling her almost roughly down from the carriage, then he seized her by both arms, forcing her to look at him.

"I've had enough of you and your obstinate and unjustified accusations, Linnet, and since Gresham no longer has a place in the scheme of things, I think after all that it's time you were put right once and for all about what happened a year ago. I meant to tell you when first you returned, but not once I realized Gresham's scheming paws were ready to seize everything. Now it's obviously necessary to bring the whole thing to a close, and to that end you'll be hearing from my lawyer in the morning. When you hear what he has to say, and read certain papers in his keeping, I trust you'll understand why I've behaved as I have. You may then live with your conscience, Miss Carlisle, and I hope both you and it can stand the stifling boredom!" His glance moved contemptuously over her, taking in her flushed and angry face, and the shocking impropriety of the citrus-yellow gown. "You've behaved very badly indeed tonight, madam," he said softly, "you've risked everything for the paltry chance of getting even with a woman like Judith Jordan. Well, since you wish to emulate one of her kind, I may as well treat you accordingly."

He pulled her close, forcing his lips brutally down upon hers. His hand moved intimately over her as he pressed her body against his, and he used no gentleness as he compelled her to submit. The rain was wet on her skin, and her hair clung to her face and shoulders. She hardly felt the moisture soaking through the thin silk of her gown, for she was only aware of the intoxicating sensuality that stirred inexorably through her, even though he used her so harshly. Her senses were spinning now, and all thought of resistance dissolved into nothing. She suddenly knew her heart once and for all; she *did* still love him, and that was all that mattered. But as she made to tell him, he froze the words on her lips.

With a cold laugh, he drew deliberately away. "You're mine still, aren't you, my dear? And I rather fancy you always will be."

The chill in his voice made her shiver, and she searched his face. "Nicholas . . . ?"

"Spare me your confusion, for if that is what you feel at this moment, it's as nothing to the way you made me feel a year ago when you came to me with your despicable accusations. I was innocent on all counts, but you challenged me to disprove what you so obviously believed I'd done. Well, tonight you've accused me for the last time, for I want nothing more to do with you. I trust that this will be our final parting, and that I never again have the misfortune to encounter you."

He turned and climbed back into the carriage, slamming the door behind him. A moment later the team was straining forward, taking the vehicle away into the rain and darkness.

She stood there numbly. If he'd physically struck her she could not have felt more full of pain and shock.

"Miss Linnet?" Mary came to her, for the maid had been waiting discreetly in the doorway from the moment the carriage had arrived.

Slowly, Linnet turned to face her.

The maid gently took her arm. "Come inside out of the rain, miss."

Linnet allowed her to lead her into the house, where she saw Venetia waiting in the hall.

25

Sommers was waiting to close the doors, and he was thunderstruck to see the complete disarray his mistress was in. Venetia hurried over, her hazel eyes large with concern, then she nodded at the butler.

"Bring a warm restorative drink to the drawing room immediately."

"My lady." He bowed, and hastened away.

Venetia turned to Mary. "Bring Miss Carlisle's warmest wrap to the drawing room, and be quick about it."

"Yes, my lady." Gathering her skirts, the maid almost ran to the staircase.

Venetia then took Linnet's cold arm. "Come and sit down, then you can tell me what's happened."

Linnet allowed herself to be ushered toward the drawing room, where the chandelier cast a soft glow, and the curtains had been drawn to shut out the appalling night. She hesitated, turning to Venetia. "Where is my aunt?"

"She apparently sent word earlier that she intended to spend the night at Lady Anne's, which is why I felt at liberty to wait here for you. Do you want me to send for her?"

"No!" The word came out sharply, and Linnet said it again, but more quietly. "No, that won't be necessary."

Venetia looked anxiously at her. "Has something dreadful happened? You look so—so . . . ."

Linnet didn't reply, for at that moment Mary hurried

into the room with the wrap. She stood quietly as the maid unhooked her wet gown, allowing it to slither to the floor, and thus the black plume was revealed, still tucked carefully into place beneath the garter. The glittering feather was crumpled and damp, but it was still very beautiful indeed, and still quite obviously the property of London's most notorious courtesan.

Venetia gasped as she saw it. "So, you *did* succeed after all! I thought when you came in that all was lost. What do you intend to do with it now? Just send it back, as you said originally?"

"I really haven't thought about it," answered Linnet quietly, for it was true. Since the moment Nicholas had seized her in Judith's bedroom, her mind had seemed to be in utter chaos. She bent to retrieve the plume, tossing it onto a nearby table. It lay there sadly, its shaft broken and its sequins winking in the light from the chandelier.

Venetia and the maid exchanged uneasy glances as Linnet then donned the wrap, but nothing more was said because at that moment Sommers knocked at the door to say that he had brought the hot drink, as Venetia had requested.

As the butler came in with a glass of hot, spiced milk which he placed on a table, Linnet withdrew a little, observing Venetia and Mary. Could it really be that one of them had betrayed her? Her glance lingered on the maid, so loyal and supportive throughout the past year. Surely she couldn't have changed so drastically that she'd give her mistress into the hands of an enemy like the Bird of Paradise? And what of Venetia? What possible reason could *she* have for such treachery? Her delight about the match with Benedict had been too genuine and honest. She quite evidently looked forward to having her closest friend as a sister-in-law, so it was inconceivable that she'd so calculatingly set about ruining that same friend. Or was it inconceivable? Linnet's head was spinning with doubts and confusion, and she didn't know what to think anymore.

Sommers was looking at her. "Will there be anything else, madam?"

"No. Thank you." Linnet nodded at Mary as well. "You may go."

"But, miss, your hair . . ."

"Can wait."

"Yes, miss." The maid curtsied quickly, and then hurried out after the butler.

The door closed, and Linnet and Venetia were alone.

Venetia went to sit down on a sofa, her hands clasped neatly in her lap. Her gown was made of a striking rose satin, and her hair was concealed by a matching turban. A choker of pearls graced her slender throat, and she looked very lovely as she smiled at Linnet.

"What happened tonight? You have the plume, so I know you gained admittance."

"Oh, yes, I gained admittance," replied Linnet softly.

"And? Oh, don't be so infuriating!"

Linnet faced her. "My every move was anticipated, Venetia. Judith Jordan knew *exactly* what I was planning."

Venetia's eyes widened. "But that cannot possibly be so!"

"I'm afraid it was very much so. Someone saw to it that I walked into a trap tonight, and if Nicholas hadn't rescued me when he did, that trap would have caught me. Only you and Mary knew every detail of my plan," she added reluctantly.

"And *I* am more likely to be the guilty party than your maid?" Venetia leapt indignantly to her feet.

"No, of course not," replied Linnet, going to pick up the glass of hot milk. "I'm merely telling you what happened, which is, as I recall, what you wished to know."

Venetia became a little more collected. "I swear to you that I didn't divulge a word. What possible reason could I have?"

Linnet gave a small, rueful smile. "None, I suppose. And the same could be said of Mary."

"Linnet, forgive me for pointing out the obvious, but servants can be bought. Someone has only to offer them a plump purse, and their tongues rattle willingly."

Linnet nodded. "Yes, but I can't believe Mary would

do it." She looked quickly at Venetia. "Just as I can't believe you would, either. Nicholas pointed out that there was the hackney coachman, and Mary's cousin, who suggested the coachman . . ."

"My wager would still be on Mary herself. Think about it, if Judith Jordan knew your every move, presumably she had to know what you'd look like tonight. Well, she would, wouldn't she?"

"Yes."

"The hackney coachman could hardly know that until you were actually in his coach. The same applies to your maid's cousin. But if you think about Mary herself, *she* knew all the details of appearance, didn't she?"

"Yes."

Venetia came to put a gentle hand on her arm. "I know that I knew it all, too, but I have no reason whatsoever for wishing to harm you. You're my dearest friend, and soon you'll be my sister as well."

Linnet pulled slowly away, drawing a shaky breath. "No, Venetia, I'm afraid I won't be your sister, after all."

"Won't be? But . . . why not?" Venetia looked at her in astonishment.

"Because first thing in the morning, I will be sending Benedict's ring back."

"But, *why?*"

"He was at the ball in Portman Street, not at any dinner in East India House, and what's more, he was with Judith Jordan in her bedroom."

Venetia was thunderstruck, so much so that for a moment it seemed she would faint. She turned weakly away, returning to the sofa. Her hands clasped and unclasped in her lap, and it was a while before she recovered sufficiently to look at Linnet. "I can't believe it. You must have seen someone else, someone who looked like him."

"I wasn't mistaken, Venetia, it was definitely him. He and that woman have been lovers for some time, it seems. I now know from Nicholas that I was courted simply because of my fortune, because contrary to Benedict's claims, he has no wealth due to him from India, but has monstrous debts that must be settled if he's to stay out of jail."

Venetia's face had drained of all color, and her shock was so evident that it was plain she'd had no knowledge at all about the truth concerning her half-brother. "You— you actually saw him with her? Beyond all shadow of doubt?" she asked in a barely audible voice.

"Yes. They shared an exceeding passionate kiss."

"So, it has been because of Benedict, not Nicholas, that that woman has been singling you out?"

"It seems so. Her intention tonight was apparently not only to ruin me by exposing my presence at such an occasion, but also to flaunt her hold upon him. I don't know why she did it, since she'd obviously been going along with it all until now, but I do know that, by the look on his face, the last thing he wanted was for the match to be snatched from under his nose."

"I knew nothing about all this, Linnet, you must believe me."

"I know you didn't."

"He's my half-brother, but I've really only known him for this past year or so. We may have been under the same roof, but we led separate lives. I believed him when he spoke of his Indian fortune." Venetia gave a wry smile. "Your great-aunt didn't, though, did she?"

"No." Linnet sipped the glass of milk. "I truly meant to make him happy, and I know that in the end, if he'd been as he seemed to be, I *would* have loved him. You do know what I mean, don't you?"

"Yes, I do know, and I also know, with hindsight, that this break with Benedict is a blessing in disguise for you. Just think how it would have been if the marriage had gone ahead, and *then* you'd found out about his liaison with the Bird of Paradise."

Linnet smiled a little, finishing the glass of milk. "Well, he may have fooled me, but fate meant me to escape."

"He'll be given his marching orders from Fane Crescent, of that you may be sure," declared Venetia firmly, a hint of bitterness in her voice. "I truly trusted him, and I thought you and he would be perfect together. I only hope you can forgive me for so diligently promoting the match.''

"Of course I can." Linnet replaced the glass on the tray, and then crossed the room, holding back one of the curtains to look out at the darkness and the endless rain. Rivulets washed miserably down the glass, and the street lamps of Charles Street were distorted.

"How will you announce the ending of the engagement?" asked Venetia, watching her.

"I don't know, but it will be done tactfully, of that you may be sure. I don't wish to offend you in any way, or cause you any distress."

Venetia smiled. "Thank you."

Linnet gazed at the rain, remembering the bitterness of her last parting from Nicholas. "Tonight, when Nicholas . . ."

"Yes?"

Linnet lowered the curtain, turning to face her. "When he kissed me by the carriage, it was all suddenly so very clear. It didn't matter what may or may not have happened in the past, all that mattered was that I loved him. I was going to tell him, but then he cast me aside, because he said I'd questioned his honor once too often for him ever to wish to see me again."

Venetia's eyes were intent. "Perhaps it's for the best. It may all seem hopeless now, but you'll find someone else, and then you'll be truly happy."

"But, I don't want anyone else, Venetia. I love Nicholas, and I have from the moment I first met him. If only I'd behaved with more circumspection and sensitivity in the past, if only I'd thought less of my apparently injured pride and more of what my heart was telling me, then none of this would have happened."

Venetia was silent for a moment. "What do you intend to do?"

"What do *you* intend to do?" countered Linnet.

"Me? I—I don't understand . . ."

"This unnamed lover who means so much to you, how much do you want him?"

"With all my heart," replied Venetia.

"Do you intend to win him if you can?"

"Yes."

Linnet smiled. "Then that is what I must do, too. If I let Nicholas slip finally from my life now, I'll never forgive myself. The man one truly loves is always worth fighting for, isn't he?"

Slowly, Venetia nodded. "Oh, yes," she said softly, "he's always worth fighting for."

"Would it be asking too much for you to stay tonight? It would be comforting to know you're here."

"Yes, of course." Venetia smiled gently at her.

26

The resolve to win Nicholas back was still with her the following morning when she awoke after several hours of restless sleep. It had stopped raining outside, and the sun shone into the room as Mary opened the curtains and shutters.

Linnet sat up in the bed, glancing at the busy maid. She hadn't sent for her when she'd retired the previous night, and this was her first proper opportunity to speak to her about what had happened. Could Venetia be right about her? Would a fat purse have proved sufficient enticement?

Mary brought her a dish of tea. "Are you feeling better this morning, Miss Linnet?"

"A little."

"Miss Linnet . . . ?"

"Yes?"

"Do you forgive me for telling Lord Fane where you'd gone? I know that I shouldn't have said anything, but he was so insistent that I was frightened for you."

"It was as well you did tell him, for he saved me from a great deal of unpleasantness."

Mary lingered by the bed, and Linnet saw tears in her eyes. "Miss Linnet, I didn't tell on you to anyone else, I swear I didn't! When Lady Hartley was going out a little earlier, she took me aside and asked me if I'd betrayed you. I told her I hadn't, but she seemed to think I had. I didn't do it, Miss Linnet, you must believe me. I love you too much to ever do anything that would hurt you."

The tears were wet on the maid's cheeks, and her hands were trembling.

Linnet knew she was telling the truth. "It's all right, Mary, I believe you."

"Lady Hartley told me what had happened, and she said that someone who knew exactly what you were planning must have told that horrid woman, but I swear it wasn't me."

"I know it wasn't, so please don't worry. Lady Hartley shouldn't have spoken to you like that."

"She thought that it had to be me, miss, because I was the only other one who knew it all. But if it wasn't me, and it wasn't her, who could it be?"

"I wish I knew. Unless . . ."

"Miss?"

"Could Tom, the coachman have said anything? Or maybe we were overheard by one of the other servants?"

Mary considered for a moment. "I suppose it's possible, miss, but I don't think any of them would be disloyal to you. We all think very highly of you."

"Thank you for saying so." Linnet smiled, sipping the tea.

"Miss Linnet . . . ?"

"Yes?"

"Lady Hartley also told me that your betrothal to Mr. Gresham is to be ended. Is that true?"

"Yes, Mary, it is."

"I hope it's because you and Lord Fane . . ."

"No, Mary, I fear not. There is an entirely different reason for the ending of the match with Mr. Gresham."

"Oh. I'm sorry, miss."

"So am I, Mary. So am I."

"I think he still loves you, Miss Linnet. Lord Fane, I mean, not Mr. Gresham. He was very anxious indeed on your account, and I'm sure he would not have been like that unless he felt . . ."

"I'd like to think you're right, Mary, but I fear you aren't." Linnet smiled a little ruefully. "I admit that I do still love him, but there are still a great many problems unresolved. Last night he told me that he was innocent of any wrongdoing last year, and yet I still persisted in questioning his honesty on one particular point. After that, he told me he didn't wish to ever see or speak to me again."

"Oh, Miss Linnet, you mustn't leave it at that, for I'm certain that he does love you."

How good it would be if that were so, thought Linnet unhappily. She was silent for a moment, before looking at the maid again. "Did you say Lady Hartley had gone out?"

"Yes, she said she had some business to attend to, but would be back later in the morning. I think she wished to see Mr. Gresham."

"Yes, she probably did," replied Linnet, remembering Venetia's vow to send him packing.

There was a knock at the door, and Mary hurried to open it. Sommers came in with a note on a silver tray. "This has just been delivered, madam. I believe it to be a matter of some urgency."

"Thank you, Sommers." Linnet took it and read. It came from Nicholas's lawyer, Sir Henry Benjamin, and requested her to call at his chambers in Lincoln's Inn at her earliest convenience. This was what Nicholas had promised her the night before. She looked at the waiting butler. "Have the carriage prepared, Sommers. I will require it directly."

"But, will you not breakfast first, madam?" he asked.

"No, I think not."

"Madam." He bowed, and withdrew.

Mary looked at her. "What shall I put out for you, miss?"

"The royal-blue lawn, I think, and I'll wear it with the black velvet spencer."

"And the black beaver hat with the royal-blue gauze scarf?"

"Yes."

"Do you wish me to accompany you, miss?"

"Yes."

* * *

Linnet decided to return the ring to Venetia rather than to Benedict, for it had been purchased through Venetia's account at the jeweler's. Given his financial problems, his talent for double-dealing, and the fact that he was being ejected from Fane Street, it was highly improbable that he'd obligingly return the ring either to Venetia or the jeweler. Intending to give the ring to Venetia later that day, Linnet chose to formally end the betrothal by writing a very final note to Benedict and sending it by a running footman.

She felt nothing as she dispatched the note. It was as if Benedict Gresham had never existed in her life. The full extent of his treachery had left her feeling empty, with none of the anguish and heartbreak that had accompanied the discovery of Nicholas's sins the year before; if sins there had been. She wondered greatly what it was that Sir Henry Benjamin would have to say to her on the subject.

There was a welcome freshness in the air as she and Mary set off in the open landau to drive across the city to the lawyer's chambers. She was conscious of some trepidation, for as yet she had no way of knowing whether Judith had made public her presence at the masked ball, but if her shocking and foolish escapade was to be the talk of society, she intended to face it with as much dignity as she could. She was glad that she'd chosen to wear royal-blue and black, for the colors weren't in the least timid or retiring. The gauze scarf on her hat fluttered as the landau drove briskly eastward across the capital, and she sat erectly in her seat, looking so much the respectable lady that she found it hard to believe she'd decked herself out like a Cyprian the night before.

There was a jam of traffic in Piccadilly, and the landau came to a standstill. Another vehicle drew up alongside, and Linnet glanced at the passenger inside. With a jolt she found herself looking at Sir Mortimer Critchley's gray-haired figure. Her heart almost stopped, for if Judith had indeed made known her excursion to Portman Street, then he, of all the gentlemen present, would know that her conduct had been anything but ladylike.

He looked very much the worse for wear after the

night's jollifications, and was obviously suffering from a monstrous hangover. His face was sallow, and his mane of hair looked dull and in need of a tonic. A pieman strolling by on the pavement chose that moment to ring his bell and shout his wares, and Sir Mortimer winced as the sound pierced his thumping head. Linnet felt no sympathy, for he well deserved to suffer, but she wished he'd look toward her, for then she'd know how she stood.

At last he turned his head, looking directly at her. There was no extra light in his eye, no knowing glint, just the usual polite acknowledgment that she'd have expected from an acquaintance. He smiled a little, adopting his usual rather sanctimonious manner, and then she knew beyond a doubt that he was completely unaware that she'd been the troublesome lady in citrus-yellow whom he had been unfortunate enough to importune at the Bird of Paradise's masked ball.

A surge of relief passed through her, and she felt much better as the jam of traffic cleared and the landau drove on toward Lincoln's Inn.

Lincoln's Inn was named after the residence of the fourteenth-century Earl of Lincoln, which had stood on the site and was one of the four great Inns of Court of the capital. The landau approached it from adjacent Lincoln's Inn Fields, which was the largest square in central London, and had been laid out by Inigo Jones. The immense gateway into the court stood in the southeast corner of the square, and opened into a fine quadrangle. Sir Henry's chambers were part of a four-story terrace of handsome classical houses, the doorways of which were approached over bridged steps spanning the drop to the basement level. There was a fountain playing in the center of the quadrangle, and Linnet could distinctly hear the water splashing as she and Mary alighted from the landau and approached the door.

One of the lawyer's clerks conducted them up to the main chamber on the floor above, and Mary stood discreetly behind Linnet's chair as they waited for Sir Henry to come to them.

He did so within a minute or so, carrying a file of

papers under his arm. He was about fifty years old, be-
wigged, and had a rather cadaverous appearance. He was
much given to sitting with his lips sourly pursed and his
fingertips resting fastidiously together, a posture that had
wrought alarm in the heart of many a felon. Now, however, he was in an obliging and attentive mood, raising
Linnet's hand to his lips and murmuring that he appreciated her prompt response to his message.

"Sir Henry, you did intimate that the matter was one
of some urgency," she replied.

"I did indeed, Miss Carlisle, because when Lord Fane
called upon me late last night, he was most insistent that I
placed certain documents in your hands without further
delay. Those documents I have here in this file. My instructions are to hand you the documents in strict order,
and, with your permission, I will so proceed."

"Yes, of course."

He took out the first item, a large document of intim-
idatingly legal appearance, with ribboned seals and formal writing. "This is the deed to Radleigh Hall, Miss
Carlisle, and if you look you will see that the property
was transferred to your name over a year ago, on the day
after your late uncle relinquished it to Lord Fane. His
lordship owned the property only very fleetingly, and was
most anxious to see that it went to you, for he regarded
you as the rightful owner."

Linnet stared at the document. It was all written there,
the dates and the names; Radleigh Hall was hers.

Sir Henry cleared his throat, relieving her of the deed,
and placing some fresh sheets in her hands. "These are
a summary of the estate accounts, Miss Carlisle. Naturally, the complete books *et cetera* are at Radleigh Hall
itself. As you will note, the entire income from the property has been made over to you, and is held in an account
at Mr. Coutts's bank. Lord Fane has seen to it that Radleigh Hall has been kept in perfect order, and you will
find it just as you would have wished."

Linnet's hand trembled as she tried to peruse the papers, but it was all too much to take in. The pain of guilt

struck through her as she remembered the bitter and untrue accusations she'd laid at Nicholas's door.

The lawyer looked at her in some concern. "Are you feeling quite well, Miss Carlisle? Shall I ask my clerk to bring you a glass of water?"

"No. I'm quite all right, Sir Henry. Please proceed." She handed the papers back.

He drew a long breath, then. "I, er, think I should warn you that the next item may cause you distress, for it is a letter in your late uncle's hand, and what it contains is an admission of certain, er, wrongdoings."

Nicholas's words rang in her head as she took the letter. *Joseph Carlisle said a great many things, God rot his pernicious soul! If ever a man deserved to be called out, he did, but his demise spared me the trouble.* Hardly daring to think what she might be about to read, she swallowed and opened the letter.

My dearest niece, Linnet,

It is with great remorse that I write this letter, and with shame, for I know that I should have the backbone to admit my misdemeanors to your face. I am guilty of having deliberately misled you, because I could not bear to know that I had been found out.

Only two things have ever meant anything to me, you are one, and Radleigh Hall is the other. I have always loved you, my sweet niece, and have long been at pains to appear all that was honorable and good in your trusting eyes, but the truth is that this particular idol has always had feet of clay, and one of my greatest weaknesses has been a tendency to cheat at cards. I have seldom been detected, but on the night I lost Radleigh Hall to Lord Fane, I was the one who had been cheating, not he, only I failed to realize that he had found me out, and that he was allowing me enough of the proverbial rope to hang myself. I fell into the trap, and I deserved to, but immediately afterward I felt goaded into retaliation. I wished to hurt Fane for my humiliation, and I chose to do so by harming his relationship with you.

Forgive me, Linnet, for I traded despicably upon your love for me, knowing that you would not expect my word to be anything less than my true bond. I told you that Fane had cheated me of Radleigh Hall, and that he was deceiving you with the woman known throughout London as the Bird of Paradise. My doctors had already told me that I did not have long to live, and that I would not therefore have to see the look of recrimination and sadness in your eyes when you found out the extent of my misdeeds.

I did not intend to confess to you, but I have received a visit from Fane, who has told me how well I have succeeded, for you have indeed faced him with the lies I've so calculatingly insinuated into your mind. My sense of guilt overwhelms me now, and I am bitterly ashamed of what I've done, but I am also still too weak and spineless to confess to you. I am taking the coward's way out, my dear, and am sending this letter to Fane, with the humble request that he does not show it to you until after my death. Even now, when I am so fully cognizant of how I have failed and deceived you, I cannot bear the thought of seeing anything less than tears of love in your eyes.

Please, I beg of you, find it in your heart to forgive me, and never believe that I did not love you dearly. Return to Fane, Linnet, for he is the man for you, and although he is at present hurt and bitter that you took my word for everything, I know that he loves you. He will make you happy, and I gladly and willingly give the match my blessing.

Think gently of me from time to time, my dearest niece, even though I know I do not deserve it.

I am, your loving and repentent uncle,
Joseph Carlisle.

Tears blinded Linnet's eyes, and she could barely fold the letter again to give it back to the lawyer. She was almost overcome with conflicting emotions; sadness that her uncle had done such things, pain that she'd continued to think ill of Nicholas for so long, and a deep sense of guilt that she'd originally given such willing credence to the lies. Oh, Nicholas, forgive me, forgive me . . .

Mary leaned anxiously forward. "Are you all right, Miss Linnet?"

"Yes. I just need a moment . . ."

Sir Henry turned to pick up a small bell that stood on his great desk, and a clerk hurried in the moment it rang. "Bring a glass of water, and be quick about it," ordered the lawyer.

"Yes, Sir Henry."

The water was refreshing, and helped to restore a fragment of Linnet's lost composure. At last she drew a long, steadying breath and looked at the lawyer again. "Have I seen everything, Sir Henry?"

"Er, no, there is one last item, Miss Carlisle, a letter Lord Fane wrote to you last night. If you wish to recover a little more before . . . ?"

"No. I'll read it now, Sir Henry."

"Very well." He handed the folded, sealed sheet of paper to her.

With a heavy heart, she broke the seal, and began to read.

Miss Carlisle,
I trust that by the time you read this, you will be in full possession of the true facts concerning past events, but should your indomitable sense of your own infallibility still be placing you under some misapprehension where I'm concerned, allow me to state quite finally that I did not use foul means to acquire Radleigh Hall, I did not take Judith Jordan there, as you suggested on your return, nor did I conduct a liaison with her behind your back. I loved you, madam, and continued to love you even when you persisted in denigrating me. I didn't wish to keep the truth from you, but under the circumstances I didn't think you warranted any more consideration than you were prepared to show me. There is one thing I will always regret, however, and that is that in the end I've been left with no

choice but to destroy the fond memories you have of your uncle.

Perhaps I must confess to another regret; that I continued to love you until this very night. You'll never know the torment I felt when, on your return to town, I realized the place Gresham had assumed in your life. I knew his true character, and that he was seeking a fortune to pay his debts, and it pained me to see you so completely taken in. It also pained me to see your uncle's lies becoming a truth after all, for now you have indeed been cheated by a lover who has been unfaithful to you with the Bird of Paradise. It was because of Gresham that I refrained from telling the truth earlier. To have given you the deeds to Radleigh Hall while he was in the offing would have been tantamount to placing them in his scheming hands, and that I would never have done.

When you first fled to Grasmere, before there was any suggestion of your liaison with Gresham, I meant to follow you, to give you the deeds and attempt to clear my name with you without resorting to showing you your uncle's letter. I knew how much you loved Joseph Carlisle, and I didn't wish to be the one to destroy him in your eyes. Perhaps I was foolish to imagine that I could persuade you of anything without using such painful proof but that is indeed what I hoped to achieve. I was delayed in leaving, however, and was then told by Lady Hartley that her half-brother was not only interested in you, but that you welcomed that interest. I therefore bided my time, in the earnest hope that Gresham was but a fleeting aberration on your part. But he wasn't, was he, madam? You persisted in clinging to him right up to the moment you at last saw him in Judith's arms.

Yes, you clung to him, madam, but you didn't love him. I've been the one you've loved, as you and I both know. But you willfully chose to accept Gresham, and even when you finally knew him for

*the monster he is, you again saw fit to accuse me of
stealing Radleigh Hall.*

*Until that moment, I had continued to love you.
That love is now dead. Take back Radleigh Hall, for
it is yours, and I trust that knowing the truth about
your uncle proves worth it all. Go to blazes, Miss
Carlisle, and pray take your all-consuming obstinacy
with you.*

Fane.

27

A few minutes later, Linnet and Mary left Sir Henry's chambers, and set off swiftly in the landau, their destination not Carlisle House but Fane House. Linnet knew she had to see Nicholas if she was to salvage anything from the wreckage left by her past actions, and by the actions of her uncle. Nicholas had every justification for being bitter and resentful, but if he'd loved her until only a few hours ago, then that love was surely not lost beyond redemption. She had to throw herself on his mercy, confess her love, and beg forgiveness for her gross and hurtful errors of judgment, and then hope against hope that he'd grant her one final chance. Oh, please God, let him grant her a last opportunity to right all the wrongs . . .

But she wasn't going to have the chance she sought, for the gates of Fane House were closed against her. The landau drove smartly enough down John Street, but as it neared the lodge and gates, it became caught up in a gaggle of other vehicles. It seemed a considerable portion of society had converged upon this part of Mayfair, and the reason was something that had occurred in the sunken garden by the statue of Nicholas's grandfather.

The coachman managed to inch the landau close to the lodge, threading the team in and out of the other vehicles. Linnet looked out and saw that there was quite a crowd gathered in the garden. She wondered what had happened, the more so when she saw that a canvas awning had been hastily erected around the statue, hiding it completely from view, except, perhaps, from the upper windows of Fane House and the crescent.

At last the coachman maneuvered the team across the road, drawing them up before the closed gates. He expected the lodgekeeper to emerge and admit the landau at once, but this wasn't what happened. He quickly came out, but shook his head when he saw the identity of the would-be visitor.

The coachman was indignant. "Open the way, for this is Miss Carlisle's carriage!"

The man's eyes slid unwillingly toward Linnet, who was rather startled to see a deep resentment written in his gaze. "No," he said firmly, "for I have strict instructions not to admit this lady, and it's an order I more than gladly carry out." Without so much as a nod of his head, he turned and went back into the lodge.

Linnet stared after him in dismay. Nicholas had *specifically* ordered that she be refused admittance?

At that moment someone in the garden happened to turn and see her. It was the omnipresent Mr. Algernon Halliday, and he lost no time at all in drawing everyone's attention to the apparently immensely interesting fact of her presence.

"I say, *mes enfants*, do look and see who's calling! It's the little brown bird herself! Come to peck a little more, eh?" He began to laugh.

Many heads turned, and Linnet was both alarmed and appalled to see the great stir her appearance was causing. A number of people she knew began to hasten toward the steps, obviously intending to speak to her about something of considerable and pressing interest, and she suddenly knew that the last thing she should do was allow them to engage her in any sort of conversation.

She looked swiftly at the coachman. "Drive off, and as quickly as you can."

"Madam."

The landau moved slowly as the team was brought about, and it seemed to Linnet that it would be surrounded by people before it could drive away. She glanced back at the sunken garden. What on earth could have happened? And why had Algernon Halliday referred to her so cryptically as "the little brown bird herself"? The landau was pulling away at last, and as it left the crowd well behind and began to come up to a smart pace, her glance moved for a final time to the strange awning protecting the statue. What was being concealed? The landau's pace took the garden from her view, carrying her safely from the press of acquaintances who were so intent upon speaking to her.

"Oh, miss! Look! It's Lord Fane!"

Mary's sharp exclamation brought Linnet's attention swiftly back to the road some way ahead, and, sure enough, Nicholas was riding toward them on his Arabian horse, the greyhounds following obediently.

He wore a charcoal coat, cream cord breeches, and a light-blue silk waistcoat. He looked as if he'd been riding hard in Hyde Park, for his face was a little flushed and his neckcloth had become undone. His hair was windswept, and his top hat was tipped right back on his head.

He saw the landau as the coachman automatically halted it in front of him, and he recognized its occupants, but he made to ride straight past.

"Nicholas?" Linnet called out urgently to him. He *had* to speak to her, he *had* to!

Still he didn't rein in.

"Nicholas! Please, I beg of you!"

He reined in at last, turning coldly in the saddle to survey her. His eyes were impenetrable, and his manner offered no encouragement at all. "I have nothing to say to you anymore, madam. This final insult is more than anyone could be expected to endure. Many things I have thought of you, but not that you were possessed of so offensive a sense of humor."

She stared at him. "I—I don't understand."

"No? Spare me your clever acting, madam."

"Nicholas, I love you."

His eyebrow twitched contemptuously. "Indeed? I suppose I'm expected to believe you, and then crush you to my bosom. Forgive me if I decline to oblige."

"Nicholas, I do love you. You were right, I've *always*

loved you, and if you want me to say how ashamed I am of all the things I've said in the past, then I willingly say it. I was wrong, wrong about everything, and I wish with all my heart that I'd shown more faith and loyalty toward you. Please, forgive me and allow me one more chance.''

His eyes flashed incredulously. ''Madam, you really take my breath away! You look so sweet and innocent, I might even say adorably innocent, when in truth you are a viper entirely without scruple. I consider myself to have had a fortunate escape.'' Without waiting for her to say anything more, he kicked his heels and spurred the horse on toward Fane House.

The coachman urged the landau forward once more and at last they reached Carlisle House, driving into the refuge of the courtyard where they found Venetia's barouche drawn up before the house, but Linnet was so close to tears that she hardly saw it as she alighted from the landau. Mary ushered her into the house, and Venetia hurried from the drawing room, her slender figure eye-catching in vermilion silk.

''Linnet, I have something very disagreeable to tell you . . .'' Her steps faltered as she saw how distressed Linnet was. ''Oh, whatever has happened? Do you know already about the statue?''

Linnet strove to collect herself. ''The-the statue? No.''

Venetia waved Mary away and put a comforting arm around Linnet's trembling shoulders. ''Sommers has just brought me a tray of coffee in the drawing room, and I rather fancy that it would do you good to take a cup with me. It's all right, it's just me, your great-aunt has yet to return.''

For the second time in less than a day, Linnet found herself being led gently into the drawing room. Venetia steered her to the sofa before which the tray had been placed on a table, and when she was seated, took a place herself and began to pour the coffee.

''I asked Sommers to bring two cups and saucers, because I hoped you would return soon,'' she said lightly, pressing a cup into Linnet's cold hands. ''Now, then, you are to tell me exactly why you are in such a pitiable state. Every detail, now, you are to miss nothing out.''

Wearily, Linnet began to relate what had occurred at Sir Henry's chambers.

Venetia's lips parted in amazement. "Your *uncle* was the one who cheated? And he deliberately told all those lies about Nicholas?''

"Yes. Oh, Venetia, I feel so dreadful that I wish I were dead. I drove to Fane House, but there was a great crowd, and the lodgekeeper wouldn't admit me. He said that Nicholas had specifically ordered that I be kept out.''

"Yes, I rather imagine that that is indeed so,'' replied Venetia quietly.

Linnet looked at her. "What has happened?'' she demanded. "All I know is that I seem to be the cause of a great new stir, and that it's nothing to do with Portman Street last night. Why did that odious Halliday toad call me 'the little brown bird herself'? And why did Nicholas then accuse me of having 'an offensive sense of humor'?''

"You've seen Nicholas this morning?'' asked Venetia quickly.

"Yes, for a moment or so in the street. He was returning from a ride.''

"But he spoke to you?''

"In a manner of speaking.'' Linnet's voice shook again, and she struggled to maintain her composure.

Venetia put her cup down and rose to her feet, going to the fireplace. She turned to face Linnet. "Someone removed the stolen plume from this room and took it to the statue in the Fane Street garden, where it was tied rather ridiculously to the horse's tail. The statue itself was daubed with tar and stuck all over chicken feathers.''

Linnet stared at her. "But, who would do such a thing?'' she breathed.

Venetia met her eyes. "Society has no option but to believe it was you, Linnet.''

"Me? But, why?''

"Because there was a verse tied to the horse. I, er,

wrote it down. It's on that piece of paper on the table
next to the tray. Turn it over, and you'll see.''

Hesitantly, Linnet picked up the sheet, and turned it
to see some hastily scribbled lines in pencil.

On this plume's owner, no pity need you waste,
For her feathers are tawdry, and she lacks all taste.
By placing her here, it's doubtless she can
Be identified by Mayfair, down to a man.
But who chose this admirable place to show her true
  worth?
Why, 'tis a sly-little, brown-little, bird from the north!

Linnet closed her eyes, her breath escaping on a long,
dismayed sigh. Now she knew only too well what Algernon Halliday had meant. The little brown bird from the
north was so simple to translate: Linnet Carlisle.

Venetia went to her, taking the sheet of paper and rip-
ping it into fragments. "I'm so sorry, Linnet, and if I
knew who'd done such a despicable thing, I swear I'd tear
them limb from limb for hurting you so. Think, now.
Have you any idea at all who it might be? Who knew
about the plume? I saw it, and so did Mary—oh, and so
did Sommers, for he brought in that tray of hot spiced
milk.''

Linnet leaned her head back, her eyes closed. "The
plume was still on the table when we retired, Venetia, so
any one of the servants could have seen it. It's becoming
more and more plain that I have someone in this house
who has been betraying me, but short of dismissing them
all, I don't know what to do about it.''

"But . . .''

"I don't want to talk about it, Venetia.''

"You can't just let it go, Linnet!''

"Please, Venetia!'' Linnet was at the end of her tether,
and the last thing she needed was pressure to do something about which she felt so utterly helpless. She got up.
"I really would prefer to be left alone for a while. I don't
mean to sound rude or ungrateful, but . . .''

Venetia put an understanding hand on her arm. "Of

course. Forgive my insensitivity. Shall I call upon you tonight?''

''Yes. That would be nice.''

Venetia went to the door, and then turned. ''Benedict received your note.''

''Did he attempt to make excuses?''

''No, for he is so demonstrably in the wrong. I believe he was indeed becoming too fond of you, however, far too fond for La Jordan's peace of mind. Anyway, it seems she is suddenly in a position to rescue him from the duns, and so losing your fortune isn't the catastrophe it might otherwise have been. I've told him he must leave, for I'll never forgive him. He didn't just use you abominably, Linnet, he did the same to me.''

As the door closed behind her, Linnet sat down again. All that had happened was just too much, and as Venetia's barouche drove away across the yard, she hid her face in her hands and gave in to tears of utter misery.

28

S he didn't know how long she wept, but at last the sobs subsided, and she sat there quietly, wondering who had worked so secretly and effectively against her. Who had informed Judith Jordan about every detail of the plan to go to the masked ball? And who had taken the black plume and used it with such devastating success on the statue? The plume was perhaps the most important matter, for who could have had the opportunity to take it from this very room in the short time it had been here? Until she'd placed it on the table, no one could even have known she'd succeeded in removing it from Portman Street. Venetia and Mary had seen it, and so had Sommers, but after that, any one of the servants could have seen and taken it. She sighed. Always it came back to the servants, and Carlisle House, like any other large residence, had a veritable army of them.

At first she didn't hear the carriage approaching across the courtyard, but as it halted at the door the coachman called out to his restive team, rousing her from her thoughts. Hope leapt into her heart that it might be Nicholas, and she got up quickly to hurry across to the window. To her amazement and outrage, she saw Judith Jordan's white landau, with the Bird of Paradise herself seated ostentatiously inside. The Cyprian looked magnificent in a clinging white muslin gown and golden velvet spencer, and the inevitable plume sprang provocatively from her golden velvet hat. The white poodle sat on the seat next to her, getting up as she prepared to alight.

For a moment Linnet was too stunned to move, but then she drew resolutely back from the window. How dare that creature call at this house! How *dare* she! Gathering her skirts, she hurried furiously out into the hall, intending to command Sommers to refuse the Cyprian admittance, but it was already too late. The butler had already opened the door, and was caught unawares as the Cyprian swept grandly past him, accompanied by the poodle.

Linnet halted, trembling with rage. "Sommers? Have this person ejected immediately."

The butler looked wretched. "Er, yes, madam . . ."

Judith's haughty eyes swept disparagingly over him. "Lay one finger upon me, sirrah, and you'll know how very sharp a poodle's teeth can be." She made a soft clicking sound, and as the poodle began to growl in a surprisingly ferocious way, she turned to survey Linnet. "You and I should talk, Miss Carlisle."

"On the contrary, Miss Jordan, you and I have nothing whatsoever to say to each other."

The blue eyes shone with a glint of humor. "Would I be right in saying that you had nothing at all to do with what was done in the Fane Crescent garden this morning?"

Linnet hesitated. "Yes."

"Would I also be right in thinking that you'd very much like to know who did do it?"

"Yes." Linnet looked more intently at her. "Do you know?"

"Shall we just say that I can make a very educated guess. Now then, do you still wish to have me thrown out? Or would you prefer to hear me out?"

Linnet drew a long breath, and then nodded at Sommers. "That will be all."

He could scarce conceal his relief. "Madam," he murmured, bowing and hurrying away.

Linnet stood aside. "Shall we adjourn to the drawing room, Miss Jordan?"

"That would be most agreeable, Miss Carlisle." The poodle followed as the two women proceeded from the entrance hall into the privacy of the drawing room.

As she sat down, Judith's glance took in the evidence of recent tears on Linnet's face. She smile a little. "I'm told that cold stewed apple is very efficacious for sore eyes, Miss Carlisle."

"I will be sure to remember," replied Linnet coolly, sitting down opposite. "Now then, Miss Jordan, if you have something to say . . ."

"Cards on the table?"

Linnet nodded slowly, wondering what was in the other's mind. "Yes, Miss Jordan, cards on the table."

"Very well. May I begin by saying that I have no wish at all to continue being at odds with you; indeed, it so happens that the very opposite is now the case."

"Indeed?"

Judith took a long breath. "I was very jealous of you, Miss Carlisle, and more than a little frightened that I was about to lose the only man I've ever truly loved. Oh, I know Benedict for what he is, but that hasn't prevented me from being monumentally unwise over him. I've always been successful in my chosen way of life, but even the sort of success I've hitherto enjoyed has failed to bring me the fortune Benedict needed if he was to escape the duns. That is why I aided and abetted him, first by keeping quiet while he awaited his aunt's death, and, when she didn't leave him her estate, by subsequently keeping quiet while he turned his attentions to seeking a wealthy wife.

"I was content enough when he decided upon you, but then I realized that he was beginning to like you too much for my peace of mind. I was angry and put out, and at first I contented myself by taunting you when you returned to town. I felt safe in doing this, because I knew you would interpret my actions as being caused by jealousy over Lord Fane, and because I knew there was precious little Benedict would be able to do about it. Everything seemed to be escalating, however, for the duns pursued him, first of all at the Theatre Royal, and then at the Hanover Square Rooms. They left him in no doubt at all that settlement had better be swiftly forthcoming or otherwise he'd find himself in jail.''

Linnet sat back. So, those two strange incidents had been because of duns. No wonder he'd looked so pale and strained when he'd returned to the box at the theater, and again after speaking to the so-called ''workmen'' at the sculpture exhibition. When she thought about those events now, she recalled that after each one he'd pressed her to marry him as quickly as possible, pretending that it was because he loved her so desperately. Dull color touched her cheeks, and she lowered her eyes.

Judith surveyed her. ''Forgive me if what I'm telling you seems to heap insult upon injury, but I'm merely explaining it all exactly as it was. As I was saying, I put up with everything, but then I realized that you meant more to him than you should, so I decided that something positive had to be done, otherwise I'd lose him forever. I have recently been importuned by a somewhat elderly and disagreeable Russian who wishes to lavish costly gifts upon me, and Miss Carlisle, when I say costly gifts, I truly mean it, for the very first thing he gave me was a diamond necklace that would have pleased the Empress Catherine herself. On reflection, it probably once belonged to that lady, for I vow it's fine enough to be part of the imperial jewels.'' The Cyprian stroked the poodle as it sat by her knee, gazing up at her with soulful, adoring eyes.

''Do go on, Miss Jordan.''

''The advent of this gentleman made my decision rather easy, for I was suddenly in a position to rescue Benedict. First of all, however, I had to separate him from you, and, I'm ashamed to say, I was so eaten up with jealousy that I needed to do you harm as well. I knew that if you saw him in my arms, you'd end the betrothal, but that wasn't enough for me, for I wished to ruin your reputation as well by exposing you to one and all at the ball. Believe me, Miss Carlisle, I'm not at all proud of myself.'' The Cyprian's dark-blue eyes rested shrewdly upon her. ''It's Fane that you love, isn't it?'' she said softly.

Linnet was about to reply that it was not any of her business, but then remembered that this was supposed to be a cards-on-the-table conversation. She nodded. "Yes, Miss Jordan, I do love him. I don't think I ever really stopped loving him. But how . . . ?"

"How do I know? Because of what was done to the statue today. It was only superficially directed at me—the real purpose was to alienate Fane from you. His high regard for his grandfather is well known, and the wanton besmirching of that late gentleman's statue is guaranteed to arouse his anger more than anything else. As I said, it was all directed only superficially at me, but the verse that was appended made it perfectly clear to one and all that you were supposed to be the perpetrator. It succeeded most exquisitely, you'll agree."

"It did indeed," murmured Linnet.

"You aren't a fool, Miss Carlisle, it must be obvious to you that it's the same person who supplied me with every detail of your plans, and I would imagine that you can only conclude that it must be one of your servants."

"Have you been a fly on my wall, Miss Jordan?" asked Linnet a little dryly.

The Cyprian smiled. "No, Miss Carlisle, I've merely considered the situation as it must appear to you. It isn't one of your servants, for a servant wouldn't have any reason for wishing to deny you all the hope of winning Fane."

"That's true."

"So, who does that leave? Who is it who has known everything all along? Which friend is it who has been close enough to . . ."

Linnet rose slowly to her feet. "Are you suggesting that it's Lady Hartley?"

"Yes."

"I don't believe you."

"She's the only person with the knowledge, the opportunity, *and* the motive."

"Motive? But she wanted me to marry Benedict, and was overjoyed that I was to be her sister-in-law, so how can you possibly say that she also wished to do my reputation as much harm as she could? It doesn't make sense.''

"It's true that she wished you to marry Benedict, and it's also true that she wished to destroy your character, but on both counts it was because she needed to see you well and truly off the market as far as a certain other gentleman was concerned. She may not have known about Benedict's huge debts, but she did know how mercenary a soul he is, so that she was sure your fortune would still prove carrot enough for him even if your reputation was less than it should be. She also hoped that by ruining your good name she'd drive a final wedge where it mattered most, and so she decided to approach me to assist her, because she knew of my hostility toward you, although, like you, she wrongly put that hostility to jealousy over Lord Fane, not Benedict.''

"What do you mean by drive a final wedge?''

"You really haven't figured it out, have you?'' murmured the Cyprian shaking her lovely head in disbelief. "*Fane* is the reason for it all, Miss Carlisle, because she loves him to distraction, although it's taken me until now to realize that that was what was behind her every move.''

Linnet was thunderstruck. "No, it can't be so . . .''

"It *is* so, Miss Carlisle, and if you pause to really consider, you'll soon see for yourself that it's all true. She exulted when you and Fane parted company last year, and was content that the way was now clear for her. Of course she promoted the match with Benedict, for with you safely married, you could never become Lady Fane. She could comfortably make a show of trying to persuade you to return to London, because she knew you still felt far too bruised to undertake such a return, and when you suddenly changed your mind, I'll warrant she virtually stood on her head in order to make you stay where you were.''

Linnet sighed, and nodded. "Yes, she did.''

"You see, a year hadn't proved sufficient time for her as far as Fane was concerned—he hardly knew she existed. Even when she moved to Fane Crescent, right opposite him, he barely gave her the time of day. I think she almost gave up at that point, and that she was actively considering accepting poor Freddy Grainger's suit, but then at a ball at Holland House, Fane arrived and smiled at her. Freddy ceased to exist for her, and she spent the rest of the evening endeavoring to engage Fane's interest.''

Linnet sat down slowly. So, it really hadn't been Mr. Coleridge, but had been Nicholas who'd been the cause of Freddy's disappointment.

Judith smiled a little. ''Things begin to fit into place, do they not?''

''Yes.'' Linnet gave an ironic laugh. ''She even told me Nicholas had taken you to Radleigh. She knew that that would hurt me deeply.''

''Fane wouldn't have done such a thing, Miss Carlisle. You've wronged him throughout, not only about Radleigh Hall and his so-called affair with me, but also about his appearance at your ball and the help he was supposed to have given me on that same occasion. He came to the ball because he really was sent an invitation, and it's my guess that it was Freddy Grainger's invitation.''

''Freddy's? Why do you say that?''

''Well, Freddy was on your list, was he not?''

''Of course.''

Judith smiled a little. ''Many gentlemen come to my house, Miss Carlisle, and quite often it is simply because I offer a sympathetic ear. Freddy complained to me that he wasn't going to receive an invitation, he was quite adamant, even though I told him I thought it exceedingly unlikely.''

Linnet stared at her. ''But of *course* he received one.''

''Did he? It's my belief that Lady Hartley chose to exclude him so that the man she really loved would be there to watch Benedict put his ring on your finger. She also wanted Lord Fane to be there to see how brilliant she'd been with the arrangements, and, therefore, how perfect she'd be as Lady Fane. As to how *I* gained admittance, well, I simply enlisted the aid of a betting gentleman whose invitation stipulated that he and 'a lady' were invited. It doesn't matter who the gentleman was, for if I told you I'd lose my reputation for being complete discreet, would I not? Lord Fane would *never* have helped me in that way; indeed, he was angry with me for telling all those malicious tales about you, so he would hardly have lifted an obliging finger to smuggle me into your betrothal ball, would he? It's clear now that he knew about my liaison with Benedict, and about the debts, and I can think of only one occasion when he may have found out. Benedict and I spoke a little unguardedly once in my drawing room, and I realized afterward that the door was slightly ajar. Nicholas was in the house at the time.''

Linnet looked away.

The Cyprian smiled. ''I see from your reaction that my guess is correct. He may have gone about things in an awkward way, Miss Carlisle, but his intentions toward you have been honorable throughout.''

Tears filled Linnet's eyes, and she tried unsuccessfully to blink them away.

''Well you might look like that, Miss Carlisle, for he has never deserved the treatment he received at your foolish hands. I'm flattered that you should have credited me with stealing him from you, for in truth he's a man worth stealing. Lady Hartley credited me with having stolen him, too, but I didn't matter to her, for a lord doesn't marry a demirep, and it was his ring she was after.'' She paused. ''I can see her motives so clearly now, and yet if it hadn't been for the damage done to the statue, I'd still have been mystified as to why she was doing what she did to you.''

''What difference did the statue make?''

''As I said earlier, it pointed the finger of suspicion well and truly at the little brown bird from the north. Lady Hartley had already worked against you, and she was the only one who could really have removed my stolen plume from this house. The fact that she then used it to such effect against you could only be on Lord Fane's account. Nothing else explains it all, and once that fact is accepted, then all the others fall sweetly into their allotted places, even down to the way she suddenly chose to cut Freddy Grainger at the Holland House ball.''

"You know what happened that night, too?''

"Yes, Miss Carlisle, because both Benedict and Lord Fane told me their versions of events. Benedict believed it was all on account of Mr. Coleridge, but Mr. Coleridge happened to spend a great deal of that evening in conversation with Lord Fane. Benedict didn't notice Lord Fane's presence, but saw only the sudden advent of the very married Mr. Coleridge. Lord Fane told me that he wished he'd never made the mistake of smiling at the lady that night, for after that she was continually at his elbow, and he really cannot abide her. That is the truth of it, Miss Carlisle.''

Linnet nodded. "I can't believe she so took me in . . .''

"An ambitious and determined woman in love can be as devious and persuasive as the serpent in the Garden of Eden.'' The Cyprian smiled. "However, you should not merely take my word for all this, Miss Carlisle, you should hear it all from Lady Hartley's own lips.''

"She's hardly likely to confess.''

"I think she will, if I am with you, for she knows I can prove her guilt. She wrote me several notes, you see, and they make it plain that she was telling me about your plans.'' Judith stroked the poodle again. "She has to be made to tell you the truth, and then Lord Fane has to be told what has really been going on.''

"You're prepared to face Lady Hartley with me? Why would you do that?''

"Because I am conscience-stricken where you're concerned. I've been a *chienne* of the first order, and have to make it up to you. I also happen to like Lord Fane, who is the most honorable gentleman it has ever been my privilege to know. He has never been my lover, Miss Carlisle, so you may put that fear from your mind, but he has always been my good friend. I value that friendship, even though I sorely tried it when I set about making life difficult for you.'' The Cyprian smiled. "Miss

Carlisle, I also wish to help you because, against all the odds, I like you a great deal. You're a lady of rare spirit, and I have to confess that if I hadn't been warned of your plans by Lady Hartley, you'd probably have pulled it off undetected at my ball. You missed your vocation, for I vow you'd have made a devastating courtesan.''

"If that's supposed to be a compliment . . ."

"Oh, it is, Miss Carlisle, a very definite compliment."

Linnet smiled suddenly. "Then I should pay you one, too, Miss Jordan. You also missed your vocation, for you'd have made a splendid lady."

"Well, since I'm determined to tie the knot with a rogue like Benedict, I doubt if I'll ever truly be a lady, but you, Miss Carlisle, can be one in every sense of the word if you play your hand properly with Lord Fane. Are you prepared to try?"

"Yes."

"Good. Then there's no time like the present." The Cyprian rose to her feet. "It's time to call upon Lady Hartley, so perhaps it would be discreet to order your town carriage. Mine is a little, er, conspicuous."

"It has also been at my door for some time now, a fact which will not have passed unnoticed. Besides, don't you think I would be guilty of a double standard if I was prepared to accept your assistance, but wasn't prepared to be seen driving with you?"

Judith smiled a little. "Then let us compromise, Miss Carlisle. We'll drive in my carriage, but with its hoods well and truly raised, and you must wear a hat with a veil, for there is hardly any point in Fane's having rescued your reputation if you immediately throw it away again for the sake of a gesture. For the moment you and I are allies, but we come from different worlds, and soon we will return to those respective worlds. It's better that way."

Linnet hesitated, and then nodded. "I fear you may be right."

"Go and change into some devastating togs, Miss Carlisle, for soon you will be facing not only Lady Hartley, but Lord Fane himself. Oh, and make sure you wear yellow, for I know he likes to see you in that color above all others.'' Judith smiled. ''But not the dress you wore last night, for that is *my* world, not yours.''

29

Linnet took Judith's advice, and wore yellow. She chose a daffodil muslin gown and matching full-length pelisse, both embroidered in white, and with them she put a high-crowned straw bonnet over which a lacy veil was draped.

She and Judith were just about to leave the house, the poodle pattering at their heels, when Great-Aunt Minton returned. Already deeply upset about the disfiguring and ridiculing of the statue, she was much affronted to find London's most infamous Cyprian with her great-niece.

Bristling with outrage, the old lady paused in the doorway, eyeing them both. "What is the meaning of this?" she demanded.

Linnet's heart had begun to sink as soon as she realized her great-aunt had chosen this untimely moment to return. "I—I can explain, Great-Aunt."

"I trust you can, missy. Well? Why is this . . . this *person* being received?"

"Miss Jordan has come to help me, Great-Aunt."

"*Help* you? Is such a complete *volte-face* humanly possible? Linnet, the creature has been endeavoring to harm you for longer than I care to remember."

Judith cleared her throat uncomfortably. "Miss Minton, I . . ."

"Be silent. I am not accustomed to having society of your kind thrust upon me!" snapped the old lady, her eyes so bright and forbidding that their glance quelled even the Bird of Paradise.

Linnet went to her great-aunt. "Please hear me out."

"Not before you answer me one question. Linnet, did you have anything at all to do with what was done to the statue in Fane Crescent?"

"No, Great-Aunt, and I'm more than a little hurt that you should think I did."

The old lady's eyes studied her for a long moment, and then softened. "Forgive me, my dear, I should indeed have known better, but I was so very upset . . . He meant everything to me," she added unguardedly, for Judith could hear every word.

"I know he did," replied Linnet, taking her hands.

"I suppose *this* person can shed light on it all?" went on her great-aunt, eyeing Judith again.

Linnet nodded. "It was Venetia, Great-Aunt Minton."

The old lady stared at her, and then drew a long breath. "Well, I suppose I should be surprised, but I'm not. I never did trust that woman."

"I know you didn't."

"If you'd listened to my advice . . . Oh, well, I suppose there's no point in saying anything. My instinct is usually right, my dear, as has been proved concerning Lady Hartley, and will yet be proved concerning her unpleasant half-brother."

Linnet glanced at Judith, whose eyes were firmly downcast. "Great-Aunt, you've already been proved right about him as well. I am no longer betrothed to him."

"Indeed? It seems that much has been in progress during my absence."

"Yes, it has. You, er, you were wrong about one person, however."

"The present Lord Fane?"

"Yes. He was entirely innocent a year ago, and I was very wrong indeed to believe to the contrary. I love him, Great-Aunt Minton, and if I can earn his forgiveness, then I will."

The old lady's fond eyes were understanding. "I'm glad to hear that he isn't a discredit to his grandfather after all, and I wish you every good fortune in your efforts to win him back, but I fail to see why this *person* is here in this house!'' This last was added with a return to sharpness.

"Miss Jordan and I are about to beard Lady Hartley in her den."

"Are you implying that you intend to *accompany* this infamous creature to Fane Crescent?" breathed her great-aunt in utter disbelief.

"Yes."

"I will not permit it!"

Linnet raised her chin defiantly. "You cannot prevent me, Great-Aunt."

For a long moment the old lady held her ground, but then she slowly nodded. "You're right, I cannot prevent you, but Linnet, are you sure you know what you are doing?"

"Quite sure."

"Then I will not stand in your way."

Linnet smiled, hugging her tightly. "Thank you, Great-Aunt."

The old lady patted her shoulder, and then glared at Judith. "You have a lot to answer for, madam, and if anything else should befall my great-niece . . ."

"Rest assured, Miss Minton, the utmost discretion and circumspection will be employed throughout."

"They had better be, madam. They had better be."

Linnet made certain that her veil was properly in place, and then she and Judith emerged quickly from the house, stepping immediately into the landau, the hoods of which were already raised in readiness. A small crowd had collected at the courtyard gates, for the Bird of Paradise's white landau was too well known for its presence to pass unnoticed. There was much whispering and speculation as to why it might be drawn up at the door of Carlisle House, especially after the matter of the statue, but their curiosity was left unsatisfied as the carriage swept out, its occupants impossible to see in the dark interior.

The lodgekeeper at Fane Crescent was caught off-guard by the landau. A barouche and four had just entered, and before he could close the gates, the conspicuous white carriage had swept by as well. The man was well aware that London's most notorious Cyprian was hardly the sort of person the residents of the crescent would wish to be admitted, but he was equally aware that Judith was Nicholas's friend, and so he pretended not to notice, closing the gates behind the landau and hastening back into his lodge.

Linnet glanced out at the sunken garden as the landau drove along the crescent toward Venetia's house. There were only a few people there now, and the men were taking down the awning around the cleaned statue. There was no sign of the plume, tar, and feathers that had adorned it earlier, or of the sly verse, which had long since been removed. Her gaze moved across the garden toward Fane House, and then quickly away again. Would he soften toward her once he knew she'd had nothing to do with the disfiguring of the statue? Would he relent and give her the one final chance she craved? Or was his love as dead as he claimed?

The landau drew up at Venetia's door, and as Linnet prepared to alight, Judith sat quickly forward, putting a hand on her arm. "You must not show your face for fear of being seen with me, so keep your veil well in place. I trust the butler knows your voice?"

"Yes."

"Then let us proceed."

Judith stepped down, and Linnet followed, being careful to conceal her face. No one walked along the pavement as they approached the door of the house, and Linnet's heart began to beat frantically in her breast. What if Judith had been lying? What if Venetia was innocent? Doubts filled her for a moment, and she almost turned away, but then common sense told her that Judith hadn't lied, and that Venetia was indeed guilty of everything.

She rapped with the knocker, and in a moment the door opened. Venetia's butler looked out, his startled glance moving swiftly toward Judith, and then the distinctive white landau.

Linnet addressed him. "Is Lady Hartley at home, Rochdale?"

Her voice took him aback, for he hadn't realized it was she behind the veil. "Miss Carlisle?"

"The same."

"Er, yes, madam, Lady Hartley is indeed at home, but . . ." He looked uneasily at Judith.

Linnet seized the moment, stepping boldly into the hall, knowing that Judith would follow. "Would you tell her ladyship that I've called?"

Looking outside to see if anyone had observed the notorious Cyprian entering the house, he closed the door and then withdrew up the stairs to the drawing room on the first floor.

It was several minutes before he reappeared, and Linnet could only imagine Venetia's alarm and consternation on hearing who had called.

"Lady Hartley will receive you now, Miss Carlisle."

With Judith walking a step or so behind her, Linnet flung back her veil, and went up the staircase. Her heart was pounding now, and she felt quite sick with apprehension. This was surely going to be the most disagreeable interview of her life.

Venetia wore a gown of a rather subdued shade of violet, and whether it was this or her great unease that made her seem so pale, Linnet really couldn't tell. She was standing with her back to one of the tall windows, and through the glass behind her Linnet could see how perfect a view there was of Fane House opposite.

The butler closed the doors, and the three women were alone. Venetia's hazel eyes moved swiftly from one to the other of her visitors. "Well, I must say that you two seem rather unlikely companions, and I can't pretend, Linnet, that I am at all pleased to be paid an open call by a demirep. I trust you have an explanation?"

Before Linnet could reply, Judith spoke. "Lady Hartley, I rather fancy that if any explanation is due to anyone, it is from you to Miss Carlisle. You see, I've been a little remiss, and have told her everything you've been up to, and I've been putting two and two together, and coming up with some sovereign reasons for your activities. Now, rather than expect Miss Carlisle to simply take

my word, I thought it best of we toddled along to see
you, so that you could explain it all yourself. I'd hate to
think I'd been less than correct in every detail."

Venetia's face was now even more pale, but she gave
no other sign of being trapped. "Miss Jordan, I neither
know nor care what you're talking about, but I would be
much obliged if you'd leave this house directly." She
reached for a handbell.

Judith tutted, and wagged a remonstrative finger. "That
won't do at all, my lady. Believe me, I'm quite prepared
to show your indiscreet notes, and broadcast my tale to
all and sundry. Now then, all you have to do is confess
that you were the one who not only informed on her
concerning the visit to my ball, but you were also the one
who removed that plume from Carlisle House and appended it to the statue we can all see from that window
behind you." The Cyprian smiled a little. "I know you
consider yourself to be a friend of the great Mr. Coleridge, but really, my dear, you aren't in his class when it
comes to poetry. That dismal little verse was such a poor
thing, was it not?"

Spots of guilty color had flared to Venetia's hitherto
ashen face, and now her eyes flashed into bitter life. "It
served its purpose!" she snapped.

"Temporarily," murmured Judith, the smile still curving her lips. "I intend to tell Nicholas the real identity
of the culprit, and after that I fear your chances of succeeding with him will be less than minimal."

Venetia's glance flew to Linnet, and there was no mis-
taking the deep loathing written in her eyes. "You don't
deserve him," she breathed. "You chose to toss him
aside, but I wanted him, I've *always* wanted him!"

Judith gave a derisory laugh. "How frustrating for you
that he hardly knows you exist."

"I'll win him yet!"

"Be sensible, my dear, admit you are defeated. He's
going to take Miss Carlisle back after all this, and you'll
be out in the cold, where you so richly deserve to be.
My, my, you did slip up, didn't you? You didn't know
your own half-brother was my lover, and you had no idea

that my intention was to end his betrothal. I vow you must have been pinched to the very quick when you realized what had happened. The business with the tar and feathers—oh, and the verse, of course—would have been a masterstroke, had it not been for the fact that it alerted me to what was really going on in your scheme of things. I suddenly knew that it was Fane that you loved, and Fane that Miss Carlisle loved as well. Your purpose suddenly became only too evident, and I'm rather afraid that I felt a good deal of sympathy for Miss Carlisle, so much that I took myself to her without delay to tell her all about her so-called friend. And here we are, and there you are, and you've admitted in front of her that you have indeed been busying yourself against her. There is nothing to be gained further from this distasteful interview, so I don't think we need bother you anymore, do we?'' Judith smiled coolly, and then turned to walk from the room.

Linnet hesitated a moment, and then looked sadly at Venetia. "I truly believed you were my friend, Venetia.''

"You're a fool, Linnet Carlisle. He would long since have been yours if you'd had the sense you were born with.''

"Will you tell me one thing? What did you say to Freddy that made him cut me? You did say something, didn't you?''

"I wished to be rid of him, and I needed his invitation card for Nicholas, so I merely told him that you intended to exclude him from the list of guests to the betrothal ball because you thought he was making a nuisance of himself where I was concerned. I told him that everyone thought he was embarrassing, and that I was entirely in agreement with you.''

Linnet gazed at her. "How cruel you are, for you know that he loved you.''

"I believe that all is fair in love and war, Linnet, but you know that now, don't you?''

"Oh, yes. I know, just as I also know what I must put in my letter to him. Any love he may have for you will cease to be after he's read it.'' Without another word, Linnet turned and walked away.

Judith was waiting in the hall. "I think her culpability is proved, is it not?"

"Yes."

"All that remains now is for me to call upon Fane and put him right on certain points. I will go there directly, and I wish you to wait by the statue."

"But . . ."

"Don't argue." Judith smiled a little. "I don't think you will have to wait very long, truly I don't."

"All I ask is the chance to earn his forgiveness."

"My dear Miss Carlisle, if I can get him to meet you in that garden, and you fling yourself upon his masculine mercy, I vow the poor fellow won't stand a chance. Every woman has a little of the Cyprian in her, so employ your wiles, as I'm sure you know how."

"I hope you're right. Oh, how I hope you're right."

"Well, let's do it, then. Oh, and as I rather think this is the parting of the ways for us, may I say that I wish you nothing but well for the future. Good-bye, Miss Carlisle."

Without waiting for Linnet to reply, Judith stepped outside, and Linnet pulled her veil forward again, before following her. The Cyprian entered the waiting landau, which immediately drove on, intending to turn into the drive of Fane House at the far end of the crescent. Its progress was observed by all those in its vicinity, and hardly anyone noticed Linnet's light figure hurrying across the road and down the steps into the garden.

The smell of tar still hung in the air, but there was no sign of it on the statue. Most of the chicken feathers had been carefully removed from the surrounding grass and paths, but some remained, fluttering gently in the light summer breeze.

Linnet paced restlessly up and down, her veil lifting now and then. She saw Judith's landau draw up before Fane House, and saw the Cyprian go inside. After that, the minutes seemed to drag on leaden feet. She felt as if she'd paced there for an hour or more, but instead a nearby church bell announced that it had only been fifteen minutes. Oh, what was being said in there? Was he listening to Judith? Or was he closing his ears to anything that might be said in Linnet Carlisle's favor?

The suspense was agonizing, and several times she felt like running away rather than face the inevitable snub, but she made herself stay. Occasionally, she glanced up at Venetia's house, and saw a slender figure in dull violet standing motionless at the window, watching her.

It was one of those brief glances at Venetia that told Linnet Nicholas was approaching. As she looked up at the window, the figure suddenly withdrew from sight, and in such a way that Linnet knew instinctively that Nicholas had appeared.

She whirled about, and saw him coming toward her. As she flung back her veil, she saw that he still wore the charcoal coat and cream breeches of earlier, but the neckcloth had been retied and was quite perfect again. She tried to read his face, but couldn't. There was no expression there, nothing to tell her what to expect.

He halted a few feet away from her. "I understand I owe you an apology, for you had nothing to do with events here today."

"I wouldn't have done such a thing," she replied, still trying to gauge him.

"I no longer know what you would or would not do, Linnet." He turned a little as Judith's white landau pulled away from Fane House, coming up to a smart pace as it passed through the wrought iron gates and out into John Street, then he looked at Linnet again. "You and Judith are a very unlikely team."

"We aren't all that unalike," she murmured in reply.

He didn't hear. "Well, since your transport appears to have left without you, I'll gladly provide you with a carriage to take you home."

"How very courteous of you," she replied, holding his gaze. "You aren't going to forgive me for the past, are you?"

"Did you ever seek to forgive *me* for *my* imagined crimes?" he countered.

"I know that I was in the wrong."

"Yes, because Sir Henry left you in no doubt."

"Do two wrongs make a right? You're doing to me what I did to you, and if I was at fault then, so are you now." She maintained an outward dignity, but inside she was heartbroken. This wasn't how she wished the conversation to go, but he wasn't giving her a chance. Even as she thought it, she remembered the times in the past when she hadn't given him a chance, either.

"If we've both been at fault, I believe we are now equal," he said.

"Equals should start again, from the beginning."

"That's hardly possible after all that's happened between us."

"Why is it impossible?" she asked. "I love you, Nicholas, and I always will; nothing has changed that *in spite* of all that's happened. And if you place such faith in us being equals, then it's only right that what applies to me should apply equally to you. In that letter you left for me with Sir Henry, you claimed to have loved me right up until last night; if you are indeed my equal, sir, then you must love me still."

"Then perhaps I'm not your equal after all, for even the brightest flame can be abruptly extinguished."

A sudden strength came to her, and she tenaciously held her ground. "No, sir, it cannot. I love you, and you love me, only now you're the one who's refusing to admit it. I've learned a very painful lesson this past year, but I've learned it well, and I won't let you down again."

"How easy it is to say that, when only yesterday you still wore Gresham's ring, and wore it willfully, even though you knew you still loved me. Being perverse comes woefully easily to you, Linnet, and although you're all sweet contrition now, how can I be sure you won't revert to your old self again when the mood takes you?"

She found herself remembering Judith's words. *Every woman has a little of the Cyprian in her, so employ your wiles, as I'm sure you know how.* She moved a little closer to him, so that there were no leaf shadows falling over her, only the full sunlight, bright on her daffodil-yellow clothes. "If you can honestly say you now despise me, Nicholas, then walk away from me, but let me tell you something first. I wasn't happy yesterday when I was still betrothed to Benedict, but I kept telling myself I was doing the right thing. You didn't offer me any hope, did you? Each time I surrendered to your kisses, you contemptuously tossed me aside, but what right did you have to show contempt? You didn't hesitate to exercise your power over me, you employed your kisses to make me betray myself, and once you'd succeeded, it amused you to cast me away. Doesn't that make you contemptible?"

"It wasn't like that."

"No?" Her voice was soft, and she was close enough to touch him. Slowly she reached out, resting her fingers against his cheek. "Then tell me how it was, Nicholas."

He didn't move away. "I wanted you to see that it was wrong to marry Gresham."

"If that was all you intended, then you need only have told me the truth about him. Your conscience would have been salved, and that would have been the end of it." Her fingertips moved seductively against his skin, and still he didn't draw away. She smiled into his eyes. "You didn't tell me outright because you wished to know for certain that I still loved you, and you wished to know that because you still loved me. That's why you kissed me, isn't it?'

His hand moved suddenly to enclose hers, and there was a different light in his eyes, a softer light. "Have you been sitting at Judith's knee?" he murmured. "I vow you've been taking lessons."

She contained her joy that he'd responded at last. "Her poodle sits at her knee, sir, I merely have a recently discovered talent for being the wanton, or so I've been told."

"Whoever told you, knew what she was talking about."

"The person is considered *the* expert in her art, sir."

He smiled a little. "So I understand, but I have no personal experience of her upon which to draw."

"So I understand," she answered softly. "You haven't replied to my question yet. Why did you kiss me, when a word or two would have sufficed?"

"For the reason you gave."

Her heart was singing, but she gave no sign. "Are we still equals? *Do* you still love me?"

"You know that I do."

"Words won't suffice now, sir. I need a kiss to prove you mean what you say."

She closed her eyes with ecstasy as he pulled her close. His lips were firm and warm, and there was no cynicism in his kiss now, just the flame of a desire that had been denied for too long.

She drew back a little, her face flushed with happiness. "Do you forgive me for everything?" she whispered.

"The past doesn't matter anymore." He looked into her dark eyes. "Will you answer me a rather intriguing question, Miss Carlisle?"

"If I can, Lord Fane."

"Just exactly where did you conceal that plume you stole from Portman Street?"

"That is a very improper question, sir."

"And a very improper place, madam," he replied softly, kissing her again.